I0638971

Interface of Cult and Culture

Essays on Inculturation, Liberation and Mission

SAMANVAYAM - Contextual Theology Series - 7

Interface of Cult and Culture

Essays on Inculturation, Liberation and Mission

SAMANVAYAM - Contextual Theology Series - 7

Author
Dr. Louis Malieckal CMI

Editor
Dr. Cyril Kuttiyanikkal CMI

2019

Interface of Cult and Culture: *Essays on Inculturation, Liberation and Mission-* published by the Rev. Dr. Ashish Amos of the Indian Society for Promoting Christian Knowledge (ISPCK), Post Box 1585, Kashmere Gate, Delhi-110006.

© Author, 2019

All rights reserved. No part of this book may be reproduced or transmitted in any form or by any means, electronic, mechanical, photocopying, recording, or by any information storage and retrieval system, without the prior permission in writing from the publisher.

The views expressed in the book are those of the author and the publisher takes no responsibility for any of the statements.

Online order: http://ispck.org.in/book.php

Also available on amazon.in

ISBN: 978-93-88945-11-0

Laser typeset by

ISPCK, Post Box 1585, 1654, Madarsa Road, Kashmere Gate, Delhi-110006 • *Tel:* 23866323

e-mail: ashish@ispck.org.in • ella@ispck.org.in
website: www.ispck.org.in

Contents

Foreword

A book is evaluated and gauged not necessarily for its distinct content but also for the authenticity and veracity of the writer especially when it deals with faith, morals, religion, theology, etc. The best and lucid way to describe the author of Interface of Cult and Culture: Essays on Inculturation, Liberation, Mission is one who puts his life, spirit, heart and soul into it and writes according to his firm convictions. He has a third eye and perspicacity to the happenings of the world and has considered and analysed everything with an attitude of inveterate optimism. Rev Fr Louis Malieckal CMI is one of the eminent authors of that genre. Therefore, it is natural that one can easily come across many creative observations, possibilities, challenges etc. in this well researched and well reflected book.

Creative and lasting changes come only through original reflection and pragmatism. This book highlights certain challenges to those who are serious about going beyond the milieu of comfortable and convenient "Passover". Those who want to maintain a 'peaceful and relaxed' life, without disturbing routine life, may not see something exquisite and exotic in this book. But those who have an acumen and sixth sense to comprehend the social transformation may be inspired, challenged, motivated by the thought patterns, reflections and realities that the author spells out in the book.

Every chapter of the book gives something unique to quench our thirst for knowledge. I strongly recommend the readers to reflect chapter three with the attitude of self-criticism because the author leads the reader to the multidimensional aspects of 'spirituality of pilgrimage'. It is an important subject which deserves to be discussed as pilgrims and pilgrimages sometimes become an end per se forgetting the core of spirituality. But this chapter gives us a new insight on pilgrimages. The Chapter titled "New Evangelization: Concept, concerns and Challenges for Indian Church" should be meditated seriously in the present context because of emerging new world views, moral outlooks, over emphasis of individualism, intolerance to divergences etc., crawl into social and religious scenarios. Our goal and means must be clear; and it is sure that this chapter will give us new insights to fulfill our mission.

The Vatican Council II, even after fifty years, is not properly understood and seriously taken by the church because of its demands for radical response from the faithful and even from the whole humanity. The author interprets worship, liturgy, rituals etc in the spirit of the Council, which will certainly inspire us to imbibe the vision of the fathers of the Council, with true spirit of openness. It is very challenging because often we are satisfied with what we have and things and thoughts which are unfamiliar to us are inevitably dangerous. The author appeals to the reader to have a radical response to the call of the Spirit.

The term Inculturation, in recent years and especially after Vatican Council II, is unimaginably adulterated and spurious as we use it unnecessarily without realising its nuances and principles. It is indeed good to read this book to know how we have to approach the reality of inculturation. An uncritical swallowing and a blind distaste of the application of inculturation are against the spirit of the Council. This is abundantly clear from the interpretation, observations and thought patterns of the author concerning inculturation. Good knowledge of inculturation will help us to maintain a careful balance between 'dos' and 'don'ts' and the book certainly will help us to distinguish and discern it.

I deeply appreciate and passionately acclaim to Rev Fr Louis Malieckal, CMI for producing such an informative, insightful and illuminating book.

Fr Peter Kochalumkal CMI
Rector, Samanvaya

Preface

There is an intrinsic relationship between culture, mission and cult in the sense of worship or liturgy. Culture plays an important role in relation to the missionary imperative expressed in liturgy. Critical reflection on these issues are essential for understanding their pastoral implications. The articles by Dr. Louis Malieckal examine the relationship between culture, mission, liturgy and inculturation. Basically they speak about the intimate relationship between cult and culture.

These articles are on the one hand, an earnest search to make theological reflection relevant to Indian cultural sensitivity and on the other hand, the ritual meaningful to the ordinary believers. Just like cult and culture feeds on each other, the gospel and culture encounter is meant for mutual enrichment, resulting in the betterment of humanity. Some of the essays delve deeply into the cultural background of certain rituals and practices to enhance the ceremonies and rituals and to add more meaning as well as bring out their liberative potential. These articles show how in the practice of inculturation the Church remains true to both the Gospel and culture and animates the process of incarnating the Gospel into different cultures and adding one more cultural expression into the Church by introducing these cultures into the life of the Church.

No Indian theologian can ignore the two important contexts of India, namely the vast number of people living under the poverty line and the variety of Indian religio-cultural traditions. The author has put in his heart and soul into these essays painstakingly striking a balance between these two realties to present a holistic and integral approach by giving them both adequate attention.

Another striking point of these articles is that they are down to earth and practical, giving a prudent well-thought out view on the issues related to mission, culture and its role in liturgy. He has also presented them not just from his long experience of living and guiding the process of inculturation efforts, but also based solidly on the documents of the Church. These articles, besides being relevant to the present era, they are a treasure for the posterity.

As someone who was in the forefront in the field of inculturation following the call of Second Vatican Council for renewal and who was instrumental in making the Order of 'Indian Mass' for the Syro Malabar Rite, and as one of the architects of contextualized theological formation in North India, the author's equanimity and poise of vision is clearly palpable throughout the articles. His influence, especially on the minds of the young generation in the ecclesial circle has been enormous.

The present work is a collection of his essays either presented in some of the theological reviews/edited books or in a seminar or a conference. My role as editor is meager and bare minimum that too limited to the technicalities of its presentation. However, I am happy to be part of this work and hope that the reader will find it an inspiring and enriching experience. I am sure this book is a must for anyone who is interested in liturgy, inculturation and evangelization.

Dr. Cyril Kuttiyanikkal
Editor

Introduction

Although etymologically the two words 'cult' and 'culture' are derived from the Latin root word *colere*, apparently they are not related semantically, at least in the popular perception. For, cult means worship, whereas culture points to an entirely new set of meanings, as we shall see below, none of them coming anywhere near 'worship'. To understand what is at stake here, we need to go to the root meanings of *colere* as well as to the two noun-forms of it in Latin, namely *cultus* and *cultura*.

Now, colere means "to worship", "to cultivate", "to refine or fine-tune"; *cultus* (cult) means religious worship or ritual, when applied to God or the gods, whereas *cultura* (culture), means agriculture when applied to soil, plants or animals, and education, refinement, when applied to humans. Thus we find that the root word *colere* is the reason for the connection between cult and culture in English, but how is this linguistic connection explained in reality?

What happens in religious worship, in praising, adoring and thanking God? According to our philosophical/theological understanding nothing happens to God. As fullness of all goodness, He is unchangeable. His glory is neither increased nor decreased. We have to remember here the famous saying of St. Iranaeus who said: *"Gloria Dei est homo vivens........"*, namely God's glory is humans fully alive. In other words, when we worship God, something happens to us: We are purified and refined internally or sanctified; our 'spiritual cultivation' takes place in every act of authentic religious worship. That is how *colere* can mean both religious worship and cultivation of land, plans, animals as well as refinement or character building of humans. In all these instances, there is development, transformation and growth, be it that of land, plants, animals or human body, mind, or spirit. Thus the interface of cult and culture is varied and subtler than we usually consider.

Let us have a closer look at culture as applied to humans. From the above discussion we see that it means cultivation of human person, or education and refinement. There is an elitist understanding of culture, which would distinguish between primitive and developed cultures, and speak about the rich cultural heritage of a country consisting of art, music, literature and also sometimes religion. This understanding of culture is very limited and partial, because it is determined based on a few people of the country, known for their skills, knowledge and erudition, whereas all human experiences, high and low, rich and poor etc. belong to culture. Culture can never be an affair of an individual at a particular moment of time, because it involves a complex interplay of perception, thought, interpretation and language. This is made sufficiently clear by the following definition of The Willowbank report (1978):

> Culture is an integrated system of beliefs (about God or reality or ultimate meaning), of values (about what is true, good and beautiful and normative), of customs (how to behave, relate to others, talk, pray, dress, work, play, trade, farm etc.), and of institutions which express these beliefs, values and customs(governments,

law courts, temples/churches, families, schools, hospitals, factories, shops, unions, clubs etc.) which binds a society together and gives it a sense of identity, dignity, security and continuity.[1]

In the following pages we shall discuss how these dynamics of culture as well as cult have given rise to manifold experiences in human life on the one hand, and how different situations of human life have necessitated a variety of cultural adaptations as well as cultic celebrations for healthy growth and fulfilment of human life and society at large on the other.

Endnotes

[1] Quoted from Joseph Chittooparampil, *A Christian Vision for a New Society in India*, (ISPCK: Delhi, 2014) p.57.

D r. Louis Malieckal, one of the pioneers in contextualized Indian theology, Indian spirituality and Indian liturgy, died of a massive heart attack on February 25 at Bhopal, central India at the age of 83, as this book was being printed for publication.

In the wake of the renewal after the Second Vatican Council he played a leading role in the liturgical experiments in the Indian Church. He is credited with the formulation of the Order of Indian Mass for the Syro-Malabar Church called the *Bharatiya Pooja* which is being currently used at Kurisumala Ashram, Kerala. Dr Malieckal introduced *Bhajans* in the Indian Church by composing the first Christian *Bhajan* (Om Jagadiswara sadapi chinmaya Jagadeeshwara vande) when he was a student of theology. Dr. Maliekal's passion for evolving Indian liturgy and Indian theology is reflected in his doctoral thesis Yajna and Eucharist: An Inter-Religious Approach to the Theology of Sacrifice.

Post-Second Vatican period also witnessed many attempts in India for contextualized theological training. The leaders of the Church were convinced that a seminary formation based on the Western style would not equip the missionaries and priests to face the various challenges in the field. Dr. Malieckal led contextualized theological formation of seminarians in central India. As the rector of Khrist Premalaya, Ashta, the regional theologate for Madhya Pradesh and Chhattisgarh, he adopted the methodology of "Action-ReflectionAction," taking inspiration from the 'Pedagogy of the Oppressed' by Paulo Freire.

Father Maliekal also took the initiative to start an inter-religious association (Sarva Dharma Sanghatan) at Ashta in Madhya Pradesh in the early 1980s. This association played a key role in preventing communal violence in Ashta town, a communally sensitive area.

When the CMI Congregation started a contextualized theologate (Samanvaya) in Bhopal in the early 1990s, Fr. Maliekal was chosen to evolve a formation process suited to the North Indian situation. The seminarians were given training in three different contexts: the tribal and rural context of Bastar, inter-religious context of Rishikesh in Uttarakhand and the intercultural context of Madhya Pradesh.

As a thinker and writer, he has published seven books and around 100 theological articles in several journals, besides presenting numerous papers at national and international seminars. Honoring his contribution in contextualized theological formation in India, a book titled Theology on Wheels: A Movement for Contextualized Theological Education (edited by Dr. Davis Varayilaan) was released on the occasion of the golden jubilee celebration of his priestly ordination.

Chapter 1

Samdhyā:
The Time of Prayer
and the Prayer of Time

Introduction

Alexis Carrel, the Nobel Prize winner in medicine says that prayer is the most powerful form of energy one can generate. "It is a force," he says, "as real as terrestrial gravity." Prayer like radium, he adds, is a source of luminous self-generating energy and when we pray we link ourselves with inexhaustible moving power that spins the universe. Probably never before in the living memory of humankind was this cosmic dimension of prayer felt more vividly by the world at large than when America's Apollo thirteenth manned space mission to the moon, ended up in a tragic failure some years ago. In spite of the advanced scientific knowledge and computer technology available at that time, the lives of the three men on board the space-ship—James Lowell, Fred Hais and John Swigert—were seriously at stake due to some irreparable technical snag which developed at some point during the onward flight. And then the hearts of men and women the world over rose as one, praying for their safe return.

Instances of prayer coupled with penance and sacrifice during the anxious and agonizing hours of human existence, regardless of nation, religion and ideology, are too numerous to quote. Somehow a 'miracle' happened, in the case of Apollo and after their safe return what John Swigert, one of the space crew, said to the crowd of media -reporters amply testifies to this. He said: "If you are asking me whether I prayed, yes certainly I did; and I have no doubt that my prayers and the prayers of the rest of the world did an awful lot for us getting back."

That was indeed a unique time of prayer as well as a great prayer of time, prayer of all that is time-bound, a cosmic prayer. This article tries to reveal this double aspect of prayer based on the concept of samdhyā, as understood in the Indian tradition and as experienced at Samdhyā prayer during the author's long stay at Rishikesh, in Uttarakhand.

SAMDHYĀ: Its Meaning and Significance

The Word samdhyä is generally considered to be derived from the prefix sam denoting cumulation, synthesis, and the root dhä, "to put/place"[1] and so these together mean "to put together/unite/meet together" etc. Therefore, the noun samdhyä literally means "holding together/union/meeting point/junction[2]. Instead of the root dhã, sometimes the root dhyai,[3] "to meditate/ ponder/pray" is associated with sam and thus the definition of the term samdhyā is given as "on what account meditation/prayer is done well—that is samdhyā" (*samyak dhyayati anaya samdhyā*). Whatever be the case, both these meanings will be of interest to us in our reflections on the concept of samdhyā as we shall see in what follows.

In a cosmotheandric perspective samdhyā is a holding together, meeting-point and junction in a variety of ways: Spatially it refers to the atmosphere or middle region (antarïksa) where the sky or heaven (dyu) and earth (prthvl) meet and merge giving rise to the horizon, the symbol of human hopes and possibilities. Temporally, it refers to the present (vartamana) where the past (bhüta) and the future (bhavin) make their point of departure. And this meeting of the three great times (kalas) present-past-future, is signified in another meeting (samdhyā) of the three juncture moments—morning, evening and noon—of every day and of every time span, since the day is an image of man's life span and the unifying element of human temporal life.[4] Further, it can also denote all dvandva's or pairs of polar opposites in nature and life, namely, sun and moon, day and night, light and darkness, man and woman, God and world etc.

Viewed in an anthropocosmic perspective the concept of samdhyā connects nature and human life in a very real way. In the words of R. Panikkar, "Samdhyā refers to the two privileged moments of Sunrise, when everything can still become everything, and of sunset, when all has been said and done and there is nothing else to do; or of dawn when man can still hope because the whole day lies in front of him, and of dusk, when he can simply live because the day is already over and nothing else remains to be done."[5] Finally, samdhyā not only refers to but really is the most suitable prayer-time, the implications of which we shall discuss presently.

Samdhyā: The Time of Prayer

We have seen that samdhyā symbolizes the meeting, union, in a variety of ways, of the polar realities in the universe. Hence we can say that it also symbolized the meeting of God and wo/man, life and death, grace and sin and thus a call to prayer insofar as prayer is essentially a meeting of God and humans. It is indeed the *muhurta,* auspicious time of prayer, —namely the "meeting" (samdhyā), when in the whole universe there takes place a series of meetings (ontic prayers: samdhyā's) at various levels, all for the happy and harmonious "holding together" (samdhyā) of the reality. That is why every pious Hindu gets up early in the morning and after his/her ablutions sits in prayer ready to greet the rising sun. In this action man/woman joins hands with the entire universe to celebrate the meeting of God and humans, and this is samdhyā: the prayer—that is a meeting. As the sun emerges majestically from behind the eastern horizon the sleeping cosmos is also awakened. There is movement, life and flow of energy everywhere. This external movement and outer awakening beckons man/woman to interior awakening and inner enlightenment which is the fruit of prayer. At the meeting of night and day or of father sky and mother earth cosmic enlightenment is effected; at the meeting of God and man/woman inner enlightenment is the result. In other words, inner enlightenment of wo/ man is the fruit of prayer, even as the rising sun is the child of samdhyā.

At every meeting there is also a crossing over from one side to the other, from one plane to the next, whether or not this meeting and crossing be real or mythical. Of all such events based on the annual cycle due to the inter-related movements of the cosmic bodies', samdhyā is the basic model at which day meets and crosses over to night, and vice versa. It is one of humanity's oldest beliefs that every 'territorial' passage, be it real or mythical, is a risky step. Every passage from the known to the unknown, from the familiar to the unfamiliar, from the old to the new, from death to life is a 'sacred' step full of challenges. Hence this passage is to be properly initiated and 'sacrificed' (made sacred) through ritual/prayer.[6] Being the basic model of these passages samdhyā necessitates some ritual/prayer. In other words, samdhyā is the auspicious time of prayer, as it is also a unique prayer by itself.

Samdhyā: The Prayer of Time

Samdhyā is equally the prayer of time, of time not considered as a series of successive chronological moments, without a 'soul' or connecting link between moments, but of time that is to be 'sacrificed', conquered and transcended in order to discover its inner core. This time springs from cult, liturgy prayer, and dies with it as well.[7] Underlying many religious traditions is the concept that man, a prisoner of time, overcomes his temporal limitation by participating in an act which in itself has trans-temporal significance. Human imitation of this act is the ritual/prayer which saves him from being drowned in the everyday 'temporocity'. For example, in Hinduism this act reaches beyond the present into the bottom of the past, even to the end of time where time itself is the creation of the original divine act, And so by positing that act man saves himself from the grip of time and reaches the 'further shore'. Similarly in Christianity, this is an act which transcends time-space continuum. It is an act which can 'forgive' past sins and treasure up future grace. Every Christian who shares in the mystery of Christ by means of this act lifts up his life into that of Christ himself. Of course, this may also serve to gain some particular earthly desire, but ultimately it differs from eve1Y other human action, as it stretches beyond the ordinary time-span and makes man shale in the mystery of the entire cosmotheandric dynamism of the universe.

Now, when man is engaged in this trans-temporal act, which we call prayer, he is not performing a private, individual action, rather he is performing a priestly action in the name of the whole of reality. He stands here as mediator, the living link between the pairs of opposites and extremes we have noted above. Man at prayer is the meeting point (samdhyā) of God and world, the Timeless and the time-bound. And prayer of time is the quest or craving of the time bound to reach their timeless core. This quest is the spiritual element which links up the otherwise disconnected moments of the temporal process. This link is the 'spirit of prayer' that unfolds in the mind and heart of man, the man of enlightenment. And then for him samdhyā is not only the auspicious time of prayer but also and more especially the prayer of time, prayer itself becoming the human action par excellence. Prayer then is not merely a mantra, a ritual but also a tantra, the right way of doing anything. That means, my sincere efforts to increase the welfare of my fellow-men, my concern for the well-being of my neighbours, my selfless actions to enhance the quality of human life in the world at large, for the transformation of social lives, for the advancement of cultures, etc.—all these are models of this action-centred prayer, prayer of the secular (not profane, however) man.

Thus, that samdhyā is the prayer of time means that in it the entire creation is involved, that in it man/woman discovers him/herself as the authentic mediator between the Timeless and the time-bound and that s/he is in communion with the rest of the universe. In this sense prayer at samdhyā, at that particular moment of 'cosmic meeting', is the becoming conscious on the part of man/woman of his/her ontic fullness; not only is s/he in the universe, but with the universe is rooted in God. Thus samdhyā as the prayer of time leads humans to a profound awareness of a cosmotheandric communion, to a sense of fulfilment and liberation

Gayatri: The Model Samdhyā Prayer

Our discussion of the samdhyā prayer in both its aspects as the time of prayer and the prayer of time may be concluded most appropriately with some reflections on the famous Gayatri prayer as a unique model samdhyā prayer. In its original form it reads thus:

OM

tat savitur varenyarñ We meditate upon the glorious

bhargo devasya dhimahi Splendour of the Vivifier divine

dhiyo yo nah pracodayat [8] May he awaken our minds.

This is perhaps the most renowned mantra of the Vedas. Manu says: "There is nothing more exalted than the Gayatri."[9] The mantra gets its name from the meter in which it is composed, the Gayatri, being a Vedic poetic meter of three lines, each of eight syllables. As it is addressed to the divine life-giver as supreme God, symbolized in Savitur (the Sun), it is also known by the name Savitri.[10] It is recited or chanted daily at the two samdhyā's (sunrise and sunset), usually with the ritual bath. As it stands now in the Hindu tradition, the prayer is preceded by Om bhür bhuvaþ svah (0M earth, atmosphere, sky) and followed by Om Santi Santi Santi (OM peace, peace, peace.)[11]

Underlying these three utterances (vyahrti's): bhür bhuvah svah is a three tiered cosmological conception. Namely, the universe is conceived to be made up of three concomitant parts or layers—earth-middle region-heaven-and their utterance is meant to evoke a sense of totality and inter-relatedness of everything.[12] Even otherwise the idea of totality is already implied in the opening syllable OM. As it is made up of three letters—(OM) AUM, to which a variety of symbolism has been ascribed by tradition [13] —to produce a single sound, this syllable 0M is identified with the entire reality as Sabda-brahman in its manifested form.[14] It is not only the sound of 0M which is significant, but the silence following its utterance and it is this ontic silence of OM which is spoken of as the soundless unmanifested Brahman. Moreover, the Gayatri mantra as such is a symbol of totality with respect to space and time. Being composed of three lines, each having eight syllables, the mantra points to the three realms of the cosmos and the eight directions thereof, thus signifying spatial totality. Because of its twenty-four syllables (three times eight), it denotes the twelve months with their bright and dark halves.[15]

Thus, we find that the entire mantra is invested through and through with the totality idea, and this undoubtedly goes quite well with the concept of samdhyā as the prayer of time as explained above. Gayatri prayer is indeed a participation in the systole and diastole of the whole universe, and when a pious Hindu on getting up early in the morning recites it, he is trying to assume, realize and become the whole reality, for "the Gayatri indeed is the whole universe, all that has come to be..... "[16] It is to be noted that this prayer originated precisely in the cosmic context of the samdhyā, when the sage first uttered it as he was overwhelmed with sentiments of wonder, praise and love, watching the marvellous effects that the rising sun (savitṛ), symbol of the supreme God, brought to bear upon the whole visible reality. And as he uttered it, it was not, for him, a mere mental and emotional act, but a real prayer, that is an existential self-disposing, a placing of his total self before God, so that he also (like the rest of creation outwardly) may be awakened from within, being filled with God's graceful light.[17]

Concluding Remarks

Samdhyā is a profound concept of prayer, where prayer is seen as an existential self-disposing of man before God who awakens man's inner self. This meeting of man and God, which is prayer, is to be seen against the background of a variety of cosmic meetings, especially at the samdhyā, the sunrise and sunset, the most auspicious prayer-times. Further, it is the prayer of time, prayer of all temporal realities,[18] in which wo/man discovers him/herself as the authentic mediator, the living link between all that is time-bound and the Timeless beyond. It may be further observed here that in a very real sense, for Christians at least, Jesus Christ is samdhyā: Prayer Incarnate. He is the perfect meeting-point of the human and the divine, of God's grace and man's weakness, of the Timeless and the time bound. The above concept of samdhyā is well exemplified by the beautiful prayer Gayatri, even as metaphors like "Light of the world" "Star of the East", "Invincible Sun" point to Jesus Christ, the Incarnate Samdhyā.

Endnotes

[1] Compare Greek *tithemi* and Indo-European *dhe*.

[2] Monier-Williams, (Munshiram *Sanskrit-English Dictionary* Manoharlal: New Delhi) 1988, p.v.

[3] Ibid. p.v.

[4] See R. Panikkar, *Vedic Experience* (DLT:: London, 1977) 781-94.

[5] Ibid. p.782.

[6] On cosmic passages and the accompanying religious rites/prayers, see Swami Sivananda, *Hindu Fasts and Festivals* (DLT: Tehri-Garhwal, 1983). On the importance of rites of passage in socio-religious and cosmic sense, see Arnold van Gennep, *The Rites of Passage* (London and Henley Routlege and Kegal Paul, 1977).

[7] On the relation between cult/prayer and time, read R.Panikkar, *Le mystere du culte dans l'induisme et le chretianisme* (C erf: Paris, 1970).

[8] Rigveda III, 62, 10.

[9] Manu II, 83.

[10] Cf. RV I,159,5;82,1; Yajurveda III,35; XXII,9; BG 10, 35.

[11] In today's India of media explosion, its chanting can be heard broadcast day and night in Rishikesh in the voice of famous playback singers like Asha Bhonsle.

[12] Already in the Upanishadic period this practice seems to have been there Cf. Br. Up. V,5,4; For later practice, see SB XI,16,3; Manu II, 78-81. Cf. Subhash Anand, "A Pre-Christian Easter Prayer," *Vidyajyoti 67/3, 1983,* pp.135-148. Recently, Kushvant Singh has attempted a new translation of this beautiful prayer as follows::OM Lord, Creator of earth and heaven, hallowed be your name. You who make the sun rise at dawn and give light and life to all things, infuse our beings with hope of enlightenment. Lord, grant us the power to cleanse our minds of dross and make them pure. Lord inspire our minds to perform noble actions." (Hindustan Times, Jan. 13, 2007).

[13] The three letters stand for the three Vedas (Rig-Sam-Yajur), three kālās (past-present-future), three divine activities (srsti-sthithi-laya), three time slots (- Ādi—Madhya-Anta) etc.

[14] Cf. Katha Up II, 16.

[15] Cf. Br.Up. VI, 14, 1. See also Subhash Anand art. Cit. p.137; R. Panikkar, op.cit. 406.

[16] C.Up. III,12,1.

[17] According to Subhash Anand, the word *dhimahi* may also be derived from the root dhā as its deponent or middle form with a reflexive meaning. In that case dhīmahi will mean "we place ourselves (before....)". Being set before the rising sun, the whole world is awakened to a new life. Similarly wo/man will dispose him/herself freely before God for interior awakening, which is prayer (see art. Cit. pp.139f).

[18] No one can see or experience time as such, except through phenomenal beings. According to Christian belief time began with creation and every created being including humans is temporal, except for his/her inner core or spirit which is eternal. Our closeness with this created earth is such that, as our late President A.P.J. Abdul Kalam rightly said, when I say I am 60/80/100 year old, it really means that I have so far made 60/80/100 revolutions (along with the earth) around the sun.

Chapter 2

Pilgrims and Pilgrimage Centres in India: An Inter-religious Approach to the Spirituality of Pilgrimage

Introduction

Religious phenomenology amply testifies that pilgrim centres and pilgrimages are in every country, be it in the West or in the East. From very ancient times the major religions of the world have their central places of worship and pilgrimage, like Jerusalem and Rome, Mecca and Medina, Badrinath and Benares (Varanasi) etc. However in this respect India seems to stand out unparalleled on account of exceedingly large number and variety of pilgrim spots and pilgrimages undertaken by devotees at different times of the year. In fact, as A. Stuart observes, "There is no numbering of holy places in this country. Almost every village can boast of a sacred tank, spring, tree, hill top, shrine or hermitage".[1] And this justifies the ancient Puranic saying: In the three worlds India is famous as a land of pilgrim centres." (*Jambave Bharatam varsham tirtham trilokya-visrutam*).

In this paper we would discuss the topic mainly from the Hindu-Christian perspectives, with occasional references to other religions. We shall consider the concepts *tirtha* and *tirthankara*, their meaning and scope, first in Hinduism, and then their parallels in Christianity, etc. Secondly the historical origins of pilgrimages will be taken up. Thereafter we shall consider the question of a spirituality of pilgrimages. Finally we shall make some critical observations and comments with regard to the current praxis of pilgrimage in Hinduism and Christianity.

Tirthas and Tirthankaras

The Sanskrit word tīrtha comes from the root tri, having different connotations[2]. Most commonly the word is given the literal meaning of "ford over water" and in fact most of the Hindu pilgrim centres (tīrthani) are located on river banks. The reason must be primitive human belief in the power of water to heal not only body but also soul (atman). Tīrtha is also the title of an Order of monks of the Sri Sankaracharya School, called Swami Ramatirtha, as also the name of any learned person, and so the Padma Purāṇa asserts that a teacher, father or chaste wife is a tīrtha. The variety of uses of the term to refer to exalted places, persons and things is due to the significance of its symbolism that lies in the notion of 'crossing over', as the site of pilgrimage is a locus of intersection between the profane and the sacred realms, where the individual interacts with the sacred space by means of many ritual exercises. In Hinduism there are liberated souls (*jīvanmukta*s) who would help those poor humans to cross the phenomenal world (saṃsāra-sāgaram), being caught up in the cycle of re-births. So, Jainism speaks of Tīrthankaras, "Ford-makers", who would do the same role. Jainism has thus twenty-four Teachers (Tīrthankaras) through whom their faith has been transmitted. Such initiated and liberated persons are able to act as the point of intersection between the divine and human planes, 'fording' and becoming 'bridge-makers' (tīrthankaras).[3]

Pilgrims and Pilgrimage Centres

The English word pilgrimage, derived from the Latin word *peregrinatio* does not by itself indicate a pilgrimage in the modern sense for which we need to consider it from historical and geographical viewpoints. Originally *peregrinatio* simply meant "wandering" and *peregrinus* a "stranger" or a "vagabond". Christian pilgrims were called *Palmieri* because they brought back from the Holy Land (Palestine) palm branches, and they were also called *Romei* because they journeyed towards Rome, the Holy City. The present understanding and practice of 'pilgrimage' only gradually entered into the Christian perspective for various reasons: 1. Some other religious groups of the Middle East indulged in it with its attendant superstitious and even immoral practices. 2, As the Second Coming of Christ

(*Parousia*) was considered as an imminent event, the idea of journeys to places connected with the earthly life of Jesus appeared superfluous. 3, During the first three centuries, because of the strictly monotheistic belief of the early Christians who were all Jews, there was no cult of saints and holy shrines during this period.

However, very soon the extreme reserve towards other religious practices diminished, the early expected *Parousia* did not take place and the number of non-Jewish/gentile Christians began to increase. And so, veneration of the tombs of martyrs and their relics, and the practice of pilgrimage, centred on the figures of Christ began to emerge. In fact B. Kotting has listed several motives for the emergence of the practice of pilgrimage in early Christianity.[4]

India: A Unique Land of Pilgrimages

In the Hindu understanding "whatever helps one to get across the sea of sinfulness is a shrine (tīrtham)."[5] Accordingly there are at least three types of sacred shrines. They are 1. Moving Shrines (*jangama-tīrthāni*), 2. Stationary Shrines (*sthāvara-tīrthāni*) and, 3. Spiritual Shrines (*mānasa-tīrthāni*). Let us have a brief discussion of them.

Moving Shrines (jangama-tīrthāni)

Sages and wandering monks (*parivrājakas*) are considered as moving shrines. For, they move from place to place, teaching and preaching the ways of salvation/liberation (*mukti*) to the ordinary faithful. Liberated as they are now, they also become the means of crossing (tarati) the sea of worldliness (*samsāra*). In Jainism therefore an Arhat is aptly called *tirthankara*.[6] Their life style is a constant reminder of the impermanence of the world. For the same reason a wandering monk is often likened to the rivers, especially to the sacred river Ganga (Ganges), which flows on and on without any stops. Like the Ganges his role is bringing everything from time into the eternity, from a state of becoming to that of being. He is the one who is present to everything and yet is bound by nothing. Just as the Ganges, in order to advance, makes use of the rock but never adheres to them, even so a wandering monk passes through the crowds of people, but is not held back by any one. No beauty and no joy can ever stop him, for he knows something more beautiful than and thirsts for some joy beyond all joy which all joy attempts to express but no joy can ever reveal.[7]

These are what we usually consider as pilgrim centres, namely sacred rivers and streams, sacred trees and forests, sacred cities and country sides, sacred mountains and hilltops. Of all the sacred rivers in India, the Ganges is undoubtedly the most revered one, because of its supposedly divine origin and mysteriously subterranean existence, apart from its surface manifestation. It is well known that the confluence of the Ganges, the Yamuna and the Saraswati (*triveni-samgam*) in Prayaga is an extremely sacred place for the Hindus. These three together with the Sindhu, Godavari, Kaveri and Narmada make up the seven-fold great Indian rivers (*saptha-mahā-nadyah*), which belong to the group of moving shrines also.

Similarly of all the sacred trees, the Pipal Banyan tree (*Ficus Religiosa*) is the most sacred one because of its mythical associations with the so-called Cosmic tree or Lord of trees (vanaspati). This tree is identified in the Hindu Scriptures as the Asvstha tree, which is conceived as standing in an inverted position (ūrdhvamūla) at the mythical centre of the universe[8]. Other sacred places as stationary shrines are so many that even to sum up in a general way is a hopeless task. Of the many sacred cities, Varanasi may be said to be the most important. Caressed by the Ganga-waters, the city is blessed with hundreds of baths, temples and shrines in a row (hence the name *tīrtharāji*). The four famous places of *Kumbhamela* and other sixty places of Srāddha are also great pilgrim centres[9]. Apart from these there are the sacred shrines in the Himalayan ranges like the Gangotri, Badrinath and the holy shrine Hemkund of the Sikh religion, whose most famous gurdwara is the Harmandir Sahib in Amritsar. It is the earnest desire of the Hindu bhakta to be able to visit one or more of these sacred shrines and die there. And blessed indeed is the pilgrim who can link in one vast tour the four centres of Badrinath in the Himalayas, Dwaraka in the west of India, Rameswaram in the south and Puri in the east.[10]

There are several very important Buddhist shrines of pilgrimages in India. One of the most important ones is at Lumbini, located near the Nepal border, the birth place of the Buddha. Another one is at Bodhayagaya, where he attained enlightenment at the age of 29 after long meditation under the *bodhi* tree. A third one is at Sarnath, in Ganges valley, where the Buddha proclaimed the law of faith. The pilgrim centre at Nalanda in Bihar is famous not only because it was blessed with the presence of the Buddha, but also because of the renowned monastic university developed there. The university also named Nalanda (meaning "insatiable in giving") played a central role in the development of Buddhism in India.[11]

Similarly, there are also at least some very important Christian pilgrimage centres in India: In the South India, we have the Mar Thoma Church at Malayattoor, central Kerala, where thousands of St. Thomas Christians go on pilgrimage, especially on July 3, the day of martyrdom of St. Thomas, the Apostle of Christ and on the first Sunday after Easter to remember the apparition of Christ after his resurrection to Thomas (Jn.20:24-29). St. Thomas Shrine, Palayur, Thrissur district is a place of great pilgrimage (*mahatirthadanam*), which is held on the third Sunday of Lent every year, attracting thousands of people from all over Kerala. The so-called Little Mount, Chennai, Tamil Nadu, immortalizing the martyrdom of St. Thomas in 72, C.E and the old church, next door originally built by the Portuguese in 1511 attract thousands of pilgrims. Besides, the Velankanni church, dedicated to Our Lady of Health and popularly known as 'Sacred Arokia Matha Church', is located 12-km south of Nagapattinam, and is visited by people of all faiths and religions.[12]

Moreover, there are also some important pilgrimage centres of the so-called "little traditions" or subaltern people (Tribals and Dalits), though there is a concerted effort on the part of the Hindutva outfits to reduce these centres into Hindu pilgrim centres either by tampering with the historical process or interpreting the religious myth concerned in tune with the Hindu religious mythology and celebrations. Yet mention needs to be made here of the famous goddess Ma Danteswari who is the local goddess (kuldevi) of Dantewada. Hundreds of people from all over Chhattisgarh make pilgrimage to this temple. It is at the confluence to two rivers Sankani and Dankani, some 80km away from Jagdalpur city. The most important event of Danteswari temple is *Navaratri in* the month of September-October, when thousands of devotees go barefoot *to* this pilgrim spot to have a darsan of the Devi. An annual festival in honour of Ma Dandesvari is held lasting for about 75 days from end of July to beginning of October, heralding the onset of the season of winter. Major tribes like Gonds, Bhils etc. of the Bastar region, dressed in brightly coloured and traditional attire take part in it. Numerous deities are brought from various parts of the region, and a massive chariot is pulled through the streets by more than 400 people.[13]

To mention one more tribal pilgrim centre, we may consider Ma Bambleśwari temple at Dongargarh, in the district of Chhattisgarh. The temple is on top of a hill about 1600ft high. Devotees flock the shrine, climbing a 1000-step stair case especially during the Navrati festival. At the peak point of celebration there is a tradition of lighting *Jyoti kalaś.*[14]

Ascetico-Mystical Shrines *(mānasatīrthāni)*

The human mind is itself a multifaceted shrine. It is there that the true pilgrimage (inward journey) begins and ends, because mind is the cause of both slavery and freedom *(mana eva manuṣ yānām kāraṇam bandha-mokṣayoḥ)*. Hence the various qualities and virtues that adorn the Atman are themselves considered *to be such spiritual shrines. Thus we read in the Skanda Purana that truth (satyam), patience* (kṣama), control of senses *(indriya-nigraha)*, compassion for all beings (sarva-bhūta-dayā), speaking only good of others *(priyavatita)*, saving knowledge *(jñānam)* and austerity *(tapas)* are the sevenfold spiritual shrines.[15] Sadhus and sages are supposed to have acquired these qualities and virtues in their Atman which render them real holy places for those who aspire to have these qualities. That is why Sri Sankaracharya has said long ago that "holiness of the mind is the greatest shrine" (tīrtham *param kim svamanovishudham)*. But much before Sri Sankara, Vyasa Maharshi has said, "Oh, Judhishtir, jump into your own river-mind, which has a bathing place of self-control, water of truthfulness, banks of good character, and waves of compassion."[16] Therefore the very sight of such sages and Rishis is sanctifying for the devotees.

Spirituality of Pilgrimage

In the above paragraphs we have discussed that in the Indian context a sacred shrine is not simply a sanctified place in nature, being associated with the memory of a salvific event or myth. It can also be human person himself/herself, if he/she has attained divine enlightenment which is not only for one's own sake but for the sake of fellow humans. Such a person can worship God not simply in material objects and places outside but inside one's person by continuing to practice the virtues like truthfulness, compassion, patience and so on, as revealed by

Jesus in his dialogue with the Samaritan woman (Cf. Jn 4:21-24). Thus a man/woman and his/her pilgrim act belong centrally to the concept of sacred shrines and pilgrimages. A person makes the pilgrimage or pilgrim act under certain religious convictions and sociological motivations both of which make up the substratum of his/her attitude in this regard, namely his/her spirituality. We shall now analyse the various factors underlying this spirituality.

Symbolic Displacement and the Resulting Change of Heart

Dupront has observed that the pilgrim act constitutes down the centuries and countless cultures and lands one of the moments of the individual or collective religious experience.[17] Now the core of this experience is a spiritual "displacement", a change of heart for better, a conversion in the Christian sense. The physical displacement or turning away from the routine circumstance towards a totally new one works as a stage setting for this turning of heart. The pilgrim leaves his/her home, kith and kin, and sets forth to an unknown, unusual and "extraordinary" place. That place, considered as an "elsewhere" is more a symbol of the divine encounter than a magic spot, a golden opportunity for change and return from there as "another" person. The sociological factor involved in the displacement makes a salutary impact on the religious factor- conversion. The displacement is not merely the action of moving from one place to another, rather it is also an act of returning to the source of one's existence. For, the pilgrim is making for a place where the Divine will be closer and more accessible to him/her since the memory of some event of salvation has charged it with a particular kind of divine presence.[18]

Discovering Fellowship

The pilgrim may well have started alone on his act of pilgrimage, but soon he/she discovers himself/herself participating in a flux which has selected the same sacred shrine. It is also seen that the pilgrim community does not make any social distinctions: classes, professions and sexes merge into a physical unity so that, at the high moments of the pilgrimage, it becomes a communion of souls.[19]And this is particularly significant in India where pilgrimage does away with even the caste barriers, which are often visible in the everyday life. In this sense the pilgrimage act has an exceptional power to introduce the pilgrim to divine forgiveness, enabling him/her to discover human mutuality and fellowship which is both a token and fruit of God's grace of forgiveness (Cf. Mt. 5:24;6:14).

Briefly there is a natural relationship between pilgrimage and conversion. Both entail a break from one's familiar surroundings, a search for peace of grace and forgiveness, and a new sense of brotherhood/sisterhood.

Praying with the Feet

We are here referring to a pilgrim act in the literal sense, namely a pilgrimage by walking and covering a pretty long distance. As in the case of a progressive mental prayer, several hardships and blessings, temptations and consolations, will be met with on the way. To get up and go, you may have to drag yourself up by the feet, and the first steps of the next stage on the way are the hardest, even as the beginners in mental prayer do always experience. Later on certain days at least, your feet pick up speed and lungs draw in great gusts of fresh air and you become quite euphoric; a stoic pleasure seizes you in the intoxication of a crazy marathon, a temptation to forget the noble end of the pilgrimage. There is a similar danger at a certain stage in mental prayer against which St. Theresa Avila has warned. Still more temptations and consolations are ahead. The monotony and boredom of certain days, heavy depression of some evenings, a feeling of inability that one is no more physically fit for walking etc. At other times, especially if you are heading towards a sacred place in nature's lap new attractions will arouse your enthusiasm: Ever new landscapes, flower-valleys, groves discovered on the edges of forests, the song of the lark, the rustle of the bushes, bubbling brooks tumbling down the slopes etc. are sources of this attraction. These can be either stumbling blocks on your way to the goal still ahead, or stepping stones, small graces beckoning towards that goal, which will have their counter parts at a higher state of mental prayer as well.

But be sure, there is the most manifest grace granted to a pilgrim on foot – a simple life style, a life of poverty and penance, and a path of childhood. Simple and plain clothes, claiming to be no person of importance and standing on the common level of the other vagrants one meets on the way, the pilgrim discovers that the world contains many other valuable things and knowledgeable persons, all, at least as interesting as one's highly qualified colleagues of one's usual habitat. Simultaneously one becomes also a poor person, a person of hunger and thirst, sometimes worried about shelter at evening fall and about the inclemency of the weather. Besides, he/ she is a "suffering person", being unable to speak the local languages. Needless to say, by this time the pilgrim will have learned the path of childhood, namely total trust in the One, for whom he/she is walking and whose hand he/she sometimes feels, he is holding as he/she continues the journey.[20]

All these are indeed great fruits of elevated mental prayer But the pilgrim's prayer with the feet has this uniqueness that in it not only the mind and heart but the whole body, the feet in particular, turns into ecstasy at the end of it, the goal of the pilgrimage, even as the strenuous earlier steps in the Yogic prayer ends up in Samadhi.

Relentless Quest for Liberation

The pilgrim act in India is a powerful symbol of a continuous search of humans for God and for liberation (*mukti*). The pilgrim makes his/her own the cry of the sages of old: "Lead me from the unreal to the Real; lead me from darkness to Life; lead me from death to Immortality."(BU 1.3.28) on his/her way to the goal, as the search for sakshatkara (realization) continues. Every step forward to the sacred shrine symbolizes a step closer to the Divine centre within oneself.[21] Thus the spiritual quest of the yogi to discover the Atman in the "interior castle" or the "cave of the heart" through single-minded attention and meditation cutting across the various body-sheaths (koshah) may be likened to the relentless onward march of the pilgrim overcoming all the barriers on the way to the goal, be it the source of the Ganges (Gangotri) in the Himalayas or the Ayyappa sannidhi in Shabari- mala, Kerala.

Harmony with Nature

Another important trait of pilgrimage, especially in India is that it is aimed at enabling the pilgrim to attain inner harmony with the whole nature, with the totality of Reality in its threefold dimension – God-Human-World. It is not for nothing that all the key centres of pilgrimage are located in nature sanctuaries – mountains, rivers, forests etc. All forms of life – bees and birds, buds and nuts, leaves and flowers, tree-branches and grass-blades, bubbling brooks and roaring torrents, softening dews and blinding fogs, mellow autumns and fragrant springs and so on – all appear in turn according to the seasons so functionally set in motion with the principle of mutuality and rhythm. Indian spirituality in general insists that it is a matter of real insight to recognize this beautiful nature's setting and cosmic order which the Lord of creation n has established to make human life happy and elevated. Our habitat is the cosmic context of our life's setting. And so in the Indian perspective the experience of unity of our life with that of our habitat is the first step towards God-realization.[22]

The pilgrim centres in India are such that humans, if they would, could enter into this harmony with nature and thus discover the presence of God. What the "mountain sage", the late swamy Abhishiktananda writes, recalling his experience during his pilgrimage to Gangotri speaks volumes for this truth. He says: "All along the way is it not OM which wells up in his [pilgrim's] heart, as it wells up from the river, the mountain, the forest, and from every living being met on the way? This OM which breaks forth from the roar of the Ganges, from the rustling of the leaves, from the twittering of the birds, and echoes indefinitely across the sheer cliff-faces, is the OM which wells up in the pilgrim's heart like an infinite echo repeating itself, increasing and finally merging into the primordial OM in the silence in which everything is said."[23]

The Practice of the Great Muslim Pilgrimage – Hajj

Although Hajj is not a pilgrimage to a place in India, we shall say a word about it because of its universal importance for a considerable number of people in India and elsewhere. Hajj, i.e. pilgrimage to Mecca, is the fifth pillar of Islam[24], and so it is the duty of every Muslim under certain conditions, to undertake the pilgrimage once in his life time. Similar to the preparations of the Hindu devotee before starting the pilgrimage to Shabarimala, a Hajj pilgrim too has to make material as well as spiritual preparations. Besides, on reaching the holy place one has to perform a number of ritual acts to perform for the completion of the pilgrimage.[25]

It can be seen that Hajj is a remarkable synthesis of sacred and secular, old and new. The pilgrimage is important for the individual as well as the whole community. It is a source of unity, solidarity, and a manifestation of the international character of Islam. For the pilgrims it is a wonderful experience of union of millions of believers from different races and cultures, an experience which they will cherish all their lives. When a pilgrim goes back home as a Hajj, he receives a new dignity and status in the community, and the fellowship of thousands becomes a fellowship of millions as they recount to neighbours what they have seen and experienced all through the pilgrimage.

Some Extreme Penitential Rites and Questionable Expressions of Devotion in Pilgrim Centres

For all world religions, pilgrimage itself is an act of penance, in addition to other good motives. Pilgrims take upon themselves various forms of penances which varied from culture to culture, from time to time, religion to religion, and region to region. Spirituality of the pilgrim's way, notwithstanding its many valuable aspects we have discussed above, is not also completely devoid of certain dubious traits and practices. Whereas some practices can be understood as genuine expressions of faith in God's goodness and penitential acts for one's sins and moral failures, others may well be judged as signs of craziness to obtain merits and favours which the pilgrim tries to count based on his /her acts of piety. For example, throwing oneself down and kissing the ground as one catches sight of the holy city of Varanasi, taking the dust from the wheels of Lord Jagannath's car at Puri and placing it on the head with signs of intense joy, shouting with joy as one gets the *darsan* of the Ganga at Rishikesh or Haridwar or of the *triveni sangam* at Prayaga – these can well belong to the first category of practices. Similarly the Ayyappa devotees of South India have a rigorous period of penance of 41 days during which they practice various kinds of abstinences. It is for them a period of prayer, introspection and self-purification hoping to get a *darsan* of Lord Ayyappa on the day of Makara-Shankranti.[26]

On the contrary, there are also some extreme forms of penance: Some Sadhus are said to practice ritual murder and prostitution, hook swinging and flagellation, noon-day sun-gazing till the eye-sight is lost, eating corpse and bathing in glaciers, etc. which seem to be motivated by egoistic desire to control nature and gain fame and glory. Thurston is said to have noted that some of the Vaishnavites and Madhavites had the custom of branding the emblem of their sect on their shoulders, and of piercing the tongue and cheeks with tiny silver spears called vel.[27] Evidently such practices will belong to the second category mentioned above. Similarly, some people travel for kilometres by measuring their body-length on the ground: They lie down and stretch their hands beyond their heads, and having made a mark by their hands, they would get up and place their toes against the mark, and again stretch themselves on the ground until they reach the pilgrim spot and/ or are dead tired. This practice also will belong to the second category. Multiplying acts of penance and physical suffering has no value unless they are genuine expressions of faith, love, sorrow for sins etc. Pilgrimage of this sort is not worth the name. It degenerates into bargaining and bartering with God in which there is least sentiments of faith and divine province.

Relevance of Christian Pilgrimages in India

We have seen that India is a land of pilgrim centres and pilgrimages. It is in these centres that Hinduism is really alive. Their role in making Hindus somewhat united and Hinduism truly a religion of the mass (not simply of the elite) cannot be exaggerated, because it is a religion sociologically less organized and it believes more in orthopraxis than orthodoxy. This context of India is a valid reason for us to accept the reality of Christian pilgrimage here and to improve its witnessing quality. In this respect, the idea that not only sacred places but also liberated persons and genuine values in life are pilgrim centres (*tirtha's*) needs to be emphasized in Christian pilgrimages. Moreover, it is quite desirable that at least some central Christian shrines in India be situated in nature sanctuaries of rivers, mountains and thick forests.

Besides, a biblical overview will show that the concept of pilgrimage outlines the trunk and branches of the Judeo-Christian tradition. Needless to say, Israel was a pilgrim people and Yahweh a Pilgrim-God. The invitation to Abraham to "leave everything ......" (Gen 12:1-4) takes later in the Exodus the form of liberation. The pilgrim-God comes down to deliver the oppressed people and to lead them to a place of freedom and peace (Ex. 3:7-8). If the Old Testament (the Torah and the Prophets) laid the foundation of the pilgrim faith, Jesus in his life time remarkably reveals its full significance. He is indeed the pilgrim par excellence, not only because he had "nowhere to lay his head" (Lk 9:58), but because we find Jesus constantly travelling to and fro between Judea and Galilee with the long ascent to the holy city, but especially because of the words of Jesus himself, "I came from the Father and have come into the world, and now I leave the world to go to the Father (John 16:23).

In this connection it is to be remembered that the true nature of the Eucharist, which 'makes the Christian community,' cannot be grasped without resorting to the concept of pilgrimage. In fact the Eucharist was born as the high point of a pilgrimage. At that time Jerusalem was full of the Passover pilgrims who had come to celebrate the memory of another pilgrimage, the Exodus, as we have seen above. And Jesus himself had come up to Jerusalem as a pilgrim for the feast of the Passover. In fact this "pilgrim's way runs through the whole of Luke's Gospel and Last Supper is the high point of this journey (cf. Lk. 22:8). All exegetes agree that during that fare well supper Jesus instituted the Eucharist in a Paschal context (if not on the Passover feast day); Jesus instituted his Passover.[28] Thus for Christians the Eucharist is the memorial of that supreme pilgrimage which associates us with Jesus' perfect pilgrimage carried to infinity (Cf. Jn. 16:28; 17:8, 11). It is to be seen as the unique pilgrimage in which we are invited to follow him celebrating the Eucharist and undergoing all the hardships of the "wilderness" to the Promised Land.

Summary and critical remarks

We have seen that in India the idea of pilgrimage/pilgrim centre (tirtham) is much deeper than we usually understands it. We have also seen that the pilgrimage spirituality carries with it certain laudable traits, like conversion of heart, fellowship experience, quest for God- realization, harmony with nature etc. Besides, we have noted that in view of the great importance of pilgrim places in Hindu tradition, the Church in India shall not only appreciate the existing practice of pilgrimage to centres like Velankanni, Malayattoor, Little Mount (Chennai), Sardhana etc., but also take steps to raise it from the present condition and improve its witness value in India. Finally we have also seen that a biblical overview of both the Old and New Covenants amply testifies that Christianity, root and branches, is a pilgrim community with Jesus as the Supreme Pilgrim, and that the Eucharist is the heavenly meal of this pilgrim community heading towards that Promised Land.

Whereas some penitential rites and practices can be understood as genuine expressions of faith in God's goodness and acts of penance for one's sins and moral failures, others may well be judged as signs of craziness to obtain merits and favours from gods. There are also some extreme forms of penance: Some Sadhus are said to practice ritual murder and prostitution, hook swinging and flagellation, noon-day sun-gazing till the eye-sight is lost, eating corpse and bathing in glaciers, etc. which seem to be motivated by egoistic desire to control nature and gain fame and glory. Surely these latter types have no place in any genuine pilgrimages.

For a Christian therefore the pilgrimage becomes something more than an edifying exercise in piety. Participating in the pilgrimage, a Christian expresses in a new way the essence of his/her life and affirms his/her longing to walk in the footsteps of the pilgrim-God. According to the Gospels a Christian disciple is the one who risks everything to follow Christ (Mt. 10: 28ff). The life of a baptized person is a continual passing from death to life (Rom. 6:4), his/her home land is now in heaven (Ph. 3:20); he/she is citizen of another Kingdom (Col.1:13) and so he/she lives as a pilgrim in this world (I Pt. 2:11),[29] doing everything looking beyond this phenomenal world to eternity.

Endnotes

[1] A. Stuart, "Pilgrimage and Holy Places", *in Religious Hinduism*, by Jesuit Scholars, (St. Pauls: Allahabad-Mumbai), 1964, p.141.

[2] Monier-Williams defines it as, "a passage", "a way", "road", "Ford", "Bathing Place", "Place of pilgrimage on the Banks of sacred streams", etc.

[3] Cf. Swami Vikrant, Indian Spirituality, (Arumbu Publications: Chennai), 2009, pp.104-117.

[4] These are the motives: 1. Burial places and memorials as pilgrimage sites, 2. Pilgrimage to living persons, 3. Pilgrimage as an ascetic way of life, 4. Pilgrimage of intercession (healing etc.), 6. Pilgrimage of devotion, 7. Pilgrimage of penance, and 8. Pilgrimage for procuring relics. (cited in Swamy Vikrant, op.cit. p.112).

[5] *Tarati pāpādikam yasmāt tat tīrtham.* Cf. Ramakrishnan Pillai, Hindudharma Parichayam (Malayalam), Ramakrishna Ashram: Trichur, 1969, p.314.

[6] Strictly speaking, only the first 24 sages, including Siddhartha are considered Tirthankaras, but in the Digambara Jain tradition, Arhats also are considered Tirthankaras.

[7] Cf. Two Pilgrims on the Way, *The Mountain of the Lord*, (CLS: Bangalore (translation by Murray Rogers), 1966, pp.29-30.

[8] These images and myths of the sacred trees are connected with the Vedic conception of the origin of the universe or the God-world relationship. The important Vedic texts concerned are RV 1.24.7; AV 10.7; Ka.Up.6.1; Bh.G.15.1. Two of the important studies are H. Aguilar, *The Sacrifice in the Rigveda*, (Bharatiya Vidya Prakashan: Delhi-Varanasi), 1976, esp. ch. 5; and E.O James, *The Tree of Life*, (Brill: Leiden), 1966, ch.5.

[9] These four places of Kumbhamela are Nasik, Prayaga, Ujjain and Haridwar. In each place the *mela* takes for a month at least. And the time of celebration for each place is fixed according to the zodiacal signs. Cf. *Srikshetre Nasik-Pancavati-Godamahatmya*, (Sanskrit- Hindi), (Vignan Mudralay: Nasik), 1968.

[10] Cf. A Stuart, op.cit., p.142.

[11] Cf. http://www.pilgrimagetourinindia.com/buddhiist.htm, accessed on 1/31/2012.

[12] Cf. http://www.pilgrimageinindia.com/churches-india.htm, accessed on 1/31/21012.

[13] http//www.tourmyindia.com, accessed on 6/24/2018.

[14] http// on line see Ma Bambleshwari accessed on 26 June 2018.

[15] Cf. Parameswaran Pillai, op.cit., p.319.

[16] *Atmā nadī samyama-punya-tīrthā satyodakā sīlatadā dayormih, Tatrāvagāham kuru panduputra, n vārina shudyati cāntarātm* (Ibid.)

[17] Cf. His article "pelerinage" in *Dictionnaire des religions*, Ed. By Paul Poupard, PUF, 1984.

[18] Cf. F. Bourdeau, "Pilgrimage, Eucharist and Reconciliation" in Lumen Vitae, 39(1984), No.4, pp.400-407. Whereas in the secularized Christian West the contemporary significance of pilgrimage is to be seen against the cultural and socio-economic infra-structures, in the Non-Christian East, especially India, pilgrimage is still principally a religious act, not much affected by the benefits or by the constraints of an affluent society.

[19] A. Durpont, art. Cit. p.1302.

[20] E.R. Lambade, "Praying with the Feet" in *Lumen Vitae*, cit., pp.432-441. Many of these experiences of a genuine pilgrim have been confirmed by one friend in Rishikesh, Fr. Stephen SJ who most recently made such a pilgrimage to the holy shrine of Gangotri-Gomukh.

[21] Cf. Two Pilgrims on the Way, op.cit. p.14.

[22] T. Manickam, "Yoga: A Sadhana for Harmony of Life in D.S. Amalorpavadas ed. *Indian Christian Spirituality*, (NBCLC: Bangalore), 1982, pp.178-182.

[23] Two Pilgrims on the Way, op.cit. p.16.

[24] The five pillars of Islam are 1. Profession of absolute monotheism (*Shahadat*), 2. Ritual Prayer (*Salat* in Arabic and *Namaz* in Persian) five times a day, 3. Almsgiving (*Zakat*), 4. Fasting (*Roza*) in the month of Ramazan, and 5. Hajj – Pilgrimage to Mecca. See. Paul Jackson, Ed. The Muslims of India : Beliefs and Practices, (TPI: Bangalore), 2001, pp.2-35.

[25] Ibid. pp.26-34.

[26] *Census of India*, 1901, Travancore Report, Part I, p. quoted in Swami Vikrant, op.cit. p.113.

[27] Thurston, *Castes and Tribes of India*, vol.V, p.399.quoted in Swami Vikrant, op.cit. p.113.

[28] Cf. F. Bourdeau, op.cit. pp.394-400.

[29] Brother John, "The Pilgrimage seen through the Bible", in *Lumen Vitae*, ibid. pp.380-93.

Chapter 3

Liberative Potential
of Christian Worship Symbols

Introduction

In this presentation the word 'symbol' is used in a comprehensive sense: It may stand for an object (object-symbol), like water, light, flower etc., it may also stand for an action/gesture (action-symbol) like washing, blessing, offering, bowing etc. Further it may refer to any ritual narration of a salvation-event which makes present that event again in a certain sense.[1]

Meaning of Christian Symbol

One may ask what is meant by Christian symbol? Are not symbols products of human experiences, more related to culture than to cult and religion? But we also know that etymologically cult and culture are related.[2] Besides, these questions cannot be properly answered without discussing the intimate relationship of cult and worship in any religion.

Now, worship may be said to be the active phase of religion as made manifest in rite and cult.[3] It involves reverence and honour paid to God, gods, saints sacred things etc. by means of devotional words and objects, gestures and postures, namely by means of symbols in general. Evidently worship can be either individual or communal, and this latter one is very much a social experience taking place at definite time and place, using a set of well-defined rituals.[4]

The form of worship in common should reflect the culture of the worshipping community, because both culture and cult or worship have a common basis in symbols. First of all symbols are not arbitrarily made, but spontaneously emerge out of life according to the felt needs of a people and their experience of life,[5] and clusters of such symbols give expression to a culture. Both cult and culture are means of communication and communion, Liberation and freedom. In both cases it is symbols that mediate between humans, and between human and God.

As it is well known, religion, whatever be its concrete form, is a major factor in the integral development of any culture. But, unlike culture, religion more easily cuts across regional boundaries and barriers, receiving new members into its fold and expands over many cultures.

From the above discussion it follows that Christian worship symbols are products of different cultures through which Christianity has spread and in which it has taken root, making these cultural expressions or symbols means of communication and union. Besides, it is through cultural adaptations that the Christian people have attained freedom and liberation from the enslaving crass ritualism of some communities. Of the many such Christian symbols, some may be called universal, in the sense that they are culturally invariant, e.g. symbols of water, light/fire with respect to their symbolic meaning in worship, whereas some others may be considered as particular, in the sense they refer only to particular socio-cultural context, for example, bowing (*pranam*), folding hands (*anjali-hasta*), use of oil-lamp (*bhadra-deepa*) in the Indian Christian worship. Moreover, if there is a symbol unique to Christianity, it is the Cross. It is unique, not only because of its universality, but also because it directly refers to the foundational event of Christianity, viz, the crucifixion of Christ. Further it may be noted that in their external ritual expressions, the Christian symbols, especially the particular ones, will have much in common with other religious symbols of a given place, because the culture of a place will be influenced to a greater extent by the pre-dominant religion of the place as well.[6]

Sources of Early Christian Symbols

In our attempt to understand the relevance and significance of common sharing in worship, a historical overview of our worship symbols will hopefully shed more light. In general three sources or provenances of these symbols may be noted. 1. Jewish religion, 2. Roman secular culture and 3. 'Pagan' religious cult

Jewish Religion

With regard to Christianity's debt to Judaism in its liturgical development, Louis Bouyer makes this general comment:

> To imagine that Christian liturgy sprang up from a sort of spontaneous generation, motherless and fatherless, like Melechiedek is from the start to reduce all reconstructions to a more or less scholarly, more or less ingenuous mass of misconception. Just as Christianity itself is an off-shoot, however fresh that be, of Judaism, so too Christian liturgy, however original it be, is very much the product of its Jewish antecedents.[7]

Several feasts of the Christian liturgical year bear the mark of the Jewish calendar. It was on the 'first day of the week' of the

Jewish calendar that the Lord rose from the dead (Mk 16:2 &lls). Gradually Sunday superseded the Jewish Sabbath completely as the weekly day of worship. In the Jewish understanding of the week, the first day commemorated creation and this symbolism was taken over by Christians. "We assemble on the day of the sun, because it is the first day, that on which God transformed the darkness and matter to create the world, and also because Jesus Christ our Saviour rose from the dead on the dame day" (Justin, *I Apology* 67). Moreover Easter, the only Christian feast based on the lunar calendar has absorbed many ancient motifs of the Jewish Passover festival. On the eve of Easter the blessing of light stems ultimately from the Jewish blessing of the lamp on the eve of the Sabbath. Similarly the feast of Pentecost is derived from the Jewish feast of Seven Weeks (Tob. 2:1) from the feast of Unleavened Bread to that of First Fruits, to which Tertulliam makes reference.[8]

Further Jewish influence is more readily visible in the case of Eastern Church architecture, iconography, liturgical texts etc. The ancient Syrian churches with Bema and with opaque curtain before the sanctuary to symbolize earth and heaven during the liturgical celebrations is a transposition of the Jewish synagogue setting with its "chair of Moses" in the midst of the people, and the "holy of holies" where the *Shekina* (Divine Presence) was supposed to reside. The earliest liturgical documents like the *Didache*, Justine's Apology, Apostolic Constitutions etc. bear the marks of Jewish textual borrowings and assimilations.

Roman Secular Culture

Ever since the famous 'Edict of Milan' of emperor Constantine in the year 313 C.E. granting to Christians full freedom of religion and worship, the Church came out in public from private houses and catacombs, and began to enter into a closer relationship secular culture. The very name basilica, "royal building" (palace) was given to colossal and magnificent structures or places of worship, worthy of an emperor. In doing so Christianity was continuing the existing 'pagan' tradition of the basilica-type of worship-place, accommodating its liturgy to the given context.

Imperial court ceremonial was a rich source from which after Constantine's 'conversion' and rejection of claims to divine honours, various customs and ceremonial practices flowed into the Christian liturgy.[9] Some symbolic gestures of the secular society, adopted by the Church into her liturgy may be noted.[10]

Pagan/Non-Christian Religious Culture

When Christianity in Europe was only a tiny vessel in the vast ocean of non-Christian religious culture for the first three centuries, all efforts were to avoid contact with 'pagan' worship forms. But afterwards in the 4th-5th centuries, when 'paganism' no longer held sway and the danger of non-Christian interpretatio0n of symbols and rites used was either eliminated or at least minimized we find a change in the attitude of the Church towards 'paganism and its worship forms. Consequently several of the Pre-Christian rites and symbols, re-christened find their way into the Church's worship forms:

Symbolism connected to the Eastern direction during prayer and worship

Most civilized people of the ancient world – the Greeks, the Romans and so on – considered the East as the place of life, warmth, power and happiness, and therefore turned eastward while praying. Towards the end of the third century the sun-cult began to spread rapidly in the Roman Empire, and emperor Aurelian imported it to Rome from the Orient and declared the SOL INVICTUS, "Unconquerable Sun" as the god of the empire. In such a situation the early Church Fathers thought it meaningful to present sun as the powerful symbol of Christ, the "light of the world" (Jn 8:12; cf. Lk 1:78f & elsewhere) and so encouraged people to turn to the East during liturgy.[11]

Symbolism connected with giving milk and honey in baptism.
In the pre-Christian practice it meant incorporation into the family and warding off demons. It was adopted into the early Church in connection with Infant baptism. For Christians it signified the ancient custom of the agape meal during Eucharistic celebration.

Another important 'pagan' rite that found its way into the Christian liturgy is connected with the burial of the dead.
The present Christian practice of mourning for 3, 7, 9, 30 or 40 days after death of the beloved ones, go back to pre-Christian traditions, especially of the Orient. The main reason for this observance in the antiquity among 'pagans' was the belief that the soul lingers about the body for some more days latest until 40 days. Christianity christened this belief, giving it a new meaning associating it with Christ's resurrection (3-day observance) and with Ascension (40-day observance). Thus the dead may be helped any of these days so that they follow the same path of Christ.[12]

Content and Dynamism of Christian Symbols

It is common knowledge that the relationship between a symbol and the reality behind it is not static but very dynamic. Symbol is reality itself in some concrete mode of existence and no symbol is fully itself except as manifestation of some reality.[13] Therefore any symbol can be a point of encounter with reality as such, namely God. And in a broad sense everything in this visible world – things, events and persons, can be symbols of this divine-human meeting. Needless to say, in the humanity of Jesus there was a visible realization of the divinity, a unique instance of symbol's becoming fully reality itself. That is why Edward Schillebeeckx says," In the dialogue between God and man[sic], so often breaking down, there was found at last a perfect human respondent; in the same person there was achieved the perfection both of divine invitation and of the human response in faith from the man who by his resurrection is the Christ."[14]

Christ is thus the *Ursakrament* or Primordial Symbol, the source and summit of all symbols and hence of all Christian sacraments and rites. The significance of Christian symbols is enhanced by their essential relationship to the unique Symbol-Reality, viz Jesus Christ, the Primordial Sacrament. Hence the major Christian sacraments and worship symbols may be seen as inseparable from the whole salvation plan of God in word and deed. As symbols impart or give us at least a glimpse of reality itself, this is more so in the cases of the major symbols called sacraments. For, "sacrament is a divine bestowal of salvation in an outwardly perceptible form which makes the bestowal manifest, a bestowal of salvation in historical visibility."[15] In the Christian sacrament of the Eucharist, this divine bestowal of salvation reaches its climax, symbol and reality being identified. In a similar way, every other Christian symbol or worship form will also do this divine bestowal in so far as it is related to the Eucharistic mystery, to Jesus Christ[16] ultimately.

Common Sharing in Inter-religious Worship

Cult or religious worship is neither something merely external and social, nor purely internal and spiritual; it embraces both these aspects uniting in itself the external and the internal, the physical and spiritual. That means, symbols are essential for religious worship, but no living religion can have exclusive symbols. In fact, a lot of common sharing in the field of worship is in the nature of things. Looking back at the history of Christian worship, we see that there has been a lot of such sharing with other cultures and religions on the level of symbols and signs. Jesus himself for whom worship was mainly spiritual in as much as it should consist in offering one's whole life to God or as worship offered to God in spirit and truth (Jn. 4:24), subjected himself to important Jewish ritual worship, like baptism from John at Jordan (Mk. 1:9) fasting in the desert (Mt 4:2), taking part in common festivals enjoined by Jewish law (Lk. 22:7f; Lk. 2:41f; Jn. 2:13 f).

While drawing on the parental form of worship, he gave new meaning and interpretation to the rite, he adopted from Judaism. A typical example in the institution of the Eucharist at the Last Supper which shows both continuity and break with the Jewish Paschal meal. Similarly Jesus' baptism at Jordan in contrast to the Jewish rite of ablusion may be considered as another example. This principle was later followed by the nascent Church, when it began to give shape to its own mode of worship. Profound Jewish influence on the early Christian prayer-forms is a well-accepted fact and it continued for some time. During the same period the Church was very negative in its approach to the worship forms of other religions for reasons we have noted earlier. Later on when the persecution ended, she began to look at the cultural values and worship forms of the surrounding religions with greater serenity and so more non-biblical and Hellenistic elements of thought influenced the interpretation of Christian liturgy and worship in general.

It is common knowledge that the Church adopted or borrowed from the religious cultures around the various rites, sacramental signs, customs and feasts. Cardinal Newmann discusses this at length in his famous book, *An Essay on the Development of Christian Doctrine.*[17] Commenting on this classical work of Newmann, the late Cardinal Parecattil says:

> Newmann shows that right from the beginning Christianity was polemical, but at the same time eclectic and unitive. It had the power, while keeping its own identity, of absorbing its antagonists, of incorporating them into itself, without being dissolved into them. In spite of the numberless influences to which Christianity exposed, it remained substantially in tact all through the centuries. At the same time it purified, transformed and took into itself the many coloured beliefs, forms of worship, codes of duty and schools of thought through which it was moving.[18]

Christian rites and symbols of various kinds connected with worship are to a great extent the result of direct and indirect borrowing from the cultures around. With regard to this point, Newmann himself notes:

> In the early stages of Christianity the use of temples and those dedicated to particular saints and ornamented on occasions with branches of trees, incense, lamps and candles, votive offerings on recovery from illness, holy water, asylums, holidays and seasons, use of calendars, processions, blessings on the fields, sacerdotal vestments, the tonsure, the ring in marriage, turning to the east, images at a later date, perhaps the ecclesiastical chant and the *Kyrie Eleison* - all these are of pagan origin, and are sanctified by their adoption into the Church.[19]

Moreover, Newmann, quoting of the 5th century C.E, explains the methodology of this process: "For the Pandian festival,...............we have the feasts of Peter, Paul and Thomas...... and of other martyrs; and for the old world and indecency of work and word are held modest festivities without intemperance or revel or laughter, but with divine hymns and attendance on holy discourses and prayers, adorned with laudable fears."[20] The story of civilization as told by Will Durant in his famous book under the same caption, has much to inform us about this give-and take, this religio-cultural osmosis down the centuries. Therefore Durant holds strongly that,

> when Christianity conquered Rome, the ecclesiastical pagan Church, the title and the vestments of the pontifex maximus, the worship of the Great Mother and a multitude of comforting divinities........and the pageantry of immemorable ceremony passed like maternal blood into the new religion, and captive Rome captured her conqueror.[21]

This dynamic process of cultural adaptation and religious dialogue by which the early church was able to grow steadily sharing and communicating through proper cultural symbols, grew weaker and weaker in the Middle Ages, when the above statement of Durant" Captive Rome captured her conqueror" became literally true. All that was Roman was now considered Christian; and all that was Christian was considered Roman to the exclusion of other cultures, ritual Churches and liturgical traditions. This Romanization and centralization policy of the Church saw its climax later in the Council of Trent. What is interesting to note is the way, the non-Roman cultural currents and worship-forms reacted in this development. We find an attempt to translate the Roman original to the religious culture and the temperament of the people. This is what happened to the simple, austere and sober Roman rite when it "migrated" to the land of the Franco-Germanic people during the 8th century: The prayer-texts, once direct and brief were adorned with a flourish, approaching verbosity, and rituals and symbolic gestures, once austere and simple, were enhanced by dramatic elements and elaborate ceremonials.[22]

In this process we may find a kind of theological impoverishment of the original material. At the same time we find in it also a spontaneous and necessary attempt to make liturgy relevant to the context, translating it into proper symbols of the cultural ethos of the non-Roman Northerners. The new culture of the Northerners endowed it with a freshness and vitality which Rome did not hesitate to appropriate in the 10th century when the new rite in its hybrid form returned to Rome as Romano-Franco-Germanic liturgy. During the later Middle Ages (also called autumn of the Middle Ages) dramatization in the liturgy continued to flourish Liturgical plays revolved around the Christmas story, Holy Week, Corpus Christi and the Blessed Virgin Mary. Some of the liturgical symbols in this development were the Christmas star that moved through the nave of the church to the crib at the sanctuary during the Gloria of the Midnight Mass, heart-rending scenes of the Passion plays, meeting of Jesus and his mother at Easter dawn before Mass etc. While drama should never replace liturgical catechesis and mystegogy, sometimes cultural exigencies may demand the revival of dramatic elements in the liturgy, e.g. dance and the use of drums in Tribal liturgies.

At the same time, if such dramatic elements do not help deepen people's understanding of the liturgy, while stealing their attention away from it, these elements may not be tolerated. This was the case with the liturgy and worship of the Baroques, as reported by Jungmann:

> Because aesthetic considerations began to hold sway, the liturgy was not only submerged under this ever growing art but actually suppressed, so that even at this time there were festive occasions which might best be described as church concerts with liturgical accompaniments.[23]

The result was a mighty façade of external forms - symbols and rituals-behind a vast emptiness.

One of the important concerns of Vat.II in its program of liturgical reform was directed against this unwholesome development over several centuries after the Council of Trent.

Therefore Vast II decreed" The rites should be distinguished by a noble simplicity; they should be short, clear and unencumbered by useless repetitions; they should be within the people's powers of comprehension, and normally should not require much explanation."(SC 34). Only such simple Christian liturgies in which local cultural expressions will have due place, will be able to cope with the exigencies of "communicatio *in sacris*" or common sharing in worship.

Concluding Critical Remarks

The foregoing discussion of the pre-Christian sources, history and inspiration behind the Christian worship symbols concern largely the early Church with its own religio-cultural back ground. As for what concerns the Indian Church it has to learn from the above historical experience of the early Church and take necessary steps to provide guidelines in matters of liturgical common sharing in the multi-cultural and pluri-religious context of India. As a first step in this direction the undivided CBCI, soon after the historic national seminar on "Church in India Today" of the year 1969, had strongly recommended the 12-point programme of liturgical inculturation, as approved by the Holy See.[24]

A related field of common sharing in worship is that of liturgical art of painting, music, dance and other sacred art forms. Soon after the Council and under its impact, Indian style holy pictures, mural paintings, window-grill designs of chapels etc. were produced by Christian artists in India, like Sr. Genevieve, Sr. Clare, Fr. Joy CMI, Mr. Jyoti Sahi and others. Similarly Bhajan-songs, liturgical dance (classical and popular/ Tribal) were increasingly introduced in Christian worship, although in recent years the Council's clarion call for up-dating of the Church in general and liturgical inculturation in particular seems to have taken a back seat.

Now, a basic question to be asked with respect to this sharing in symbols – forms of music, art & architecture, gestures and postures etc., of Indian cultures and religions is this: Can we simply restrict the sharing to the outward form or external style of the symbol concerned? For example, for us Indians representation of Jesus in Indian art forms would mean so much, because we are familiar with Indians, not with Palestinians, Africans or Europeans. And yet creative artists think that this is a very imperfect way of understanding the implications of inculturation and hence of the question of common sharing in worship.[25]

Here lies the crux of the problem when we think seriously about sharing in Hindu worship symbols, namely, can we go deeply into their inner symbolic vision? Is this vision in harmony with the Christian vision of reality? To what extent does the incarnational self-emptying of Jesus offer at once a challenge and an ideal in this crucial connection between form and content, when we consider the question of sharing in the worship of other religions? One safer approach in this matter seems to be this: We may surely accept those symbols of Hindu (non-Christian) religious worship which are also part of the social culture of the people. Action-symbols of welcoming, offering, praying etc. and object-symbols of incense, water, fire/light etc. belong to this category. For the same reason, replacing the symbol of the Cross (Christianity) with that of OM (Hinduism) in any art form may be avoided.

Endnotes

[1] For example, the rite of the Passion Narrative from the Gospel of John on Good Friday.

[2] See Introduction pp.1-2.

[3] Encyclopaedia of Religion and Ethics, Vol XII, under "worship."

[4] Cf. A. Pushparajan, "The Christian Perspective of Worship and Culture" Journal of Dharma 3(1978)373-94.

[5] For example, take the colour yellow in Philippines: When Benigno Aquino was murdered in Manila in 1983, he was wearing a yellow shirt. From then on an already existing powerful movement for justice among the people almost spontaneously adopted yellow as the symbol of freedom...........Cf. Gerard A. Arbuckle, "Communicating through Symbols", Human Development, 8(1987)7-10.

[6] This is one major reason why often inculturation in India appears to be Hinduization; we shall speak more about it later.

[7] Eucharist, Notredame, 1968, p.15.

[8] Cf. Ch. Jones et.al, ed., The Study of Liturgy, London, 1978, p.411.

[9] Cf. J.A. Jungmann, The Early Liturgy, London, 1980, pp.129f.

[10] Kissing as a sign of greeting and welcome/incorporation into the community of the secular culture was adopted for Christians immediately after baptism. Kissing also as a sign of reverence/homage in the antiquity towards holy objects/persons was adopted into the Church thus the priest kisses the altar in the beginning and at the end of the services. Similarly, The Latin expression ITE MISSA EST said earlier at the end of the Holy Eucharist is also a custom derived from the ancient Roman culture: "Go, this is the dismissal" was said at the end of any public function, to announce the dismissal of the gathering, after the session of the court or religious service. See Jungmann op.cit. pp.128-29.

[11] Other reasons for the importance of the Orient (East) may be noted: The picture of Paradise painted in the Genesis story stands in the East (Gen 2:8); the angel of the Lord in the Apocalypse comes from ab ortu solis, "from the place of the sun" (7: 2), as Jesus called himself "light of the world", people applied to him passages about light and sun(Lk 1:78f) moreover in the OT Malachi speaks about the Sol Justitiae (4: 2). See Jungmann ibid. pp.133-13).

[12] Cf. Jungmann, ibid. pp.141-143.

[13] Cf. Louis Malieckal, "Symbolism in Hindu Worship", Journal of Dharma, 9(1984)261-73 (266).

[14] *Christ the Sacrament of our Encounter with God*, New York, 1963, p.13.

[15] Ibid. p.15.

[16] Cf. Louis Malieckal, op.cit. pp.261-71.

[17] J.H. Newmann, *An Essay on the Development of Christian Doctrine*, London, 1914.

[18] Cardinal Parecattil, "Paganism in Christianity" Convocation Address, Alwaye Pontifical Seminary, # Dec. 1974.

[19] Newmann, op.cit. chapter VIII, p.373 above.

[20] Ibid. p.376.

[21] Will Durant, *Caesar and Christ*, New York, pp.671-72.

[22] For a description of the earlier form according to Roman genius, see Edmund Bishop, "The Genius of the Roman Rite" *Liturgia Historica*, Oxford, 1918, pp.1-9.

[23] Jungmann, *Mass of the Roman Rite*, N. York, 1961,p.112see also Jungmann, "Liturgical Life in the Baroque Period", in *Pastoral Liturgy*, pp.80-101.

[24] For the said 12 points of "adaptation" (inculturation), their explanation and careful implementation see D.S. Amalorpavadas Ed. Towards Indigenization in the Liturgy, NBCLC, Bangalore (not dated), pp.31ff.

[25] Jyoti Sahi, for example holds: "This approach ignores the real connection between inner and outer, between form and content. Forms are not just indifferent. They arise organically out of an inner content; what is said is very closely connected with how it is said.......Experientially I became more and more conscious of the fact that Indian images point to an Indian experience and an Indian spiritual vision. The form has led me to the content." (See Jyoti Sahi, Stepping Stones, Bangalore, 1986, p. 2. Speaking further about the intimate relationship between form and content he adds: " ....What is inner to experience has its natural expression in external form......I feel, we cannot just approach Indian culture as if it were an ensemble of visible forms and practices which the Christian can take from and apply to his own faith expression regardless of the inner experience of Hinduism." (Ibid. p.4).

Chapter 4

Liberative Potential
of Religious Rituals

Introduction

Ever since human life appeared on the face of the earth and humans began to be overwhelmed by the overarching might of the powers of nature like roaring seas, deafening lightning-thunders and earth quakes, ferocious wild animals of the 'black forests' etc. fear and trembling gripped them and they began to brood over the possibility of a supreme power, hidden behind these explosive phenomena, which need to be acknowledged and made peace with by whatever way possible so that their life become safe in the midst of these inimical forces. Gradually arose by force of the circumstances middle men, called shamans, soothsayers, magicians and later religious practitioners or priests who would propose means of dealing with such higher powers or gods.

In the process of growth and development humans felt the need of affirming their existence and of giving greater meaning to life itself. But this was hampered by their own inability to assert themselves, grappling with situations around, which seemed to take away meaning from life. Thus one of the roles of religion has been to liberate humans from these obstacles and evils.

Evils, and Rituals to Deal with them

There seem to have been two types of evils that prevented humans from arriving at fullness of growth – moral evil, or sin caused by evil inclinations, which could be corrected by moral prescriptions and ascetical practices, and physical evil, caused by external forces. Humans tried to liberate themselves from these by means of rituals proposed by religious practitioners. Thus they got power to withstand the evil forces. Sometimes moral and physical evils are considered interchangeable, and consequently the remedies also, namely moral laws and ritual practices were applied indiscriminately to remove obstacles and obtain liberation. In all these it can be seen that the ritual practices had their origin in the need of humans to be totally free; for, it is in this total freedom that man/woman become truly him/herself. Thus the sense of freedom, at least to some extent, made man/woman enter into the sphere of the Unbounded or the Divine realm or life. This entry into communion with God is human salvation. In what follows we shall discuss the history of the ritual process of salvation and assess their value today as liberative actions.[1]

Religious Rituals in the History of Human kind

Odo Casel who has studied deeply the pre-Christian sources of the NT form of the Church's worship has discovered that the Graeco-Roman world of Jesus time has been permeated by [2]the so-called mystery cult. In our discussion of the religious rituals we need to have at least a bird's eye of this cult.

Mystery Cult

Casel himself has defined mystery cult /religion thus: "The mystery is a sacred ritual action in which a saving deed is made present through the rite; the congregation, by performing the rite, take part in the saving act, and thereby win salvation." Two points stand out in this definition: a) acceptance of a saving event or an intervention of God in the past *(in illo tempore)* in favour of humanity, namely God entering into human struggle on earth, fighting and suffering for humans whose sorrow in pain is brought together in a mourning for the God who dies for them; but he returns to life somehow so that the whole humanity indeed the entire nature revives and lives on. This story is narrated in mythical terms and enacted in sacred rites and ceremonies.[3] b) The second point is that the saving event revives through the ritual enactment of it and hence the effect of divine intervention continues. In other words, ritual worship is the way, the divine saving and healing action continues in creation. The aim of the ritual action is a sharing in divine action and thus final liberation and union with God.

In the development of human race, primitively we find two types of societies – Agrarian Society and Hunting Society. The former began to worship hero-figures of nature, like the sun, moon, earth, seasons, whereas the latter chose to worship beasts, birds, fishes etc. The various rituals or rites performed in worship were to effect a sharing or communion with the hidden divine power which controlled nature. This process would enable humans to overcome the hurdles against his freedom which is his path to salvation.[4]

The Vedic Theory of Sacrifice

The first truth about sacrifice as a ritual consists in that in the beginning of every being there is a sacrifice that has produced it. This means that the core energy of sacrifice is the creative force, the power of becoming which is called Rta in the cosmological sense.[5] In this sense the ritual sacrifice is the externalization/visibilization of the invisible Rta which is inherent In all reality, which may be called divine power. Looked at in this way, the sacrificial ritual is the re-enactment of the creative action.

Soon this creative action is rendered inactive by the forces opposed to it. This is the story of the struggle for immortality between *deva*s (gods) and *asura*s (demons), which is one of the richest myths concerning the constant battle being waged between the two opposing forces operating in human beings. Now the correct performance of the sacrifice is the only solution for this as reported by the Vedas:

> It was by the perfect accomplishment of the sacrifice that the gods proceeded to the heavenly realm; and it was due to their defective performance of the sacrifice that the asuras were conquered.[6]

Thus by performing the ritual sacrifice, humans enters once again into the original dynamism of becoming; he is liberated from his powerlessness at the mercy of natural forces.

The Liberative Power of Rituals in the History of Religions

From the above two instances – of the Mystery Cults and of the Vedic Sacrifices, the liberative potential of religious rituals stand vindicated. In the first case, whether it is an agrarian or hunting primitive society, the performance of various rites in worship was meant to effect a communion with the hidden divine power which controlled nature, thus enabling humans to overcome the obstacles to the freedom, which is the way to his salvation. In the second case, we see that the sacrificial rituals are liberative in as much as they lead humans to the original Rta of becoming. It may be noted that "To perform the sacrifice is not to participate in a good act or to do good to the gods, the mankind or oneself; it is to live to make one's own survival and that of the whole universe."[7]

Biblical Concept of Sacrifice

For the Jews in the OT the sacrificial act was the memorial of their liberation from Egypt. Participating in the ritual action was considered a re-enactment of that original event of liberation in one's life (Ex. 13:3-16) The Jews kept alive the messianic hope of final liberation, through the commemorative ritual of the original liberation from Egypt. The specificity of this OT concept of liberation consists in that the original event which is re-enacted ritually was a historical event, while in the above two cases we have mythical and cosmic symbolisms.[8]

In the NT concept of ritual sacrifice, the memorial concept is continued, but with a difference. The original act of liberation is a personal act of love and self-gift. Jesus Christ re-placed the OT Paschal ritual with a fraternal meal (*Agape*), implying self-sacrifice in symbols which was fully realized in Calvary on the Cross by his death and resurrection. Therefore St. Paul later described the Christian ritual as a memorial of this liberating act of Christ (Rom 6:6-11), and for the Church the Eucharist (1 Cor. 11:23-27) became the continuation of this ritual. In the case of the NT the liberative force of this ritual is manifested in making humans free from selfishness, enabling them to love others to the extent of sacrificing life for them out of love. Thus, one becomes totally free for universal love. In this way one becomes fully saved and liberated, entering into full communion with God who is so lovable and loving. [9]

The Double Nature of Religious Rituals: Their Enslaving and Liberating Characteristics

When the ritual operates for obtaining favours, it loses its liberative potential, and instead becomes a cause of enslavement, just as human effort for attaining freedom may lead to further slavery. This is also the case of uncritical use of certain rituals in worship without reading the signs of the time. One of the important reasons for cultural adaptations in liturgy is also to liberate worshippers from the clutches of conservatism in the use of signs and symbols. We may now cast a look at the history of religious worship to understand the veracity of the above statement

The practice of the mystery cult in the Graeco-Roman world soon degenerated into many abuses. The religious experience accompanying such celebrations at times was transformed into erotic enjoyment. Instead of leading the worshiper to true liberty, sometimes it made him/her belong to secret groups of orgies, thus depriving him/her of the true freedom. Such instances also appear to have happened in India as well, when the priest (pujari) presiding at a sacrifice would assume a certain divine character, tempting him to exploit the ritual act for his own selfish motives.

In the Bible, particularly in the Old Testament, the very ritual acts that were supposed to lead the people of God to liberty, made them slaves of such rituals, making them obstacles to the practice of the covenant, the summit of the liberating act of God.

In the Christian practice of ritual worship also such eventuality cannot be ruled out: This would happen when the ritual become the act of the priest as a means of gaining heaven, without giving due importance to the commitment to build community of love.

Briefly, it would appear a paradox that the very ritual act, meant to effect true freedom, should turn out an alienating force among people. In the efforts for organizing inter-religious worship, it is at the level of rituals that worshipers of one religion often experience insurmountable problems in communicating with their counter-parts in other religions. Jesus during his earthly life was very wary of human rituals for this reason, as can be seen from the gospels. Therefore it is indeed sensible to believe, like Louis Bouyer and others, that the Last Supper of Jesus which is the basis of the Eucharist, the highest Christian ritual action, was [10]most probably not a traditional Jewish paschal meal, but an agape, a friendship meal.

In conclusion, humans cannot avoid rituals completely, not only because they are an authentic medium for communion with the rest of humanity and with God, but also because of man's/woman's symbolic nature as embodied spirit or spirit-filled matter. But these rituals should be such that make humans truly grow in freedom. This is possible, only if we not domesticate them for our own selfish interests. Otherwise they become magical acts and superstitious practices leading to man's/ woman's enslavement, instead of liberation.

Endnotes

[1] Cf. Paul Puthanangady, "The Liberative Power of Rituals", Journal of Dharma 9 (1984) 208-215.

[2] O. Casel, *The Mystery of Christian Worship*, London, 1963, p.54.

[3] Cf Ibid. p.53.

[4] Mircia Eliade, *Rites and Symbols of Initiation*, Harper, 1958.

[5] Rta is the cosmic and sacred order, the universal law, the ultimate dynamic and harmonic structure of reality (See R. Panikkar, The Vedic Experience, Pontichery, 1983, p.88.7.

[6] Taittiriya *Samhita*, 1,6,10,2.

[7] R. Panikkar, op.cit. p.353. It may also be noted that in the case of the mystery religions, the ritual leads humans to the saving act of God which is represented in terms of a myth, whereas in the Vedic ritual of sacrifice, it leads humans to the saving act of God in the form of a cosmic act of creation; and the symbols used in the rituals, namely agni, soma juice, etc. indicate the return of humans to the original state of creation.

[8] Paul Puthanagandy op.cit. p.212.

[9] Paul Puthanangady, op.cit. p.213.

[10] Ibid. p.214, esp. fn.13 there.

Chapter 5

Cultural Currents and Emergence of Many Cults and Sects

Introduction

Murray Rogers observes that in the history of religion and culture,

> When the relationship between God and the world changes in the minds of men [sic] then there follows a shaking up, a crisis in man's understanding of worship; the Old Testament bears witness to such crises, as when Israel, for example, ceased to be nomadic tribal society and became an agricultural society, and the Church in the history of the last two thousand years has from time to time experienced disturbing changes of this sort involving radical thinking and a new expression of her relationship to God in worship and prayer. [1]

This is probably what we have been witnessing since the post-war second half of the 20th century, especially during the last quarter of it – a proliferation of what may be called informal groups and sects which possess a certain common morphological characteristics, rooted in the dynamics of culture and interpersonal relationships. At the same time it may not be correct to see in it only a simple repetition of the past. It may be more sensible to link this new tendency with the specific problems of the modern growing techniculture that rouses in people both a desire to control their own destiny and a feeling of reserve and even apathy towards large-scale organizations.[2] This phenomenon is not peculiar to the western society alone; whereas it is very conspicuous in the West, it is surely taking shape in the East as well.

Faced with proliferations of these comparatively small worship groups of many forms, we are required to search for the factors that give rise to them, and to enquire into their meaning and relevance for modern humanity. A few years ago sociologists, journalists and theologians prophesied not only a 'death of God', but also a slow death of religion and worship. Meanwhile, what we saw a revival of religion and its varied ritual expressions, not only in the Christian West, but in the Communist world: From Indian mysticism to orgy-like drug festivals; from Protestant monastic orders to Catholic Pentecostals; from new totalitarian religion in Japan to spontaneous new churches in Africa; from Pentecostal mass meetings in the woods of Siberia to small house groups to Soviet and American Intellectuals.[3] This awakening in religious worship meets a human need, however differently one might evaluate its many coloured manifestations.

Method of Presentation

Worship as a human and personal dimension can be the subject matter of different human sciences – sociology, psychology, ethnology, history of religions etc. Each of these approaches is bound to be incomplete by the nature of the phenomenon called worship. Therefore the tools of our enquiry and reflections are not restricted to any particular science. We would rather follow a complementary approach drawing insights and inspirations from more than one of them. We shall first a present brief inventory of the religious groups with their new life styles and worship forms that have cropped up in the past few decades. Then we shall analyze their raison d'etre in terms of socio-cultural principles and finally go further into the anthropological nature of and function of religious rites and worship that necessitate such acculturation and socialization in concrete human life. We have to be selective in their choice because of the multiplicity of forms and the limited scope of our study.

Special Groups Assemblies and Religious Unions Since 1950[4]

Scientology Church

This peculiar church appeared in America in 1950's. One Ronald Hubbard, a leading science-fiction writer is said to be its innovator. His famous book "Dianetics – The Modern Science of Mental Health" is considered to be the inspiring source of it. Soon this 'religion' spread to Europe, especially Germany, by the year 1970. Scientology is said to be an applied religious philosophy, borrowing ideas from different religions like Buddhism, and human sciences like Psychiatry. Its ultimate goal is to put man/woman in a new and absolute state of freedom. And for this it proposes a sort of religious praxis consisting of a rather complicated system of courses and a precise technique of spiritual counseling using some electric gadget. The praxis also includes a freely accessible liturgical service.

Union of Free Missionary Communities

This is also called the Evangelical Brothers Society, founded in 1967 by Frit Berger. Later arose a difference of opinion among the members regarding the content of their faith.

The progressive group took a free attitude in interpreting the biblical content of faith vis-à-vis the other religious followers as well as the contemporary world.

Zen-Buddhism

This 'religion' of Japan is already well-known both in the East and the west. From time to time new centres are opened in different parts of the world. One of its recent exponents, from the Christian point of view is H.M. Enomiya-Lassale. According to him, for the accomplishment of "Zazen" (sitting-meditation) three things are essential – the posture, the breathing and the mental attitude.[5] Apart from its ultimate goals of enlightenment and transcendental existence, it increases self- control and interior freedom, which provide man/woman a better chance to become a useful member of the human society. One of its recent form may be found in the "Circle of Zen-friends of Roshi Nagaya" that appeared in Hamburg in the year 1972.[6]

Ananda –Marga

Ananda-Marge (Way to happiness) was founded by P.R. Sarkar (Ananda Murthi) about the year 1955. In recent years Karunanada, as its first spokesperson, went abroad and formed several groups of followers in different parts of Europe. The Margis for their religious worship stand in the tradition of Yoga with suitable exercises and bhajan-singing. They have borrowed elements from Christianity, Marxism, and natural science. The members are said to organize action to remove individual and social misery.[7]

Divine Light Mission

Its founder is said to be Sri Hansji Maharaj. About the year 1960, he announced the new Light or divine Knowledge to the people of different social strata of India. Its recent history is well-known.[8] As for its life style, the followers of DLM live in Ashrams professing vows of poverty, chastity and obedience. Satsang, meditation and service are its three important components.

Divine Light Centre

Its founder is Swami Omkararanda, a follower of Swami Sivananda of Rishikesh, India. It had its origin in Switzerland in the late 1960's. DLC devoted itself to the message of "spiritual-religious work according to the teaching of the Gospel". According to its founder, man [sic] is from and in God, and our task is to translate the Divine in us to reality. This is made possible especially through meditation and above all through mantra meditation.

Hare Krishna

This movement is also known as International Society of Krishna Consciousness. It was started by Swami Prabhupadananda in New York in the late 1960's. Soon it got wide currency in Europe with its centre in Frankfurt opened in the year 1973. Its ultimate aim is the attainment of Krishna consciousness, which is proposed for the salvation and redemption of the world. Its worship style is incessant chanting of the mantra "Hare Krishna". It consists of 16 words and the followers of the movement have to chant it 1728 times daily. By its very nature of worship it stands in the Hindu Bhakti tradition.

Ahamadiya Movement

Although a century old, this movement is considered here for its new European centre started in the year 1963 with the erection of a big mosque in Zurich, having several branches in

Hamburg, Frankfurt, London, Hague etc. This religion teaches about Jesus, that he, after an apparent death, was resurrected and wandered toward Kashmir, India, where after announcing the Gospel died at the age of 120.

Free Bahai-follwers

(World Union for Universal religion and Universal Freedom). This is an offshoot of the century-old Bahai-religion, with its new branch in Switzerland which came into existence in 1974. The so-called sect of carvan of East and West has been inspired by this. The life style and worship form are oriented to the evolution of a world religion, world brotherhood, a world Bible, made of texts from the spiritual books of various religions.

Pentecostal Churches and Movements

Pentecostal Movement began about a century ago as a revival movement or charismatic movement in the existing churches. It has also a considerably long past among the 'black churches' in Africa and America. Here we shall point out only the more recent development especially with respect their patterns of worship.

New Pentecostalism among the Protestants[9]

Since 1950 a revitalization has appeared especially in the Anglican and Protestant churches of USA and the Baptists churches of Russia. These are called Neo-Pentecostals or Charismatic Movement in the Historical Churches. This spirituality also spread quickly to the Historical Churches of both the Americas and Europe. Their liturgical expressions are too well-known to require any description here. In passing we may only note that, generally they claim freedom of the Spirit, creativity and spontaneity in the worshipping of God.

Hence in many cases they differ from the traditional patterns of worship. 'Speaking in tongues, giving free expression to one's prayer experiences, being baptized in the Spirit, healing through prayer etc. form part of their charismatic jargon. We shall discuss later their socio-cultural significance.

Catholic Pentecostalism

Perhaps this is the latest among the Pentecostal movements. By 1962 there were already some contacts between Catholics and Protestants in this matter in Holland and USA. The Breakthrough however came only in 1967, when several Catholic lay people – all members of the faculty of Duquense university, Pittsburg were drawn together in a period of deep prayer and discussion regarding the validity of their faith. Not satisfied with a life of ivory tower scholarship, they concerned themselves with the problems of the renewal of the Church. In recent years they had been involved with the liturgical and ecumenical movements, with civil rights and with the concerns of world peace.[10]

This movement had a rapid spread into many countries not only of Europe and Americas but also of Asia and Africa. As for its liturgical expressions, these have many elements common with other Pentecostal movements. But in Catholic circles (especially in official circles), the expression "Renewal in the Spirit" or "Charismatic Movement" was preferred to "Pentecostal Movement". This option perhaps signifies a more modest claim to the effusion of the gifts of the Spirit in congregational gatherings than was evident at the first Pentecostal gathering, described in the Acts chapter 2. Consequently perhaps the expressions of the prayer-experiences in groups through body movements, gestures and prophesying are less obtrusive and less numerous than in other such prayer gatherings.

Black Pentecostalism

In the context of the revival of Pentecostal movements in various churches, special mention must be made of such movements among the 'blacks' of Africa and America. For, the Pentecostal movement in America began in the same milieu in which the spirituals, jazz and blues emerged. Yet, while black music has gained recognition as a contribution by the Negroes to the universal culture, the black influence on the Pentecostal cult movement has been almost forgotten. Black Pentecostalism affirms that liberation is always a consequence of the presence of the Spirit. Authentic liberation can never take place apart from genuine Pentecostal encounter, and likewise, authentic Pentecostal encounter cannot occur unless liberation becomes the consequence.

Opinions vary concerning the origin and function of the Negro Spirituals.[11] However they do not provide enough evidence to prove that the black people reconciled themselves with human slavery. On the contrary, there are black freedom songs which emphasize black liberation as consistent with divine revelation. We shall see below that from the socio-cultural point of view black Pentecostalism and the emerging black power are both movements of social transformation. Their worship-forms are typical of their socio-cultural milieu. That is why with respect to the Kimbanguists of Zaire, Prof. Hollenweger observes that that cult or worship ritual admits no strict division between sacred and profane. The social get-together, the profane singing, making music and palavering, giving and receiving gifts etc. has as much religious character as the 'religious ' singing, praying, making music, offering gifts and the stylized dancing.[12]

Dynamics of Cult and Culture

The above worship-forms (cult/ritual of whatever kind) emerging from their particular cultural contexts lend themselves to different interpretations in the light of insights from human sciences. Different, but complementary interpretations from different angles appear to be necessary to explain in a satisfactory way the connection between the complex phenomenon of worship-forms and their socio-cultural contexts

A Psychological Approach

This approach to interpret the above cult-cultural dynamics uses the data regarding forms of worship in question and tries to find the unconscious motivations that stimulate the external visible patterns of behavior in worship. Thus it would explain the proliferation of informal groups of the type we have seen in terms of anonymity and isolation of modern man/woman. [13] Behind the apparent spontaneity and intimacy of personal relationships, which are more conspicuous in the Pentecostal type of gatherings, a psychological exploration of individual participants may discover 'concealed motivations', not perceived by the individuals themselves. It may reveal, for example, that the majority of the participants are immigrants and socially marginalized citizens, thus confronted by social and economic problems.[14] They will oppose the society that has isolated them, and the churches or religious organizations that have connived with the former in this strategy of their isolation. In such situations the new-found worship –groups will function as a substitute and compensate for their social frustrations and isolations. And this will in turn multiply the number of groups within which they can communicate, share and be appreciated for their own sake. Thus according to this view, the liturgical expressions (cultic forms) will symbolize a pathological condition of the participants.

It is evident that this interpretation, though not totally wrong, cannot adequately account for the wide range of worship-forms evidenced by the foregoing inventory. The western society, especially its urban environment, is characterized by the multiplication of functional relationships, distinct from personal relationships.[15] Such contexts stimulate informal groups of the type we have just mentioned. In the given context of the techniculture, these groups may function in two ways: They may provide affective protection to the members, while training them for a life marked by risk and lack of love, characteristic of a society structured on functional relationships. They may also function as useful 'energy source', one can periodically resort to, in order to recuperate oneself, whenever one feels uncomfortable and insecure in the anonymity and functional quality of modern city life.

Socio-Cultural Approach

In this approach there are several alternatives which will be helpful to pick up the particular features and concerns of the worship-forms or cultic rituals, we have encountered above.

A. From Big Religious Organizations to Small Groups: One of the notable features of the groups considered is their emergence as fragments of some big churches and religious organizations. Everywhere there is a tendency to fall back on comparatively small group-worships, as against the large congregational worship of earlier times. Apart from the psychological explanation already offered for this, there is also a relevant sociological reason behind it. The present day cultural evolution is undergoing a process of transformation from a culture of mechanical solidarity into one of organic solidarity.[16] And by its very nature mechanical solidarity is built up and maintained through collective social[17] rites. Because they will guarantee the necessary collective function of the society. At the next stage these social rites will assume the role of religious rites, which are supposed to enable the society to organize itself with respect to certain uncontrollable forces, on which it depends. Thus the decisive rites become automatically religious rites or liturgies to be performed always collectively in accordance with a unitary and hierarchical vision of the universe.

B. Symbolic of Mystico-Aesthetic Vision of Life: Some of the emerging worship patterns appear to be totally withdrawn from socio-political involvement. Some varieties of the so-called charismatic movements, especially among the Catholics, as well as some Hindu Christian syncretic worship forms may be said to belong this type. How can we explain this phenomenon in socio-cultural terms?

The peculiarity of a society built on organic solidarity, as we have seen, is its fragmentation into specialized groups according to the mode of insertion of individuals. Now, this insertion is motivated by interests of self-establishment in the society, which may be achieved in various ways. One way is through socio-political commitment, which then is expressed in the symbolic of religious rites (certain type of liturgies do this as we have seen above). Another way to achieve this goal is through mystic-aesthetic vision of life, withdrawing from socio-political commitments, which in turn is expressed in the symbolic of some other type of liturgies.[18]

C. Disregard for Space-Time Factors in Worship: Worship gatherings in improvised situations – temporary sheds, private houses, sometimes even in the heart of a buzzing city life, as well as unilization of 'sacred places' for 'profane purposes', without attaching special significance to a particular time (Sunday) as time of social coming-together, against a 'work time (Weekday) of dispersed activity are some special features of the new patterns of worship. This change of perspective springs from a marginalization of the difference between the sacred and the profane.[19]

The collectivistic vision of the mechanic solidarity had projected itself into all the realms of religious life – spatial and temporal, radicalizing a dichotomy of sacred/profane and its correlatives centre/periphery, Sunday/Weekday, work/leisure etc. The disruption of the unitary world view structured on hierarchical centrality, which is now brought about on account of a societal transformation, is at the root of this change of perspective. Diverse projects of different interests cannot naturally come together in the same place to give symbolic expression (worship/liturgy) to their concerns and preoccupations. Thus the significance of Sunday for collective life has been reduced, and the same applies to towns and village centres.[20]

D. Disregard for Rule of Thumb in Ritual Worship: Not only with regard to time and place but, but also regarding the very liturgical action (celebration) there is a change of perspective in the new forms of worship. There is a relativization of 'Rule as something to be conformed to'. The new tendency is to consider rite in the style of "feast," a conception which springs from one's pre-occupation with self-establishment in the worship. Instead of viewing worship as morally obligatory, these groups take it as an occasion for 'concelebrating' the experiences and preoccupations in diverse socio-cultural contexts.[21]

Thus we find that in the sociological approach of interpretation there is an appreciable degree of correlation between the proliferation of new worship-forms and the modern cultural evolution. At the same time there are still questions for which we require some other type of approach, questions, for example, regarding the conservative nature of social rites which resists changes.[22] Or questions about what is happening in the so-called liturgical improvisations? What is really being changed? Or again why does a sacred ballet make sense in a cathedral but not in a modern chapel Or why does a lay dress for the celebrant appear meaningful in a family worship, but not so in a big church? It seems that some other approach is required to interpret the very anthropological nature and structure of rite in order to be able to shed light on such important questions.

Cultural-Anthropological Approach

In modern times various human sciences have drawn attention to the significance of rite in human life. In what follows below we shall concentrate on the positive aspects of rite in human life, leaving out its negative aspects,[23] namely rite as something intensely personal to man/woman in his/her cultural and religious self-actualization.

A.   Rite and Symbolic Expression

Symbol is constitutive of human 'being-in-the-world', and his/her 'being-with-the other'. It is inherent to his/her being that he/she 'expresses himself/herself in symbolic systems – verbal language, sign language, body language etc. which are not instrumental actions.[24] They are symbolic actions, because they always connect body attitude with intentionality. Every such gesture unites man/woman with the spatio-temporal world.

Now, rite may be said to be 'operative expression', namely in it, sign and meaning coincide; there is no functional subordination of the sign to something exterior to the meaning. Otherwise a rite becomes an instrumental action, as explained above, or a religious magic. Thus it is quite natural to man/woman to have recourse to rite to operative and expressive symbols in order to signify 'his/her being-in-the-world'. In fact, to be human is to symbolize existence.[25] Human nostalgia for ritual symbolization of his/her privileged moments of existence can be seen in all ages and cultures. The so-called rites of passage[26] are not mere ceremonies of insertion in the society. They are highly symbolic celebrations of the essential dimensions of existence. It is interesting to note that such symbolic celebrations are of the body-dimensions of existence are manifested in the Yogic patterns of prayer, in the diverse charismatic prayer-forms as in the hippy style of life with its protest against a monotonous life style. This human need for ritual symbolization of existence is displayed in another form in the craziness for modern ballets.

B.   Symbolic Realization and Cultic Expression

From the above brief discussion of the anthropological meaning of the term 'expression' and its relation to rite, it must be clear that rite in its true sense is operative in itself. It is an operative expression; it realizes what it signifies – a power which is in the nature of every symbolic sign. However there is a tension between signification and realization in every ritual expression. There remains always some surplus signification (meaning) or an experience of the 'beyond' in the very process of its realization. We shall try to make this idea clear by an example. When a husband and his wife embrace each other, this is an expressive gesture in the true sense, i.e. expression of an inner disposition. But in the very gesture of embracing and all that accompanies it, there is something that escapes them. They cannot fully accomplish all that they would, namely the intentionality beyond. In other words the two things - expressive gesture - and inner disposition (signification/meaning) - are not always co-terminus, co-extensive. Similar is also the case with cultic or ritual expression: In the ritual is created an opening, a void entailing surplus signification.

Thus from the anthropological standpoint, every religious rite and liturgy or worship- form takes man/woman through his/her body-bound subjective 'expressive' experiences to the brink or threshold of something' beyond' or to a 'void' in which is experienced the irruption of an Other, the Divine. It is the juncture of 'presence-absence, 'the emptiness' created by the symbolism of the rite which is filled by the irreducible alterity of the sacred, the divine. For, instance, we may consider the rite of offering. The cultic gesture of offering is first of all a negative rite, because, to offer is to separate from common and profane use.[27] Secondly, the rite carries also the idea of mediation between two asymmetric poles of exchange – human and divine. However it does not evoke the DO UT DES (I am giving so that you may give back) business concept. And whenever this latter idea (business idea is present offering loses its symbolism; whereas as a symbolic gesture it 'represents' a 'presence in absence'. This negative moment is essential to it, because it transforms what is immediate in life and in the experience- data into a signifier of what is being re-presented – existence and all that it means. The efficacy of the rite of offering means lies in this that through its negative moment it opens the human world and in the void (absence) thus created, it allows the divine to present itself. In this sense every liturgical rite is operative by itself (opera operato). This is the type of divine-human operation inscribed in the scheme of Christian sacraments, so well typified in the Incarnate Word.

From the foregoing analysis of the structure and meaning of rite and its capacity for symbolic realization of human existential experiences opening out for a divine-human encounter in every ritual expression properly so-called, it may not be difficult to understand the importance of having recourse to every possible means that would make a worship ritual 'expressive'. In the following paragraphs we shall make a few observations on this aspect. The horizons of these observations are limited to Christian liturgies, even though in a broad sense they may be applicable to any religious worship.

Emerging Worship-forms in Suitable Cultural garments

A Preliminary observation is in order: To make a worship-form 'expressive' (meaningful) is not to clutter it with unnecessary details - secondary signs, ceremonies and rubrics etc. In fact such encumbrances will only render a rite less expressive and revealing to the irritation of intelligent participants. It is good to know that present-day distaste of people for liturgical participation springs not so much from the obsoleteness or antique nature of the rite in question as from its ceremonialization and 'pontificalization'.[28] We shall now deal with a few points which will highlight the need for making worship and liturgy truly expressive, by bringing out the intimate connection between worship-forms and the cultural contexts in which they emerge.

Texts, Actions and Gestures in Worship

There are three areas of liturgy to be taken care of, namely texts, actions and gestures, if we want to make liturgy truly expressive, with all that it implies anthropologically speaking. Texts include written forms of prayers, readings and hymns in worship. Actions mean sacramental and ceremonial actions. Gestures mean every symbolic body-movement in the liturgy – bowing, prostration, yoga-praying posture, dance postures etc. Liturgical texts are expressive, as a whole, with specific illuminative force at work according to the theory of "speech acts."[29] Liturgical actions are also expressive in so far as they form part of the rite in question, but degenerate into magic, when devoid of any symbolism. Gestures as symbolic body-movements are always expressive. A happy concurrence and coordination of these three dimensions are necessary in order to make liturgy fully expressive. Unfortunately the third dimension has not been sufficiently taken care of even in the present-day worship services, not to speak of the earlier ones. The post-Vatican II liturgical reforms and renewal programmes in diverse churches have mainly centred on the first two dimensions. Even here the so-called 'simplification' of rite has often led to the suppression of the essential and elementary gestures and the addition of a lot of singing in and out of place. The dimension of gestures plays only a negligible part in the liturgical celebrations, even though it is the most basic and primitive of human expressions.

Symbolic play is at the root of our expressive gestures and body movements, above all the dancing gestures and postures. To those who look with suspicion at dance being introduced in liturgy, we have to say that cult or worship is not dogma but action and actualization of faith, that liturgy has to be put in the category of art rather than of science. As E. Tinsely has rightly remarks: "The liturgy is a composite, art and form which contain what is specifically human- his word, his gestures, his singing and dancing before God."[30]

Since cult (worship) and culture are closely related not only in life but also in linguistics, as we have seen at the beginning of this book, this dimension (all the three above-mentioned dimensions for that matter) has to assume cultural 'incarnation'. If a 'Beat-Mass' of the 2nd half of the 20th century with its thundering rhythmical 'Gospel Songs' and the 'Spirituals' are more appealing to the cultural ethos of Africa and America, and perhaps of Europe,[31] it may be mere deafening noise to the Indian ears. Indian culture has produced its own specific forms of dance – Bharatnātyam, Kathakali, Kathak, Manipuri etc. and their variations,[32] which are highly symbolic and devotional. Indian Christian liturgies have to assume this movement dimension in order to make them expressive according to the genius of the native culture.[33]

We cannot resist natural cross-cultural fertilization in worship patterns, which are concomitant of socio-cultural interdependence. Such may be considered, for example, the 'Spiritual' and the 'Hare Krishna'; not that these were perfect models of such fertilizations, but only that they were pointers to an awakening in religious worship, which could assume global proportions, meeting a specific human need, not covered by other areas of life and endeavours.

Concluding remarks

Phenomenology of modern religious worship has revealed a proliferation of groups of diverse nature. Human sciences have tried to explain their emergence and their worship patterns from their respective stand points. These are valid but incomplete explanations because of the complex nature of the worship rituals which are rooted in human cultural ethos. Consequently we are led to a study of the structure and meaning of rite itself. The anthropologically key word here is 'expression', which may be thought of as an act uniting a symbolic gesture to an inner disposition, a concurrence of the two without any logical priority.. Understood as operative expression, religious rite then opens the way for a divine-human encounter through its capacity for symbolic realization of human existential experiences.

This insight into the nature of worship immediately makes its demand on us to search for every possible means that would make worship, Christian liturgies in particular, truly expressive, and thus helping us to understand the multiplication of worship forms as so many incomplete attempts for self-expression in accordance with the cultural ethos of the people. Body-movement, including dance-postures, has yet to find enough space among such possible means for making liturgy inculturated and expressive. This movement-dimension which belongs to the essence of elementary human expression would help them to pray with body as well as mind. However, its integration into worship will have to take different forms according to socio-cultural contexts.

Endnotes

[1] C. M. Rogers, "Worship and Contemporary Asian Man ...Some reflections," *Religion and Society*, Bangalore: 1969, pp.52f.

[2] According to the late Prof. Ramond Panikkar, This is characteristic of the present-day human consciousness achieved by the secularisation process: a quest for 'profane autonomy' (see *Worship and Secular Man*, London:DLT,1973, pp.28-44).

[3] Cf. W. Hollenweger, Pentecost between Black and White, Belfast:: Christian Journals Ltd. 1974, p.98.

[4] For this inventory we mainly depend on Oswald Eggenberger, *Die Kirchen, Sondergruppen und religiösen Vereinungen* (Zürich:: Theologischer Verlag, 1978).

The author treats the groups under different heads as churches, sects, catholic, non-Catholic, non-Christian etc. But for the purpose of our study we shall not make such confessional and denominational distinctions in order to avoid any value judgement of them.

[5] Enomiya Lassale, "en-meditation" *Studia Misssionalia*, 25(1976)29ff.

[6] Eggenberger, op.cit. pp.131ff.

[7] Eggenberger, op.cit. p.131f.

[8] Namely, after the death of Hanji the widow Mathaji entrusted its task to her younger son Guru Maharaj Ji who took to the West and very much westernised. Later when he married a Californian girl Matha Ji disowned him and thus the movement took a new turn, being split into two branches. The Eastern branch is headed by the elder brother Bal Bhagavan JI and the other by Guru Maharaj Ji himself.

[9] For convenience sake we use the expression "Protestants" to designate different non-Catholic confessions like Episcopalians, Methodists, Presbyterians, Anglicans, Baptists etc.

[10] Hollenweger op.cit. p.76.

[11] Hollenweger, "Spirituals", G.J. Davis Ed. *A Dictionary of Liturgy and Worship*, SCM, 1972, pp.394ff.

[12] Hollenweger, *Pentecost between Black and White*, p.67.

[13] J.Remy and I. Voye, Informal Groups in the Present-Day Church – A Sociological Analysis", *Concilium* (1974), 86.

[14] A case study among Pentecostal groups in USA is said to have revealed the above-mentioned characteristics of the participants. Cf. A, Vergote, "Regard du Psychologue sur le symbolisme liturgique", *La Masson-Dieu*, 91 (1967, 129).

[15] Functional relationship is always on a utilitarian basis, whereas personal relationship is on an affective basis.

[16] For more about the process of this transformation see J. Remy et.al "Form liturgiques et symboliues sociales", *Social Compass*, 22 (1975)177f.

[17] About the nature and function of social rites, see below.

[18] Remy et.al, article cited pp.188f.

[19] The concept of a sacred heteronomy or hierarchical structure of reality is at the root of this dichotomy sacred/profane which is characteristic of primitive societies – See M. Eliade, *Le sacreet le profane*, Gallimard, 1965.

[20] Remy and L. Voye, op.cit. pp.88f.

[21] Remy and Others, op.cit. p.185f.

[22] For example the court of justice: The tribunal, judges, and advocates in their official costume, stock phrases, speeches etc. do they not really make up a ritual, which remains unchanged? We may also consider table ritual, theatre ritual etc.

[23] In the negative understanding of rite in human life, its stereotype behaviour, obsolete ceremonial etc. will be the focus.

[24] Instrumental action is an action which produces an effect outside the action or it has a goal outside action, whereas in the science of signs, human 'expression' is a symbolic action, whose effect is not outside, but within itself. For example, pressing an electric switch to give light, or to press the accelerator of the bike to increase speed etc. are instrumental actions, not symbolic ones, on the contrary, offering a gift, shaking hands with another person, embracing somebody – these are symbolic actions, not instrumental ones.

[25] For the symbolization dimension, se among others, C. Levi-strauss, *Anthropologie structurale*, Paris, 1958.

[26] Rites of passages are rites connected with birth, initiation, marriage, death etc. Cf. A. Van Gennep, The *Rites of Passage*, London : Routledge and Kegan Paul, 1977.

[27] A.Vergote, "Dimensions anthropologiues de l'eucharistie", *L'Eucharistie Symbol et Réalité*, Paris: Gembloux, 1970, p.36.

[28] By these terms we mean the undue ceremonial display of liturgical vestments and things, and the clerical fanaticism over-emphasizing role-differences in liturgical celebrations.

[29] Cf.J. Ladrière, "The Performativity of Liturgical Language," *Concilium* (English), 1973, pp.54-55.

[30] "Liturgie et art", *Concilium* (French), 62 (1971)71.

[31] As for its questionable character when introduced into Europe and White America, cf. Hollenweger, op.cit. p.23.

[32] To these classical dance forms may be added some relevant popular dance forms of the Tribal people of India, notably of the North East, Jharkhand and Chhattisgarh areas.

[33] For a meaningful attempt at the adaptation of such classical dance forms for Christian liturgies, cf. A. R. Sequerira, *Klassische indische Tankunst und christliche Verkündigung*, Freiburg, Herder, 1978.

Chapter 6

A Liturgy for Mission that Proclaims Jesus Christ to all Peoples and Cultures

Introduction

More than half a century ago the Council of Vatican II in its historic document on liturgy declared: ".....Liturgy is the summit toward which the activity of the Church is directed; it is also the fountain from which all her power flows." (SC 10). Elsewhere in the same document the Council emphasizes that "it is through the liturgy, especially that the faithful are enabled to express in their lives and manifest to others the **mystery of Christ and the real nature of the Church.**"(SC2, emphasis added). Moreover Pope Paul VI who carried forward the Council after the demise of Pope John XXIII, and completed it, is reported to have said that liturgy was not only the first subject treated by the Council but the "very first in intrinsic worth and importance in the life of the Church."[1] All this shows that, liturgy, Eucharist in particular is intimately related to the Church as well as its important role in proclaiming Christ to the World.

This is an exalted position and vision of liturgy; but at the same time it is ambiguous and, one may add, dangerous like a double-edged sword. Negatively, it can lead to an *apotheosis* or deification of a ritual ridden cult, a purely sacral vision which may not admit of any change according to the time and place, and may be unaffected by conditions human life.. In fact it is such a vision that resists any serious effort at cultural adaptation, thus crippling liturgy in its otherwise powerful proclamatory function. Positively, what the vision should mean is already implied in the conversation of Jesus with the Samaritan woman when he said: "Believe me woman, the hour is coming, when you will worship the Father neither on this mountain nor in Jerusalem.....God is spirit and those who worship, must worship him in spirit and truth." (Jn 4:21, 24). In other words, Jesus makes the point that God is spirit and freedom, not a localized thing; that he is not bound to any place in nature like a mountain or to any place of worship like a temple or even to any geographical direction like the East. In fact, the Psalmist gives expression to an intense experience of God's omnipresence (Ps. 139:7-12) which is also shared by the Apostle Paul in another context (cf. Acts 17:24-25). Such basic biblical perspectives would help us grasp the true meaning of liturgy and get behind inane debates on ritual trivia, on gestures with no clear meaning or vital message, which befog and block the celebration.[2]

Authentic liturgies spring from and lead to commitment and struggle for justice, freedom and human dignity.[3] That is why when the liturgical concept of Vat.II was interacted in the Latin American context, the local bishops declared that "the liturgical celebration crowns (combre) and nourishes (fuente) a commitment to the human situation, to development and human promotion."[4] Therefore we have to explore the deeper meaning and significance of liturgy with regard to its ability for authentic proclamation.

Worship Beyond Worship

Jesus' invitation to the Samaritan woman to "worship in spirit and truth" is indeed a challenge before his disciples of all times and places. In his reply to the woman he was revealing and unveiling the mystery of worship. He was not simply re-defining the temple, but repudiating it together with the cultic system, replacing it with his own body (Jn 2:20-22).[5] As the word 'worship' (worth+ship) implies, it is the act of acknowledging the supreme 'worth', value or dignity of God by his creatures, accepting in all humility and truth our utter dependence on him. The creation is to offer this worship, this liturgy. Authentic human worship is nothing but human appropriation of the 'spirit of worship' pervading the entire nature, and humans should do this worship not simply in signs and symbols (bowing, prostration, ārati etc.) but through their lives (lived in obedience, honesty simplicity etc.). Long ago the late Vandana Mataji wrote:

> As there is a Silence beyond sound to which the sound is meant to lead us
>
> As there is a Stillness beyond movement which the dance is meant to hold
>
> So, there is a Worship beyond temples, beyond mountains – a worship in spirit and truth.[6]

What Mataji would tell us is this: There is a deeper dimension of all external ritual forms of worship and liturgy. We are so used to the external form of it, and 'both training and tradition have instilled it into us that *pujas* and *samskaras*, church-going and sacraments are a necessary characteristic of a religious person.' But in the process we often mistake 'religious' for the 'spiritual'.[7] Those who seek to worship on this mountain or in that temple, or turning toward the East may be called 'religious people'; but they may not be 'spiritual 'persons, who live by the Spirit, namely who listen to and obey the voice of the Antaryāmin.

Religious worship versus Spiritual Worship

The Greeks, the Romans and most ancient peoples worshipped turning towards the East, as they regarded the place of the rising sun as the source of light and life, power and happiness. Temples were so built as to let the rays of the rising sun fall upon the idol when the door of the temple was opened in the morning. Christians also at least from the second century prayed facing the East, and this practice got momentum when Christ began to be symbolized by the sun.[8]

But the truth is that Christ is also symbolized by the lamb, the bread, the vine, the way, the door, the shepherd and so on. The risen Lord is not just localized in the East; he promised to be with his disciples as they go in all directions, proclaiming his word to all the peoples. Wherever two or three meet in his name, he is there irrespective of the direction they face together or they face one another (Mt 18:19-20). Commenting on this passage, Fr. Rayan adds that Christ is in every starved man and deprived woman and hungry child, and in all the stripped, the despoiled and the broken, regardless of what the compass says. The Eucharist which is the supreme act of Christian worship, he says, is not a procession led by the priest and moving toward the sun, but a shared meal with historical roots in Jesus' fellowship meals with the impoverished and the outcast of the society.[9]

God is surely in the East, though that is not his only address; in fact his ineffable presence everywhere is the theme of

Ps. 139, and this experience of the Psalmist is equally shared by our ancestors in India, who said, "This whole world is pervaded by the Lord......" (īśāvāsyamidaṃ sarvaṃ..... Is.Up 1). The Creator of the world does not need for his home shrines and basilicas made by human hands (Acts 17: 24f). In whatever direction we turn we are face to face with him. Indeed in him we live, we move and have our being (Acts 17: 28). Therefore if we would express his presence face-to-face with us most symbolically, the finest symbol will be the human person. Facing East rests on religious cosmology, facing Jerusalem or Mecca or Varanasi hinges on salvation history, but facing one another is rooted in the mystery of the body of Christ, the community of bread-sharing.[10]

Such insights help us grasp the difference between religious worship and spiritual worship. In his discourse on sacrifice and Sabbath, on fasting and ablution etc. Jesus made it clear that what pleases God is not ritual sacrifice, but acts of justice, mercy and faithfulness; not observance of minute Pharisaic rules of exclusion but compassionate acceptance of the outcast and the sinner (Mk 2:23-23; 3:1-6; Mt 9:1-12; Hos 6:6). Jesus attacked all formalism and verbosity in prayer; he insisted very much on worship by praxis, that is more by deeds than by mere words. Sharing, not fasting is the attitude that befits the newness of the reign of God (Mk 2:18-22 6:30-46; Is.58). The words of the late ardent Gandhian Vinoba Bhave, "Religion divides, spirituality unites" may be applied here and say, "religious worship divides, spiritual worship unites." In the context of all kinds of atrocities in the name of religion and religious worship in India to day, what we need most is an authentic 'spirit of worship' beyond all sundry forms of worship.

Liturgy of the Church versus Liturgy of the World

Karl Rahner's theology of worship is rooted in the basic vision that worship is not primarily what happens when we gather together in prayer, but what happens when we cooperate with God in history. He makes a distinction between what he calls liturgy of the world and liturgy of the Church. The former, he says is God's continued self-communication and our free response, a process that takes place throughout our life and history. History of the world is the original history which gives the primary content and meaning to our concept of liturgy, he says. He reiterates that the human community's ongoing communion and co-operation with God in history is the liturgy, the primary and original liturgy.[11] Rahner's intention is not to explain history in terms of liturgy, but liturgy in terms of history. In his work, "history of the World and Salvation History" he upholds the unity of the two histories, and says that salvation history takes place right in the midst of ordinary history.[12] Therefore we can say that the history of salvation is co-extensive with the history of the human race, though the two are not identical because the latter also includes guilt and rejection of God. For Rahner the history of the world is liturgy in the sense that the explicit history of salvation reveals that there is a perpetual interaction between God's gracious self-communication to us and our free self-donation to God, lying hidden within all human history.

Now, we have difficulty in recognizing this liturgy of the world, not because it occurs so rarely, but so frequently and because of the vast amount of evil we witness in the world. Nevertheless this liturgy is celebrated not only by those who rejoice in the beauty of life, but also by those who persevere in all its ugliness. Human history is liturgy, not despite its dark moments, but even in its darkness. Liturgy is not originally the praise we give to God when we pray; it is rather what happens when we freely immerse ourselves in the abiding absolute mystery during the great and small moments of life. For, when we worship God, by adoring, praising, thanking etc. nothing happens to God, to his worthiness, honour etc., but happens everything to us – we are made holier, are sanctified, are made worthy to be closer to God etc. which itself is God's glory (Iranaeus).

Not only human history but also the entire creation is drawn up into this liturgy of the world, because the material world also takes part in this graced exchange with the Absolute Mystery. Not only the human community but the whole cosmos participates in the life of God, as this is taken up and transformed in human history. Viewed in this way, the universe does not simply provide the stage for the liturgy of the world; it actually participates in it through us.

Now, if our life and history are already a liturgy, why do we need organized ritual worship? Surely we need because the liturgy of the Church gives dramatic expression to the liturgy of the world. When we participate in Church's ritualized worship, we are explicitly focusing on the deepest meaning of those activities, though we are not doing anything quite different from them. In other words, the liturgy of the Church is the explicit manifestation of the implicit liturgy of our lives or liturgy of the world.

Rahner's view that all of human life can be implicitly an act of worship is not so evident to us. Normally we are conscious of our communion with God only when we explicitly ritualize it in our liturgical gatherings. By mistake we identify our relationship with God exclusively with those few ritualized moments, and think that this relationship is a rather limited part of our life. And this relationship is taken as one among many others – with family, with friends, neighbours, colleagues and so on. In a similar way we arbitrarily reduce liturgy to those times in which we intentionally offer praise and thanks to God, and so we tend to see worship as just one of many activities. But as Rahner suggests our lives are much more deeply intertwined with the absolute mystery than we could ever imagine. And the more attuned we become to our active participation in the ordinary wonders of the liturgy of life, the less important the liturgy of the Church would appear.[13] Any human activity is an implicit act of worship to the extent that we experience and accept the gracious self-communication of God in it. Worship then, says Rahner, is not fundamentally something we need to take extra time for, in our daily schedules; we should rather allow the activities we are already involved in, to be transformed into acts of worship. Therefore the liturgical renewal most urgently needed is not the renewal of the liturgy of the church, rather it is the renewal that will take place, when our daily lives become an implicit and unself-conscious affirmation of God.[14]

The value of the ritual liturgy (liturgy of the Church) lies in that it is not the original liturgy. This allows us to step outside the liturgy of the world, reflect on and rehearse for the liturgy of the world. The relationship between the two is that of a symbol and the reality, it conveys or of a unity-in-difference. We should not therefore separate the liturgy of the Church from the liturgy of the world; they complete each other. As Skelly puts it beautifully, explaining the position of Rahner, "The liturgy of the world will engage us as fully conscious and free persons only if it is given explicit expression in the Church's worship. And if the liturgy of the Church were not manifestation of a liturgy that already successfully pervades our lives, it would not have the power to transform us."[15]

Liturgy and Mission

The Council which declared that the activity of the Church is centred on liturgy as its source and summit (SC 10), has also stated elsewhere that "liturgy marvelously fortifies the faithful in their capacity to proclaim Christ" (SC 2). These two texts SC 2 and SC 10 make some significant statements connecting liturgy and mission: First of all, 'the activity of the Church is mission or proclamation of Christ or the good news of the reign of God, because the Church is the eschatological continuation of Jesus' mission (missio Dei) on earth which was indeed to proclaim the arrival of the Kingdom (Mt. 3:3 Lk 4:1-2) Secondly the spiritual power for the Church to accomplish this mission she derives from the liturgy.

Mission, Yesterday and Today

The Council inaugurated a great paradigm shift in the concept of mission: First of all the expression, 'missions' was replaced by 'the mission'. Namely, for a long time before the Council, those countries or territories were called missions, where the (Roman) Church had not been established, and where consequently the then Propaganda Fide (presently Congregation for Evangelization) used to send regularly its chosen missionaries to do that work. In this perspective mission was not understood as an ecclesial act, as a faith-community's common witnessing and sharing the Good News. Rather, it was considered the task of individual zealous Christians for the expansion of the (Rokan) Church.

The Council on the contrary re-discovered the true nature of the Church and declared: "The Church on earth is by her very nature missionary, since according to the plan of the Father, it has its origin in the mission of the Son and the Holy Spirit (AG2). Thus the whole Church is in mission everywhere through concrete acts of faith-communities, namely individual as well as local Churches. Mission is the basic duty of the entire people of God (AG35 EN 43).

The bishops of Asia meeting in Taivan in the year 1974 described mission or evangelization as the local Church being in dialogue with the Asian realities. They spelt out these realities consisting of three categories: the poor, the cultures and the religions.[16] And since then mission would be described as a threefold dialogue with the poor, with the cultures and with the religions of Asia. However these are not to be taken as three different activities of mission. The truth is that they presuppose and involve one another in a process of integral mission.

> One cannot authentically liberate the poor from the poverty by changing economic and socio-political structures without transforming the way they look at God, the human and the world as well as the value system that guides their relationship to them - that is without a cultural change. Similarly one cannot profoundly change culture without the help of religion that speaks of ultimate concerns and values. In the same way dialogue with other believers is meaningless if it does not lead everyone to realize the presence and action of God in their life and community, and to listen to God in challenging culture and religions themselves and in doing justice through defense and promotion of common human and spiritual values. One cannot also change the way people think and the values they live by without changing the economic and socio-political structures that keep them enslaved. Briefly, an integral evangelization has to engage in the liberation of the poor, through the transformation of culture in collaboration with believers of other religions.[17]

The Shape of a Liturgy for Mission

A liturgy for mission in the above sense involving a three-fold dialogue with the poor, the culture and the religion is indeed challenging. Such a liturgy has to own up and express in symbols (liturgy of life and liturgy of the Church the process of building the new community of freedom, fellowship and justice which is the primary goal of mission or evangelization. In principle every liturgy, Eucharist in particular, symbolizes the NT assembly of the people of God, called by and sent by him with a mission. Just as liturgy is the community celebration of the saving act of God in Jesus Christ, so also mission is the community proclamation of the same salvific act. Celebration and proclamation are both rooted in the day today life of the community. In every liturgical gathering of the faithful there is also a sending or mission. In the liturgical gathering the faithful listen to, participate in and experience the *MIrabelia Dei*, wonderful works of God: And this ecclesial Christ experienced is shared, recounted and proclaimed to others, which is authentic mission. When the word is listened to, broken and shared in the liturgy, it imparts a twofold experience of the Paschal Mystery – sinfulness and brokenness of the human person on the one hand, and the divine forgiveness, compassion, love and fellowship on the other. Every liturgical celebration is meant to deepen this twofold experience so that the departing community at the end of the celebration become a "missionary people", a people, living a personal experiential message to share and proclaim, similar to the experience of Paul on his encounter with Jesus on the road to Damascus.

The context of (mission) proclamation is the first hand Christ-experience, as is also testified by John the Evangelist (I Jn 1:1-5). This experience is ritualized and sacramentalied realized and communicated in liturgical celebrations. Whereas Christian dogmas and doctrines try to articulate Christian faith in appropriate categories thought, liturgy imparts and keep alive this faith for personal fulfillment and communal proclamation.

It was in the liturgical action of "breaking bread" in memory of Jesus' action at the Last Supper (I Cor. 11:23-27) that the disciples' faith became alive as in the Emmaus episode (Lk. 24: 13-25). The Eucharistic liturgy which is the communal prayer of the "new people" (a people who are converted toward Christ or who have accepted his mind in accordance with Ph. 2:1-6, is to be celebrated in the new temple, which is not built of brick and mortar, but spontaneously emerges, where people gather in the name of God, wherever communities are created by sinking divisions and factions, uprooting evils of injustice and exploitation. When ritual celebrations of the Eucharist takes place in all such situations, these will become authentic expressions Christian fellowship. And in this vision of mission rooted in liturgy in depth, a missionary's priority may not be to ritualize the Eucharist wherever he/she goes proclaiming the word, but to give shape to basic human/ Christian communities which will eventually call for the liturgy of the Church (ritual form of the Eucharist) as their authentic symbol and holding centre.

Viewed in this way the Eucharist is the marvelous epiphany of the mystery of the Church and the fulfillment of the mission. Consecration of the Eucharistic elements is not simply the transformation (transubstantiation) of the bread and wine into the body and blood of Christ; it is also the transformation (transignification) of the whole universe into the Body of Christ; an assumption of all material realities and human lives into Christ to be consecrated to the Father. In Rahner's theology of worship, liturgy of the Church is a real symbol of the liturgy of the world. And this is what Eucharist is in its double dimension as symbol and reality. It is both the 'body of Christ' glorified, and symbol of the cosmic or universal body of Christ or the eschatological community which is the final goal of all mission.

Inculturated Liturgy and Proclamation

The sign value of the Church that is "raised above the nations", to become the "universal sacrament of salvation", will be clearly manifest to all peoples only when she has undergone the 'purifying'/'refining' (cultural) process of inculturation, a total inculturation, covering all aspects of the Church life and activities of which the ritual way of worship of liturgy of the Church is certainly a prominent one.

Ever since the mission planning and action was shifted from Rome to local/individual Churches, the question of inculturation has assumed top priority for all Churches. Hence the Conciliar document on liturgy speaks about liturgical renewal in terms of cultural adaptations of signs and symbols. "The liturgy is made up of unchangeable elements divinely instituted and of elements subject to change. These latter not only but ought to be changed with the passage of time......" (SC 21). Therefore liturgical inculturation may be understood as that necessary process of giving the liturgy the required cultural shape so that it is capable of expressing and communicating the authentic content of Christian faith. Liturgical celebrations are not neutral experiences; they are symbolic affirmations of the life and history of a people (Liturgy of the world) assumed into the Paschal mystery of Jesus Christ. They influence our feelings and thoughts, emotions and aspirations, and they are the ways in which we are open to God's saving action, responding to it in faith. However this task of the liturgy will be effectively realized only if its celebration is properly inculturated, only if the signs and symbols gestures and postures, language and settings etc. are in tune with the given culture of the people concerned.

The Council has given general guidelines to all Churches on this task of inculturation. The Council also desires that wherever necessary the rites be revised carefully **in the light of sound tradition,** and that they be given new vigour **to meet the present day circumstances and needs (SC4)**. In the above statement, the two highlighted sections are worth considering in this context;

a)   In the light of sound tradition

This means that the criteria for judging the soundness of a tradition are in the capacity of the rites to communicate the original apostolic experience of the risen Lord; their mere antiquity alone has no much importance if the condition of "communication capacity' does not exist.

b)   The rites be given new vigour to meet the present-day circumstances and needs

This surely gives an unequivocal invitation to the program of renewal and updating or inculturation. These two directives a) and b) refer to two aspects of the same action: a tradition unearthed need not be sound by its mere restoration it may require updating and inculturation; so the two cannot be separated. Only when both actions take place will there be a renewed liturgy according to the Council.

Besides, the Council in the same article 4 of SC makes this telling statement: "…….in faithful obedience to tradition the sacred Council declares that Holy Mother Church holds all lawfully recognized rites to be of equal right and dignity….." The phrase "lawfully recognized rites" *(ritus legitime agnitos)* is an amended text. Before the amendment the text read thus: ".....lawfully existing rites...." (*ritus legitime vigentes*). As the late Fr. Paul Puthanangady rightly remarks, this amendment is purposeful. Without it, the text would limit the nature of the rites in the Church to those that existed before the Council, whereas, with the amendment, there is a possibility open for new rites to emerge, as the Gospel encounters other cultural groups in the world. The only condition for it is the official acceptance and recognition by the Magisterium.

Although inculturation of liturgy of the Church in the spirit of articles 4, 21 and 37-40 of SC is certainly important in particular contexts of the celebration, we must go beyond and relate liturgy to the history and life-struggles of the people. A liturgy that claims to proclaim Christ, will do so only to the extent that it identifies with the history or plan and purpose of the people. That is why, about the so-called 'protest Mass' of the Latin American people, Raphael Avila says: "In reality the mere proclamation of the Lordship of Christ does not change anything. But if the lordship of the people is proclaimed, then repression immediately follows."[18] It is a fact that we do not really hear God speaking to us in the word proclaimed during the liturgy, as long as we are deaf to his calling us in the voice of the voiceless. Similarly we do not really partake of the one bread and drink from the same cup to become one body of Christ (I Cor. 10:16), if we are not sensitive to the glaring inequalities and injustices in the parish community and of the society at large. So let us expand our vision of such inspiring forms of worms, woven out of rite and life, mystery and history of people that would be capable of 'proclaiming the death of Christ' and of many others with him, until the Lord comes.

The kind of liturgy that would fit in a mission context must also face the challenges of the Asian realities, we have noted - liberation of the poor through transformation of culture in collaboration with believers of other religions. Christian liturgy, above all the Eucharist, is the 'subversive memory' of Jesus' total commitment to the culture of the poor against the ruling class of his society. Jesus has shown that in a world that is essentially political, worship cannot be nonpolitical and neutral. In fact a neutral liturgy is a prop for the status quo, and implicitly denies that Jesus was crucified and that the Kingdom he preached is a transformative force. Therefore we may hold with Avila that "the only persons edified to participate in the celebration (of the Eucharist) are those working for liberation, and for suppression of objective conditions which make exploitation possible."[19]

Concluding Remarks

In the above few pages we were trying to discover the salient forms and features of a liturgy that would be capable of presenting Jesus Christ to the multi-cultural and multi-religious context of the modern world, which is beset with many problems, especially poverty and exploitation. In the first instance we have seen that true worship and liturgy is a far cry from the many kinds of ritual forms being paraded in numerous cult-centres. We are inspired to make a strong critique of cult by none other than Jesus himself. In his reply to the Samaritan woman, he repudiates the temple together with the entire cultic system, priestly authority, its political power and its accumulated capital. Instead of acting as a re-distributive system to secure socio-economic justice within the community of Israel, the temple accumulated capital and directly oppressed the poor by cultic obligations, which they were not able to fulfil

(See Mt. 23:4ff). By a series of words and actions Jesus made it clear that obedience is more pleasing to God than cultism, what would proclaim him better in the midst of the people is the *worship of praxis*, not the worship of words (Mt. 7:21).

This is also the meaning of Paul's exhortation to the faithful in the Church of Rome (See Rom. 12:1). When Jesus said "The Sabbath as made for man [sic], not man for the Sabbath"(Mk. 2:27), he implied that Sabbath is best celebrated in the practice of mercy and justice, or that the so-called worship of God will be hollow if it is not accompanied in a parallel 'worship of humans' who are in need. Jesus also declared elsewhere similar teaching emphasizing fellowship as the indispensable pre-condition for making an offering (See Mt. 5:23-24). Moreover he strongly condemned the evil practice of making a promissory offering to the temp le by children to evade their responsibility to the needs of their parents. (See Mt. 15:1-9). Concisely put, Jesus' approach to worship teaches us, as Rayan rightly expressed, "[His] struggle against debt and hunger, against exploitation and inequality, against hierarchism and domination of every kind his feeding and healing ministries, his socializing with the outcasts, his repudiation of oppressive power systems; and his consistent dissent from the subversion of the dominant culture are as much part of his worship of the Father as are his prayers on lonely mountains and in solitary hours, or his loud cries and tears in the watches of the night and his suffering and death."[20]

Briefly, the whole of our life in its small as well as great moments can be a liturgy that proclaims and makes present Jesus to the world. This liturgy has no time or place, no temple or priest set apart exclusively for the purpose. It can be realized at all times and places; the whole world is a temple for it and every human person is a priest who can offer the sacrifice of his work in the sanctuary of his workshop, study-room, office-table, laboratory, operation theatre, family-kitchen and so on. All these human activities can be implicit acts of worship, to the extent that we experience and accept the gracious self-communication of God in them. Our relationship with God should not be reduced to those few moments we are in the church/temple/mosque at prayer; this is a wrong way of understanding our relationship with God, as if it were one among many others. The truth is that our lives are much more deeply inter twined with God our worship embraces a much larger part of life than what is spent in the shrine/chapel during the early hours of the day. And the more attuned we become to our active participation in the ordinary wonders of the liturgy of life, the less prominent would appear ritual worshiper the liturgy of the Church.

Therefore, in order to make our liturgy, our Eucharist in particular proclaim the Lord until he comes, we have to celebrate it as a memorial to inspire us to what we can do, as a prophecy to challenge us to attempt what appears impossible, and as an imperative for our conscience to work relentlessly to secure daily bread and a measure of human dignity for all.

Endnotes

[1] C.J. Mcnapsy, "Liturgies", *The Documents of Vatican II*, New York, 1966, p.133.

[2] Cf. Avila Raphael, *Worship and Politics*, Orbis Books, Maryknoll, New York 1981, pp.79-80.

[3] Samuel Rayan, "Worship in Spirit and Truth", *Jeevadhara* 23 (1993) 247-60.

[4] English Translation CELAM, *The Church is the Present-Day Transformation of Latin America in the Light of the Council, Vol.II Conclusions*, Washington D.C., 1968, p.4.

[5] Rayan, op.cit. 249.

[6] "Worship Beyond Worship", Paul Puthanangady Ed. *Sharing Worship*, NBCLC, Bangalore, 1988, p.88.

[7] Paul Puthanangady, op.cit. p.94.

[8] Cf. J.A. Jungmann, *The Early Liturgy to the Time of Gregory the Great*, London, SCM Press, 1959, pp.134-137.

[9] Cf. Rayan op.cit. p.248.

[10] Cf. Rayan op.cit. p.249.

[11] Skelly Michael, *Liturgy of the World: Karl Rahner's Theology of worship*, Liturgical Press, Minnesota, 1991, pp.85-105.

[12] K. Rahner, *Theological Publications*, vol.5, Cross road N.Y.1963, pp.97-114.

[13] Skelly, op.cit. p.101.

[14] Ibid.

[15] Ibid. 104.

[16] G. Rosales & C.G. Arevalo, *For All Peoples of Asia*, Orbis, Maryknoll, N. York, 1992, pp.14f.

[17] M. Amaldoss, *Beyond Inculturation: Can the Many be One?*, Vidyajyoti, Delhi, 1998, p.48.

[18] Op.cit. p.86.

[19] Op.cit. p.105.

[20] Op.cit. p.253.

Chapter 7

Holy Mass Turning to the People or Away from the People?

Introduction

As this seminar has been organized to celebrate the Centenary of the birth of the late Archbishop, Joseph Cardinal Parekkattil, an illustrious son of the Syro-Malabar Church, I am extremely happy to take part in it, presenting this s paper on a subject which was one of the major concerns of the Cardinal in his relentless fight for renewal and adaptation of the Holy Eucharist in the spirit of the Second Vatican Council.

Questions like "should the Holy *Qurbāna* (Eucharist) be offered turning to the East or turning to the Altar or turning to the faithful" etc. are, to my mind, questions wrongly put. Such questions cannot be detached or de-linked from more vital questions integral to the Council's vision of liturgy and the Eucharist in particular. Besides, it may be remembered that this liturgical vision of the Council had, to a great extent, set the tone and temper of the general renewal (*aggiornamento*) of the Church as envisaged by the visionary Pope, Blessed John XXIII of happy memory. This is evident from the fact, in God's providence[1], that the first of the sixteen documents to be discussed, voted upon and passed as well as issued by the Council was the one on the "Sacred Liturgy", *Sacrosanctum Concilium* (SC hereafter). As we all know it was promulgated on December 4, 1963, "the first fruit of the Council"[2] and offered to the entire Church as the road map to liturgical renewal "in accordance with the Council's principles of fidelity to tradition and openness to legitimate development."[3]

Therefore, before we take up the precise and pointed issue "Holy Mass turning to/ facing the people" we need to attend to the following larger issues: 1. Theology of the Church of Vat. II, 2. Theology of the Ministry/Priesthood of Vat.II and Theology of the Eucharist of Vat. II, not elaborately, but at least in their bare outlines as far as required for our

Elements of the Council's Ecclesiological Vision

Fully convinced of the ancient wisdom, "The Church is to be constantly reformed" (*Ecclesia semper est reformanda*), the late Pope John XXIII wanted a top to bottom reform and up-dating of the Church to make it relevant and timely in its encounter with the contemporary world. He had indicated that the Council's task would be to concern itself with a two-fold search of the Church – *ad intra* relating to its internal structure and institutions and *ad extra*, relating to the contemporary world. In this respect his famous catch word *aggiornamento* projected a three-fold action plan: Church's (1) self-discovery, (2) self-realization and (3) world-mission[4]. Keeping in mind this three-fold process, if we analyse the contents of the 16 documents of the Council, they may be classified under the above three heads – **Church's**

self-discovery, self-realization and world-mission[5]. From the above classification it can be seen that the most important document under the first head, namely Church's self-discovery, is **Lumen Gentium [LG], which scans most effectively the true nature and structure of the Church**. The original schema of the Church had its opening chapter with the title "Hierarchy" presenting it as a concrete historical reality, as an institution in terms of visible structures, rights and powers of its own. This schema was radically modified in the Council hall and the final text passed gives us the opening chapter with the title "Mystery of the Church", followed by the next chapter with the title "People of God", and **then only comes the title "Hierarchy" as the third chapter.**

Church as the 'People of God': Its Implications according to Vat.II

Since the Council, it is quite common to describe the Church as the 'people of God'. However it seems that for the Council "people of God" was a favourite term, not simply because it was quite convinced about the communitarian nature of human salvation (cf. LG 9; AG 2). But more importantly "Vatican II wished to stress **the basic equality of all the members of the Church**. That is why *Lumen Gentium* speaks of the Church as the people of God, before it deals with the functional differences in the Church,"[6] treated in the next chapter entitled "Church is Hierarchical". Therefore it is clear that according to the mind of the Council Fathers, **the concept of Church as people of God underlines the fundamental dignity and equality of all members, irrespective of their offices and positions in the community, like bishops, priests, deacons, religious, lay persons etc.**

A New Way of Being Church according to the Council

From what has been said above, it can be seen that, the Council, playing down the traditional institutional and hierarchical models of the Church, wanted to introduce a 'new way of being Church'. This new model would not be fully democratic and never autocratic, but very much dialogical and communitarian. The various ministries in such a Church would be considered as functions within the community of the people of God. They are meant to foster the growth of the entire body of the faithful, while respecting and safeguarding the dignity and freedom of each one as Vat. II expresses it (cf.LG 18).

Emergence of Basic Christian Community (BCC) Model Church

This Vatican spirit of 'new way of being Church' that wafted gently across the globe, began to echo and re-echo from continent to continent starting with Latin America in the 1980s and under different nomenclature like BCC, SCC, BEC, BHC and the like. And this 'spirit' is being kept alive by feed-material created by different institutes and movements, like **Lumko institute of S. Africa, House Church Central movement of North America, At Your Word, Lord program of England** etc.[7] Let us try to draw up below the Post-Vatican II 'People of God' model Church contrasting it with the Pre-Vatican II 'Hierarchical' or Institutional model Church:

From Pre-Vatican Model Church to Post-Vatican Model Church

Perspectival Differences

1. A sacramentalist Church   →   A service-oriented Church

2. A clerical Church   →   A people's Church
3. An individual-salvation   →   A community salvation
    centred Ch.   centred Ch.

Shifts of Emphasis

1. From a stress on structure →   To life-spirit-growth/
    /institutions   charisms
2. From administrative task   →   To personal charisma
                                    & service
3. From hierarchical Order   →   To people's welfare
4. From being inward looking   →   To outward looking to
                                    the world
5. From being a judging   →   To being a Church
    church   in dialogue

Self-image of the Church

1. From ark of salvation   →   To symbol of salvation
2. From perfect society   →   To Pilgrim people
3. From Church of holiness   →   To Church of sinners
                                    as well as holy people

Elements of a Theology of Ministry in the Church according to Vat. II

The Council has underlined the scriptural basis of the common or people's priesthood and its implications for authentic Christian living. **Before Vat. II the lay people were overly dependent on priests to the point of remaining passive and voiceless.** They were able to do little in the religious sphere without the help of priests. They used to seek the priest's approval for everything and would not move if priests did not lead and guide them from the front.

Now, the enlightened laity knows that the ministerial priesthood (due to the sacrament of Holy Orders) is ordained to activating the priesthood of the faithful (due to baptism and confirmation); that the lay faithful also possess the Spirit and can animate the Church and have the responsibility of ministering to others. **I Peter 2:9 helps them to reflect on these truths**: In this letter St. Peter tries to console and strengthen the Christians in Asia Minor who face persecution from the surrounding people of other faiths, by pointing out some implications of their baptism. **All the four titles used in verse 9** – chosen race, royal priesthood, holy nation and God's own people, having their OT back ground (chosen race to Is.43:1; other three titles to Ex.19:6) **refer to the faithful as a whole, and not to ordained ministers alone**.

Priest: Spokesperson of One Priestly People

The picture of an ordained minister that emerges from the foregoing discussion is that he is the animator, coordinator and spokesperson of a people who are by their call priestly. He is to be their leader not by domination, but due to the quality of his service, of coordinating the efforts of all and directing them toward a common goal, while respecting the God-given dignity and freedom of every one (see LG 18). This service is rendered not only to individual members but to the community as a whole (LG 20). And on this question, Y. Congar, citing Bonaventure Kloppenburg says, "This 'service of the community' is not just a function; it is **the function** of those who receive priestly ministry through the sacrament of holy orders."[8]

Priest: Leader/President at a Participatory Liturgical Celebration

A 'participatory liturgy' may be defined as one in which all members of the celebrating community enjoy their proper vocation and fulfil their proper role[9]. According to the mind of the Council Fathers liturgy is a **communal celebration** of the whole Church as 'one priestly people', presided over by an ordained minister, in which **all are supposed to participate** actively and consciously by making use of vocal responses, bodily movements as well as moments of silence. **If the roles of the priest as leader and that of the community 'gathered in Christ' are properly understood, it is meaningless to make the distinction that the priest celebrates, whereas the people participate**. In the liturgy all are participating and all are celebrating; but certain defined ritual actions and accompanying prayers are reserved to ordained ministers, by virtue of their sacramental ordination.[10]

Elements of a Theology of the Eucharist according to the Council

Sacrifice, meal and presence: all three aspects of the Eucharistic mystery are united by an indissoluble bond. During the Council of Trent the Reformers challenged the sacrificial value of the Eucharist, which, they feared would detract from the uniqueness of Christ's sacrifice; instead they began to lay emphasis on the meal aspect of this mystery. Ever since Trent, Catholic Church began to oppose the Protestant position over emphasizing the sacrificial aspect of it to such an extent as to belittle the meal dimension. If we examine the manuals of Eucharistic theology of almost 400 hundred years between Trent and Vatican II, this impoverishment of the theology of the Eucharist can be seen.

In our own day after the Council of Vat. II, the Church is seeking to establish a balance between the various facets of this mystery and the Post-Vatican renewed theology of the Eucharist seems to have re-discovered from the Bible and the early tradition the great importance of the meal aspect without detracting from the sacrificial dimension. In fact the earliest two names given to this mystery – 'breaking of bread' (Acts 2:42) and 'Lord's Supper' (I Cor.11:20) by the Church remind us very well of this meal dimension.

The Eucharist and Community

In whatever way the Eucharist be interpreted theologically[11] there is no doubt that its basic symbolic action is a **shared community meal taken in memory of Christ, celebrating his paschal mystery**. The agent of this symbolic action is the community led by the priest, **which becomes and acts as the Body of Christ with its head Jesus Christ**. The priest prays and acts in the name of the community. **The community is part of the action; is the celebrant, not merely a participant as a kind of observer**. It is not outside it or only drawing benefit from it. Besides, Eucharist is not a meal that follows a sacrifice, nor a meal that replaces the sacrifice. It is the memorial meal of the Last Supper, anticipating the sacrifice on the Cross. Hence as such a sacrificial meal. All this means **that the meal is a high point of the life of a community to express love for one another by sharing their goods**. And St. Paul makes it clear that a Christian community cannot celebrate the Eucharist meaningfully without sharing also their goods (Cf. Acts 2:42-47). Sharing a meal of food and drink is symbol of sharing life and all that it demands not only with Christ but also with one's brothers and sisters.[12]

Law of Orientation in Worship: Insights from the Council's Theological Vision

We have discussed very briefly in the foregoing pages the Council's vision of an ecclesiology or theology of the Church, a theology of the priesthood or ministry in the Church and a theology of the Eucharist. We shall now try to gather the main insights from these three discussions that would hopefully lead us to an objective assessment of the question of, which way we need to turn in liturgical worship, in the celebration of the Eucharist in particular.

1. St. Paul makes an intriguing connection between the Church and the Eucharist, in terms of the metaphor of the Body of Christ: Church is the **ecclesial body of Christ**, namely a community of Christ's disciples convoked by God himself, as the word '*ekklesia*' connotes against its OT background,[13] so that God is in their midst; he speaks his Word to them, and the 'assembly that is the church' (Mt. 16:18) comes to an end with a covenant sacrifice.[14] In other words, in the New Testament, Church is the liturgical assembly convoked by Christ in which his manifold presence is assured, of which the presence in the eucharistized bread and wine is unique (*modo singulari*).[15] And here we have in that 'Eucharist', namely the **sacramental body of Christ, the Church**. "The Church makes the Eucharist, even as the Eucharist makes the Church", so goes the Patristic wisdom.

The Council's theological vision of the Church as the 'people of God' has been surely inspired by this Pauline insight. At every Eucharistic gathering **top priority is for the experience of Christ's presence in the midst of the community through the fourfold action**: turning to one another as a community, turning to the Word of God, turning to the priest-celebrant and turning to the Lord in the sacrificial meal. **What other community model but the BCC can graphically picture to us the face of such a Church!** In such a Church the basic equality of all members is guaranteed and at the same time a functional leadership role of a particular member as the coordinator & president is taken for granted.

2. As we have seen, the Council's theology of priesthood underlines the common priesthood of the faithful, that the basis of ministerial priesthood is the common priesthood, that the people are not only participants in, but also celebrants of the liturgy. Besides, In the document of the 'Life and Ministry of Priests", *Presbyterium Ordinis* stress is made on their being collaborators with the bishops in carrying out the Church's mission rather than the exercise of the individual's *potestas ordinis* (power of Order). And this should give each priest a greater sense of being part of the people God (See PO 2). Moreover, "PO 9 envisages a Church in which the laity has a place of respect and a responsible role to play."[16] Again this way of understanding priest-laity respectful collaboration in the context of the Eucharistic celebration can be achieved only in a BCC, circular understanding of the Church, without endangering the hierarchy'[17] and not in a 'leader-followers' model, which is the picture drawn by a Mass turning away from the people or worse still turning back to the people. In this circular understanding of the Church, "There is a collective leadership in which the priest is the spiritual leader who inspires and animates the community."[18]

The Eucharist as Memorial Meal: Insights from Vatican II

From the Council's emphasis on the Church as a 'people of God' and from its re-discovery of the biblically rich meal-dimension of the Eucharist, arises the spontaneous picture of the Eucharistic assembly in a BCC circular model under the 'servant-leadership' of an ordained minister. The underlined basic symbolic action is a shared community meal taken in memory of Christ, celebrating his paschal mystery.

1. A synchronized symbolism of a community, called by the Lord (*Ekklesia*), of the word of God proclaimed, broken and shared, and of the communion of the 'food over which thanks has been said' (Justin the Martyr), under the servant leadership of an ordained minister powerfully evokes the picture of a 'Lord's Supper' model of the Eucharist, envisaged by St. Paul.

2. The origin and evolution of the rite of the Eucharist speak volumes of its meal dimension: The Eucharist grew out of the context of the Passover meal of the Jews (commemorating the events of creation, sacrifice of Abraham, Exodus and the coming of the Messiah). After the Passover meal, Jesus took bread and cup of wine, praying and giving thanks... (The rest is history and mystery).

Among the disciples of Jesus after the Resurrection, the Eucharist was celebrated at the end of a common meal (I Cor. 11: 17-34). Due to abuses the meal Eucharist was shifted from actual meal, and evening meal (supper) was shifted to Sunday morning. Liturgy of the word used in the synagogue was integrated in the Eucharist. It is thus, the Eucharist became more of worship and sacrifice of praise and thanks. The table used for meal was changed over to altar of 'sacrifice'. Bread became thin white wafer due to economic reasons and increase of the number of faithful. But the basic character of the Eucharist as meal (gathering, greeting, bonding, strengthening relationships etc.) still exists and has been re-discovered by the Council of Vatican II.

The Eucharist Versus *Populum/Altare*

Let us now take up the precise question at issue: Mass Facing the People as it has been put in the title. The Greeks, the Romans and most of the ancient peoples worshipped turning to the East, as they regarded the place of the rising sun as the source of life, power and happiness; temples were so built as to let the rays of the rising sun fall upon the idol when the door was opened in the morning. Christians also at least from the 2nd century C.E. prayed facing the East, and this practice got momentum when Christ began to be symbolized by the sun[19].

But **the truth is that Christ is also symbolized in the Bible by the lamb, the bread, vine, and way, light, door, shepherd** etc. The risen Lord is not just localized in the East; he promised to be with his disciples as they go in all directions proclaiming his Word among all the peoples. Wherever two or three meet in his name, **he is there irrespective of the direction they face together**, or they face one another in a circle (Mt. 28:19-20; 18:19-20). Commenting on these passages Samuel Rayan, SJ adds that Christ is in every starved man and deprived woman and hungry child; and in all the stripped, despoiled and broken, **regardless of what the compass says**. The Eucharist which is the supreme act of Christian worship, he says, is not a procession led by the **priest and moving towards the sun**, but a shared meal with historical roots in Jesus' fellowship meals with the impoverished and outcaste of the society.[20]

God surely is in the East, though that is not his only address; in fact his ineffable presence everywhere is the theme of Ps. 139, and this experience of the Psalmist is equally shared by our ancestors who knew that this whole earth is pervaded by the Lord (*īshāvāsyamidam sarvam*), that the Lord dwells in the heart of every created reality (see Is.Up.1; Bh.G. ch.10). The Creator of the world does not need for his home shrines and basilicas, veiled sanctuaries and hidden tabernacles made by human hands (Acts 17:24-25). In whatever direction we turn we are face to face with him. Indeed in him we live, we move and have our existence (Acts 17:28). If we would express his presence and our being face to face with him most symbolically. **The finest symbol is human person. Facing East rests on religious cosmology; facing Jerusalem or Mecca hinges on salvation history, but facing one another is rooted in the mystery of the Body of Christ, the community of bread-sharing.**[21]

Other Views and their Critical Assessment

That the Council did not say about Mass facing the people [22]
First of all, the Council in general did not make any 'executive' decisions regarding the programs of renewal of the liturgy; rather it has given principles and norms for the reform of the liturgy, based on which practical norms should be established by the competent bodies, as clearly mentioned in article 4 of SC. And as for the Roman Church this practical decision was established by the Congregation by Divine Worship when it published the *General Instruction of the Roman Missal and General Norms for the Liturgical Year and Calendar*, 1970, (here after referred to as GI) in which we read thus:

> The main altar should be freestanding, so that the ministers can easily walk around it and Mass can be celebrated facing the people. It should be placed in a central position which draws the attention of the whole congregation (no. 262)

Besides, while speaking about the position of the "celebrant's chair in the sanctuary", it is said that "...the proper place for the chair is in the centre of the sanctuary **facing the people, unless** the structure or other circumstances are an obstacle..." (no. 271; emphasis added)

That never in the history of the Church until 1969 was a tradition of celebrating Mass facing the people[23]

This is a hyperbolic statement. There is enough evidence to show that in the apostolic and post-apostolic community of Jesus disciples, the celebration of the "Lord's Supper" (St. Paul) was as memorial meal of Jesus' Last Supper. *Didache* chapter14 as well as Justin's Apology 65-67 give sufficient indications of the situation of celebration in the middle of the 2nd century. Of course, we need to understand that in the early Church the meal aspect of the Eucharist was quite spontaneously understood and accepted. In the GI, nos. 2 and3 perhaps for the same reason, the meal aspect is mentioned first, and as J. H. Emminghaus has rightly suggested, "the Mass is a rite derived from a meal, not from a Eucharist as sacrifice. As a memorial of his pasch, the Lord left his Church the Eucharist, that is the prayer of thanksgiving over bread and wine as elements of a meal.......It is therefore important that in celebrating the memorial of the Lord we give careful consideration to the meal aspect of the Eucharist. Behind and above this meal form, however lies the reality of the sacrifice of Christ and the Church. "Sacrifice" here must doubtless be taken in a rather broad sense as self-giving. And we must not read into it all the implications of a later theology.[24] This understanding of the Eucharist in its 'meal form' and use of the following expressions, like "When we finish praying, we greet one another with a kiss. Then bread and a cup containing water, and wine mixed with water **are brought to him who presides over the brethren.........**" can help us to infer that the assembly is not oriented to East or West, that is in any particular direction, but faces one another in a circular direction – the BCC church model we have noted above.

That Mass is part of the Pilgrim Church on the way to her heavenly home land, the priest leading the people who follow him[25]

This view is due to the Pre-Vatican perception of the Church mainly as a hierarchy. But in the Post-Vatican perception of the Church as 'people of God', we have 'a new way of being Church', discussed above as BCC model, in which the leadership of the ministerial priesthood is understood as service in terms of the principle of collegiality. Besides, yes, the Church is a pilgrim people led by their priest-servants towards the *eschaton*. Now, the Eucharist is the 'bread broken and shared' as a meal on the 'day of the Lord' on their way, in memory of His redemptive death. Hence a celebration facing the people or rather Mass around the altar is more fitting than the one turning away from the people.

That the Mass facing the people makes the priest 'the performer and the people spectators'[26]

This seems to be a rather silly or childish objection raised by some people who have probably psychological problem to face people. In fact the centre of concentration in Mass turning to the people is not priest or any particular person, but the cross which is obligatory to be placed on the altar between the priest and people. Hence GI says: "There should also be a cross, easily seen by the congregation either on the altar or near it." (no. 270). In fact in Mass facing the people, priest in his servant hood is not a performer, but a humble minister, well integrated with the community, and the people not a mob watching a show (which may be the case if the priest keeps his back turned to them), but a real community of persons with 'full, conscious and active participation' in the celebration assured.

Concluding Remarks

Pope Emeritus Benedict XVI in recent years seems to have spoken or written in support of Mass turning to the East and about the 'theological significance of priests and people facing East towards the Lord to come.'[27] The Pope is considered a strong supporter of turning to the East in our prayer and naturally in offering the Mass. However, for him "East" is not exactly a geographical location, but rather a symbol of the Cross, which itself is a unique symbol of our salvation. For, in his book *Feast of Faith* and under the title 'East or Westward –Facing? A correction' he argues that what is most important is not 'East' or 'West', but looking towards the cross, which is the symbol of our salvation. Besides, elsewhere he proposes a solution to the controversial question of Mass versus *altare/populum*, suggesting that wherever turning to the actual East is not possible, the Cross may be taken as the interior 'East' of faith, which should stand in the middle of the altar as the common point of focus for the priest and the people. And this position of the Pope comes very close to what we noted earlier with regard to Mass facing one another, if we simply change it as 'Mass around the altar.'[28]

The context of this study on "Mass facing the people", as we know is the celebration of the birth centenary of Cardinal Parekkatil of happy memory, who loved so much to reform and update our liturgy in the spirit and theological vision of

Vat. II, because he strongly believed (and there is much truth in it also) that what SC, no.3 says regarding the application of the principles of liturgical reform concerns not only Roman Rite, but to a great extent other Rites, including Syro-Malabar Rite also. The Council's vision of *aggiornamento* is two-fold – restoration and renewal. If restoration is the thrust of OE, and it should be rightly so, as far as the Orientals are concerned, that of SC is renewal, without at the same time neglecting either the question of renewal in OE and restoration in SC. And so an integral vision of liturgy according to the Council need to take into account not only OE but SC as well. The restored liturgy of the Syro-Malabar Church, especially in its solemn forms, does not seem to have taken this point seriously. In its present form, with priest and people completely turned to the East/ altar,[29] is more suitable for a well-established stagnant Church; it fosters rather the status quo of whatever kind, but offers no challenge to a pilgrim people and a missionary community; does not inspire especially the youth for liberative social action. It may be more appealing to retired, ethno-centric and middle-aged aristocracy, as it prepares them well for their final journey of hope in the Lord.

Let me conclude this discussion, quoting the words of J. H. Emminghaus, a trusted. Follower of the late Pius Parsch, at the Vienna university. Emminghaus, after having scanned the history and practice of the 'law of orientation' in the Church, concludes:

> The principle of orientation admittedly disappeared from the popular consciousness in the Middle Ages and in modern times; yet on the grounds of tradition, though frequently with no grasp of the real point, it continued to be observed in the constructions of churches and location of altars. In our day, the logical conclusion has been drawn from the change of consciousness, and the altar is again being placed in the centre between the priest and people. In other words, the "ideological" law of

orientation, by which the original natural relationship between celebrant and congregation had been distorted and become unfamiliar, has now been given up in favour of the older and, functional view point, certainly more correct face-to-face position of priest and people.[30]

Endnotes

[1] Whatever be the extrinsic circumstances under which the Council had to begin its first session, discussing SC and getting it passed along with a second document on IM (Communication Media), it was indeed God's providence.

[2] John Paul II, Vicessimus Quintus Annus [VQA], no.1.

[3] VQA, no.4; also SC, no.23.

[4] Here step (1) means this: By a thorough self-examination of the Church's origin and growth through the vicissitudes of time and history, she would re-discover her authentic nature, step (2) means this: She would re-affirm this true nature through a programme of reflection, prayer and action and thus actualize herself in tune with the discovery made; and step (3) means that this 'new way of becoming Church' itself would make herself 'missionary' of the Good News to the modern world.

[5] Classification of the 16 Documents of the Council of Vatican II into the Councils Three-fold Objective:

(1)	Church's Self-Discovery Documents	1. Lumen Gentium (LG) 2. Orientalium Ecclesiarum (OE) 3. Unitatis Redintegratio (UR) 4. Dei Verbum (DV)
(2)	Church's Self-Realization Documents	1. Sacrosanctum Concilium (SC) 2. Perfectae Caritatis (PC) 3. Optatam Totius (OT) 4. Apostolicam Actuositatem(AA) 5. Presbyterium Ordinis(PO) 6. Christus Dominus (CD)
(3)	Church's World-Mission Documents	1. Gaudium et Spes (GS) 2. Nostrae Aetatae (NA) 3. Ad Gentes (AG) 4. Dignitatis Humanae (DH) 5. Gravissimum Educationis (GE) 6. Inter Mirificum (IM)

For details about the rationale of this classification and its meaning see my article "Church: the Sign of Prophetic Love and Service – the Focus of Second Vatican Council" in Third Millennium XIII(2010)3, July-September, 26-45.

[6] Kurien Kunnumpuram S.J., The Indian Church of the Future, St. Pauls: Mumbai, 2007, pp.113-123 (117). Emphasis added.

[7] Cf. Joseph G. Healey, Small Christian Communities Today: Capturing the New Moment, Claretian Publications: Bangalore, 2005.

[8] Y. Congar, The Lay People in the Church, London: Geoffrey Chapmann, 1965, p.43. Emphasis added.

[9] We have here imitated Ecclesia in Asia in its definition of a Participatory Church as in no. 25.

[10] See my article "The Role of the Laity from the Perspective of the Syro-Malabar Liturgy" in Paul Puthanangady Ed. Together in One Priesthood, NBCLC: Bangalore, 1991, pp.48-58.

[11] Usually three different ways it is understood: primarily as a sacrifice followed by a meal or a sacrificial meal or a sacrament of Christ's bodily presence which becomes food and drink for the community.

[12] Cf. M. Amaldoss SJ, "The Eucharist and the Christian Community", in VIDYAJYOTI: Journal of Theological Reflection, Vol.68, No.10, 2004, pp.721-733.

[13] The Greek word ekklesia from the Hebrew word qahal brings out the first characteristic of the assembly of the people, namely that it was convoked by God himself. See A.G. Martimort, The Church at Prayer, Vol.I: Principles of Liturgy, Liturgical Press: Minnesotta, p.92.

[14] Ibid.

[15] S. Congregation of Rites, Eucharisticum Mysterium, 1967 shows how in the unfolding of the Eucharistic celebration, the various modes of Christ's presence in the liturgical assembly are progressively revealed. See no. 1585 in Neuner-Dupuis, ed. The Christian Faith, TPI: Bangalore, 1981.

[16] Errol DD' Lima, "Priestly Formation for the Service of the World", in Vatican II: A Gift and A Task, Ed. By Jacob Kavunkal et al, St. Pauls :Mumbai, 2006, p.234.

[17] Msgr. Bosco Puthur, "Vision of the Vatican Council II and the clergy of the Syro-Malabar Church", in Pauly Kannookaedan Ed., Syro-Malabar Church: Forty Years after the Vatican Council II, LRC publ. 14, Mount St. Thomas, 2007, p.175.

[18] Ibid.

[19] Cf. J. Jungmann, The Early Liturgy to the Time of Gregory the Great, SCM Press: London, 1959, pp.134-137.

[20] Cf. Rayan, "Worship in Spirit and Truth', Jeevadhara, Vol.23, 1993, pp.247-60 (248).

[21] Louis Malieckal, "A Liturgy For Mission that Proclaims Jesus Christ to all Peoples and Cultures", in Third Millennium II (1999)2, 8-24; see Rayan, op.cit. p.249.

[22] J. Ratzinger, The Spirit of the Liturgy, San Francisco, 1999, 9.78; also quoted by Bishop Thomas Elavanal, "Influence of the Vatican Council II on the Syro-Malabar Church", in Pauly Kannookand Ed. op.cit. p.111.

[23] Joseph Fessio, "The Mass of Vatican II", in Catholic Dossier 5, no.5, 2000, 12-20.

[24] The Eucharist: Essence, Form and Celebration, Liturgical Press: Minnesota, 1978, p.xx; A.G. Martimort op.cit. Vol.II, p.14.

[25] Joseph Fessio, work cited.

[26] Joseph Fessio, ibid.

[27] Bp. Thomas Elavanal in the book ed. By Pauly Kannookadan, p.111.

[28] Cf. Fr.Antony Narikulam, in Pauly Kannookadan, ed. op.cit. p.129, where he refers to the book of the Pope mentioned.

[29] I can still find some justification for the option of turning to the altar for the anaphora part of the Eucharist, called liturgy of the faithful, although even this cannot be considered unchangeable.

[30] Op.cit. pp.47-50 (50).

Chapter 8

Participatory Liturgy in the Vision of Vatican II

Introduction

As the Central theme of this Colloquium is **Vatican II: A Gift and a Task**, it is indeed fitting to discuss a topic of the kind addressed in this presentation namely **A Participatory Liturgy in the Vision of the Council**. For, when the Council finally entered into its second phase of Celebration,[1] its deliberations began surprisingly not on a document on the Church (which would have established the locus of all others including the liturgy), but on that of the Liturgy: its Reform and Renewal in particular, hoping that this would be the most effective approach in order to attain the Council's fourfold goal, namely, 1. To impart an ever increasing vigour to the life of the faithful, 2. To adapt more closely to the needs of our age those institutions which are subject to change, 3. To foster whatever can promote union among all who believe in Christ, and 4. To strengthen whatever can help to call the humankind into the Church's fold.[2]

Moreover, of the sixteen Documents of the Council, the one on the Liturgy *Sacrosanctum Concilium* (SC) was the first to be promulgated on Dec.4, 1963 which is also very much pastoral in its tone in tune with the saintly Pope John's original vision and purpose regarding the Council.[3] Therefore while celebrating the 40th anniversary of the Council's closure in 1965 by organizing this Colloquium, the need and relevance of this presentation can hardly be exaggerated.

The following will be our method of presentation: **First** we shall go straight to the texts of the liturgy document (SC) to know what the Council has said on the matter; **secondly** we shall analyze and comment on the texts based on important commentaries and thus bring out the full meaning and implications of these texts regarding a participatory liturgy, **thirdly** we shall examine how far the vision of the Council on this matter has been realized, especially in the Indian Church, and **finally** we shall conclude the discussion touching on what may be called the **'unfinished agenda' of the Council** on this matter.

What the Council has Said: A Textual Excursus on Participatory Liturgy

It can be seen that SC repeatedly makes use of the expression "full, conscious and active participation" in a number of places in the document[4] In order to achieve such a participation some of the means proposed are "acclamations, responses, psalms, antiphons, hymns, and actions and gestures and bodily postures."(SC30). This is made explicit in the next article, saying that "When the liturgical books are being revised, the people's parts must be carefully indicated by the rubrics (SC31). Further, SC proposes that the liturgical rites be simple, short and clear without useless repetitions and within people's power of understanding (Cfr. SC34). Evidently these measures are meant to ensure people's active participation as is made clear elsewhere as follows: "The rite of the Mass is to be revised in such a way that the intrinsic nature and purpose of its several parts as well as the connection between them may be clearly manifested, and that devout and active participation by the faithful may be more easily achieved." (SC50). Besides, the Council, even while favouring Latin as the language of the liturgy, adds this significant note: "But, since the use of vernacular...... may be of great advantage to the people, a wider use may be made of it....." (SC36; see also 54).

The Council Fathers, representing a host of cultures and traditions of the universal Church[5] were aware of the pressing need of cultural adaptations in the liturgy in order to take it closer to the people. That is why the Document says: "Even in the liturgy the Church does not wish to impose a rigid uniformity in matters which do not involve the faith or the good of the whole community. Rather does she respect and foster the qualities and talents of the various races and nations....." (SC37). After impartial study and discerning process genuine values and ethos of these peoples may be incorporated into the liturgy (Cfr. Ibidem). Dealing especially with the Holy Eucharist, the Council says that it "earnestly desires that Christ's faithful when present at this mystery of faith, **should not be there as strangers or silent spectators**.....they should take part in the sacred action, conscious of what they are doing, with devotion and full collaboration offering the immaculate victim, **not only through the hands of the priest** but also together with him, they should learn to offer themselves..." (SC48)[6]

The importance of reading the Word of God in the liturgy more lavishly is highlighted in order to provide a "richer fare for the faithful" (Cfr. SC51). In particular a homily to break the Word properly is highly recommended at those Masses which are celebrated with the people assisting, and on "Sundays and holidays of obligation….it should not be omitted except for a serious reason." (SC52). Another instance of the Council's view of a participatory liturgy may be seen in its decision to restore "the common prayer "or "prayer of the faithful" especially on Sundays and holidays of obligation, because in them the people are actively involved. (Cfr.SC 53). Similarly the Council "warmly recommends" communion of the faithful from the same holy Mass which would demonstrate a "more perfect form of participation in the Mass." (SC55). The Council has also suggested structures and training centers which would initiate God's people, including those under formation for better and more active participation in the liturgy (Cfr. Nos 17, 19 and 43)

Liturgical Celebration versus Participation

Before proceeding to examine the implications of the Conciliar texts on the matter, we need to clarify the above two concepts – celebration and participation as related to liturgy. The document *Ecclesia in Asia* has defined a 'participatory Church' as one "in which all members enjoy their proper vocation and perform their proper role."[7] Similarly we may understand a 'participatory liturgy' as one in which all members of the celebrating community enjoy their proper vocation and fulfil their proper role.

Vatican II makes clear that liturgical celebrations are the action of Christ and of the Church or of the whole Body of Christ. They concern also individual members in different ways, depending upon the diversity of orders, ministries and their actual participation in them (SC26; see also *Redemptionis Sacramentum* –RS 36). Moreover, the Council has observed that the people should be encouraged to participate actively by means of acclamations, responses, psalms, antiphons and hymns as well as bodily gestures and postures and even by reverent silence (SC30).

From these and similar texts of the Council documents, it can be seen that according to the mind of the Council Fathers, liturgy is a communal celebration of the whole Church as 'one priestly people' (cfr. I Pt.2:9-10),[8] presided over, of course, by an ordained minister, in which all are supposed to participate actively and consciously by making use of vocal responses like readings, prayers and acclamations, bodily movements, gestures and postures as well as moments of silence. In other words, the concept of 'Celebration' evokes in the first place the external and action-oriented aspect of the liturgy, whereas that of 'Participation' expresses primarily the internal attitude and deep wonder before the great mystery being celebrated. And both are necessary for any meaningful liturgy.

Briefly the concept of participation goes beyond external and loud cries, noisy singing and praying. It means first and foremost, understanding and becoming familiar with the Bible, responding to the Word and committing oneself to it through the sacraments for renewal of hearts and fraternal charity. **Hence in the liturgy all are participating and all are celebrating; but certain defined ritual actions are reserved to ordained ministry.** On the contrary in the case of non-liturgical celebrations, for example popular devotions, the aspect of celebration can become more pronounced with the active involvement of the laity, which, if properly guided by pastoral prudence, can contribute towards active and meaningful celebration of the liturgy as well. Thus if we keep this unity as well as distinction between the two concepts, we can avoid any possible confusion in the use of terms like "celebrating community"[9] or "Celebrants All,"[10] etc.

Inferences and Implications of the Concerned Texts on Participatory Liturgy

Already in the opening paragraph of SC, one of the four declared objectives of the Council is 'to impart an ever-increasing vigour to the Christian life of the faithful', and this objective is to be attained through 'reform and promotion of the liturgy' (Cfr. SC 1). The Council was painfully aware of the distance between liturgy and the life of the people that existed for several centuries since the Council of Trent and Reformation. One of the main reasons for this awful situation was the rigid liturgical laws and regulations to safeguard unity and stability in liturgical celebrations. However, it is common knowledge that this pre-occupation for unity and stability soon imposed uniformity and conformity in all matters concerning liturgy, leading to fossilization and immobilization of both liturgical theology and liturgical practice. There was loud cry and clarion call from below for liturgical reform and restoration, renewal and adaptation from the time of the great Liturgical Movement towards the end of the 19th century which actually paved the way for the liturgical thought of the Council. Hence it is obvious that its document SC on liturgy is very much in favour of a people-friendly or participatory liturgy, and not for one alienated from them.

SC 50, second paragraph needs to be cited before its historical back ground and prophetical vision are elucidated:

"For this purpose [of people's active participation] the rites are to be simplified, due care being taken to preserve their substance. Parts which with the passage of time came to be duplicated or were added with little advantage, are to be omitted. Other parts which suffered loss through accidents of history are to be restored to the vigour they had in the days of the Holy Fathers, as may be useful and necessary."

The question here concerns revision of the Roman Missal which was in use for the past about 400 years ever since its promulgation in 1570 by Pope Pius V, following the decisions of the Council of Trent. Two trends were visible among the Council Fathers on this issue. Some of them favoured it citing the pastoral benefit of active participation and liturgical advantage of restoring the Roman rite to its original simplicity and splendour. Others however feared that the proposed revision, in spite of its pastoral benefit of people's active participation, might cause scandal, impair the sanctity of the Mass and eventually do away with this very ancient rite inspired by the sobriety of ancient Rome. In the wake of these two views, some strongly recommended moderation in introducing changes so that the text could be passed. And this was achieved by inserting into the draft text Pope Pius V's revered phrase "in keeping with the pristine rule of the Holy Fathers" *(ad pristinam sanctorum patrum normam)*, and thus we have the present text SC50 passed by the Council. Besides, the text of SC23 which speaks about retaining sound tradition, while keeping the way open to legitimate progress, and SC33-36 which assure that restoration does not disregard pastoral needs, were also passed by the Council to keep balance between the two views of classical restoration and pastoral exigency expressed in SC50.

In particular, the articles SC 33, 34 and 35 underscoring simplicity, brevity and clarity of liturgical rites would certainly lead to the improvement of the quality of active participation of the congregation. As for article 36, while it makes mention on the use of Latin, does in fact recognize that use of vernacular "frequently may be of great advantage to the people," and so along with SC 54 it really supports extended use of vernacular within the Holy Mass. Thus restoration of the classical shape of the Mass was not meant to retard progress of liturgical *aggiornamento*, rather its ultimate aim was to achieve more readily devout and active participation of the faithful.[11]

New Order of the Roman Mass and Its Cultural Adaptation

The revision and restoration of the classical form of the Roman Mass envisaged in SC 50 perhaps did not have a vision very much beyond that of the 1570 missal of Pope Pius V, to produce a new Order of the Mass. Perhaps at the time of the Council the idea of alternative Orders of Mass was regarded as deviation from the long-standing tradition of the Roman rite. However the programme of classical restoration called for in SC 50 opened up new horizons of liturgical creativity, and a new Order of Mass was prepared in light of the decrees of the Council; it was formally approved and promulgated by the late Pope Paul VI by his Apostolic Constitution *Missale Romanum* of April 3, 1969 and introduced by the Congregation for Divine Worship on March 26, 1970 by its decree General Instruction on the Roman Missal.

This new order of the Mass is a great step forward, compared to the 1570 missal of Pope Pius V, regarding proper revision and restoration to the tradition of the early Church

Fathers, because the discovery of more important and more ancient manuscripts on the matter took place only after the 16th century. Both the Apostolic Constitution and the General Instruction have contributed towards cultural adaptation of the new Roman missal of 1970, as mentioned above. AS for the former, Pope Paul VI, having welcomed his predecessor Pope John XXIII's initiative towards restoration of the Paschal Vigil and the Holy Week, makes this remark in *Missale Romanum* that it can be considered as "the first step towards adaptation of the Roman Missal to the new outlook and spiritual mentality of our own times." He must have been aware that the Roman simplicity, brevity and sobriety of the text, might find it difficult to resist cultural adaptation when introduced into local Churches in the world over.

On the other hand the other document General Instruction (GI), which introduced the New Order of the Mass, is more explicit and forward-looking in this matter of cultural adaptation. It admits that "the single faith has been expressed in quite diverse human and social forms prevailing in Semitic, Greek and Latin cultures." (GI, Intr.9). GI thus seems to hold that diversity in cultural expressions was partly responsible for diversity in liturgical forms. It further adds "how the Holy Spirit keeps the people of God faithful in preserving the deposit of faith unchanged, while prayers and rites differ greatly." (Ibidem). That is why GI sponsored the most innovative decision and said: "In accord with the Constitution on the Liturgy, each conference of bishops may establish additional norms for its territory to suit the traditions and character of the people, regions and various communities." (GI, ch.I.6). It is significant that GI in a foot note makes reference to SC 37-40. The inclusion of article 40 suggests that it endorses radical adaptation of the new Order of Mass to the culture and traditions of various peoples. And it further points to possibilities of alternative orders of the Mass, as hinted at also by SC4 (11A).

Briefly, SC 50 has set the stage for people-friendly liturgy by restoring the order of Mass to its classical shape before 8th century. This has provided the local churches with an ideal *terminus a quo* of cultural adaptation. Moreover, the entire Conciliar document SC through several of its numbers like 14,19, 21, 27, 30, 36, 41, 48, 50 etc. has given top priority to full, active and conscious participation of the people. The basic criteria and *raison d'etre* for revision and adaptation in the final analysis is the Council's concern for promoting genuine participation of the people. Since GI cites all the four articles 37-40 on inculturation bearing on the new order of Mass, future possible variations in it may not be confined to pastoral relevance. In particular, inclusion of article 40 on radical adaptation can lead to drawing up new orders of Mass for local Churches, which is also favoured by a general principle maintained in article SC4. Nevertheless the passage from the Roman Order of Mass to alternative Orders is a tremendous task ahead for local Churches. Important points to remember in this matter are (i) fidelity to the sound tradition, (ii) sense of creativity tempered by prudence, and (iii) respect for authentic culture and tradition of the people.[12]

Level of Implementation of the Council's Vision of a Participatory Liturgy

Prof. Jaroslav Pelikan, a Reformation scholar as observer at Vatican II, is reported to have said as follows on the Liturgy Document immediately after the Council: "That the Document can be translated into action still remains to be seen".[13] In spite of the professor's minimal expectancy about SC's implementation, the last 50 years' history tells us a different story. Joseph Cardinal Cordeiro puts it this way: "If we alight on some random spot where the Document has been taken seriously and pick for example an average or even unlettered Catholic; let him see on a video tape his own comings and goings and doings at a Sunday Mass of the early 1960's; then expose him to a corresponding video tape of the way he fits into the Sunday celebration of today, he could be startled out of his wits. Without realizing it, without keeping tag of the intervening stages, he finds that he has been through a revolution in his mode of worship."[14] How did this 'revolution' come about? On reflection we discover some outstanding features, which made the Post-Vatican liturgy people-oriented.

A Life-sustaining Worship

We discover in the first instance a life-sustaining liturgy. The Document presented a liturgy that touches life, springs from life and flows into rough and tumble of human life. The renewed liturgy has brought humans to worship God in gratitude. He hopes to carry there from the inner reserves he needs to meet the mounting pressures of daily life. Briefly, worship now can work out to be the "source and summit of Christian life and mission.'

A Relaxing Church at Worship

This is the second discovery that we make: As against a Church in a state of siege, tension and insecurity as well as concern to 'hold on 'at the time of the Council of Trent, which reflected in the worship of the time,[15] SC presents us the Church not only at worship, but relaxing at worship, relaxing to be herself regardless of all else. And this relaxing mood has spilled over to three positive notes of the worshipping community:

A Sense of Community

Worshippers can now enter the Church, not as second class citizens, but as living members of the 'people of God', called to celebrate the New Covenant of Jesus, knowingly, actively and fruitfully. This sense of community has blossomed impressively in small communities at worship. Whereas it is still a far cry in big parish gatherings and celebrations.

An Absorbing Presence of the Risen Lord

The relaxing posture of the Church shines well when the community slips into the absorbing presence of the risen Lord, mentioned by the Document. Namely the fourfold presence of Jesus in the community, in the word spoken/ proclaimed, in the symbol of the Priest-president and in a unique way in the Eucharistic elements. These progressive encounters with the Lord call for deep inner responses that lead the people to experience the transforming power of the Spirit as happened at the first Pentecost.

A Discovery of the Scripture and the Spirit of Ecumenism

This is the third feature of the relaxing Church. SC 24 opened the way for the discovery of the Scripture. It acknowledges the Scripture as the fountain and inspiration of so many liturgical elements and so earnestly appeals for the promotion of 'that sweet and living love' for it. SC 24 along with UR 15 also promotes the spirit of ecumenism in the celebration of the Eucharist, by acknowledging 'the sweet and living love for the sacred Scripture of the venerable Eastern and Western traditions', and 'with what love the Eastern Christians celebrate the sacred liturgy, especially the Eucharistic mystery.'

Implementation: National and Regional Levels

In the foregoing paragraphs we have made some general observations about the implementation of the Council's vision of liturgy in the Church at large. Perhaps it is more relevant and useful to consider the same question as applied to the Churches in India. The late Fr. Gerwin, who was closely associated with NBCLC and its Post-Vatican liturgical movement from its beginning till 2000, gives us a very objective assessment in his article "Liturgy in India After Vatican II."[16] He treats the subject mainly with regard to the Latin Rite. We shall present his report briefly, and then add some remarks as regards the other two Ritual Churches in India.

Shortly after the National Seminar on Church in India To day of 1969, took place the solemn inauguration of the NBCLC in 1971. And for the following 20 years the history of liturgical renewal in India coincided to a great extent with that of this National Center. The late Fr. Amalorpavadas, its Founder-Director, was deeply convinced that liturgical renewal was an ecclesial movement a people-oriented programme. For its actualization he made use of two methods.

All India Liturgical Meetings (AILM)

From 1968 to 1989 eight AILMs were conducted for the actualization of the Council's vision of liturgy on a national level. The AILM was composed of members of the CBCI Liturgy Commission (consisting of bishops, a knowledgeable and representative body of consultants and advisors) and the secretaries of the Regional and Diocesan Liturgical Commissions. Thus the whole Church, as it were, was involved through representatives, which made the liturgical renewal an ecclesial process or a people-friendly movement.

Manifold Liturgical Diakonia of NBCLC

This was the second method of actualization of the Council's vision enshrined in SC. This was done as follows:

1. By organizing animation seminars at NBCLC and in many dioceses with their cooperation.

2. By conducting such animation courses of three months at NBCLC in order to train regional/diocesan leaders of liturgical renewal. Quite a number of religious also took part in these courses and became trained liturgical leaders in their respective Congregations.

3. By publishing the relevant ritual books and liturgical documents in English, as soon as they became available through NBCLC's warm relationship with ICEL.

4. By publishing the review "Word and Worship" which kept the readers abreast of the latest developments in liturgical renewal in the country.

5. By promoting study and experimentation particularly in the field of liturgical inculturation.

In this way a serious effort was made in India for implementing the thrust of the Council's vision of liturgy. The most notable steps taken in this direction may be listed as follows:

1. vernacularization of the Latin texts of the reformed liturgy, sacraments and sacramentals.

2. new disposition of the altars in the churches and chapels towards the people.

3. construction of new churches according to the new directives.

4. use of the lectionary and preaching homily especially in the conventional Masses.

5. adopting regional language and music in liturgical singing which is to be more congregational than choral.

6. adoption of postures and gestures within prescribed limits and in keeping with the cultural and social patterns of life in the given area.

These various reforms and renewal programmes introduced in the liturgy contributed largely towards making it participatory and people-oriented

Implementation of the Vision of a Participatory Liturgy: Oriental Rites in India

The above-discussed steps of implementation initiated by the NBCLC were directly applicable only to the Latin Rite in India, although they have also indirectly helped the other two Rites, especially the Syro-Malabar Rite in implementing the Vatican vision of participatory liturgy mainly by means of the Regional Liturgical Centres like POC, Kochi and MOC Kottayam. Another point to be noted here is this: In some of the things concerned, these liturgies, compared to their Latin counter-part, were closer to the people's lives, even before the Council. For example, liturgical texts were in local language, liturgical singing was in local language and cultural forms. Communion already existed in both species at least to some extent. By their very nature, these liturgies have many dialogue-prayers alternating between the priest and the people/ deacon etc. We shall consider now how these two Rites went about making their liturgies more participatory following the vision of the Council.

Implementation by the Syro-Malankara Church

The implementation process for this Church is rather slow and beset with some problems. Namely, it cannot entertain the question of further inculturation of the liturgy in the spirit of the Council to make it closer to the people, mainly because "this Church exists and aims at the re-union of the separated brethren. They in general, the Jacobites in particular, are very conservative in their liturgical practices. Therefore any important change in the text as well as in the manner of celebration without their cooperation would be detrimental to our mission",[17] says one of its spokesmen. At the same time the wonderful ashram movement started in Kurisumala, Kottayam, by Fr. Francis Acharya, a member of this Church, following the vision of Mar Ivanios, the pioneer of the re-union movement to integrate the Eastern Christian monastic life with the Indian tradition of sannyasa and develop a new form of monastic life in India, has in it many elements of cultural adaptation of liturgy and life of the people envisaged by the Council.[18]

Implementation by the Syro-Malabar Church

The period of implementation from 1966 had a fast pace initially under the late Joseph Cardinal Parecattil till about 1975. But thereafter the process slowed down mainly because of a polarization of opinions among the Bishops and priests of this Rite on whether the liturgy needs further reform and adaptation to translate the vision of the Council.

Whatever one might say on this question regarding its home context of Kerala, no one can deny its urgency in the mission areas outside the proper territory of this Rite, where it is rubbing shoulders with several shades of Indian culture – Tamil, Kannadika, Telugu, Marathi, Gujrathi, Kashmiri and Hindi as well as several sub-cultures of the vast Tribal belt.[19] The text of the Sacred Liturgy, after its de-latinization and restoration to the Chaldean pure form as well as vernacularization into local languages, has not undergone any meaningful renewal process in the vision of the Council which says that "....wherever necessary, the rites be revived carefully in the light of sound tradition, and that they be given new vigour to meet the present-day circumstances and needs." (SC4).

The restored liturgy, especially in its solemn forms seems to be more suitable for a well-established/ 'stagnant' Church; it fosters status quo of the Church, but offers no challenge to a pilgrim and missionary people; does not inspire, especially the youth for liberative social action. It may be more appealing for retired and middle-aged group of people, as it would prepare them well for their final journey of hope in the Lord.[20] Of late, however there are some signs of improvement as visible in the recent publications of the revised sacramentary and 'propria' of the Holy Liturgy which augurs well for the future.

The Unfinished Agenda of Vatican II

The Council introduced new concepts and participatory methods in the understanding as well as celebration of the liturgy, as we have highlighted in the foregoing pages. At the same time the Council cannot be the last word in these matters, because liturgical renewal and up-dating is a movement, intimately related to the life and mission of the Church, which, as the saying goes, "is to be ever reformed" *(ecclesia semper est reformanda)*. Hence the implementation of the Liturgy Constitution SC has to take place in the context of an on-going ecclesial renewal. Hence fidelity to the Council's spirit and vision, going beyond the letter of the Document is to be expected. In fact this has already happened in a few cases. For example, it is common knowledge that the pronouncements of the Constitution SC regarding the use of vernacular and the practice of communion under both species have already been surpassed Similarly some new practices, not explicitly mentioned by the Council have been introduced, like communion in the hand, communion more than once a day, composition of new Eucharistic prayers, Mass facing the people etc.

The process of de-centralization in liturgical matters has been going on at a rapid speed, be it official or unofficial, even though higher authorities also have put restrictions and regulations as safe guards from time to time. Consequently, we cannot assert even today that we have achieved the goal of 'full conscious and active participation' or a fully participatory liturgy; rather we may say that people today respond better to the prayers of the priests, are more aware of their rights and obligations at the liturgical celebrations and understand better the connection between 'the liturgy of the Church and the liturgy of life', between ritual celebration and actual life.

Any attempt to enter into a movement, especially a living and active movement, cannot remain without a vision about the direction it takes. If such has been the case with post-Vatican liturgy, what is the direction, this movement is heading for? We shall indicate briefly some aspects of this question:

1. The Council's basic insight that liturgy is not merely an act of worship, but also a powerful symbol of fellowship has to be given wide currency and better acceptance among the people...

2. The Council's teaching that liturgy is the expression of the 'true nature of the real Church' (SC2); that liturgy is 'the Source and Summit of the Church's life and activities' (SC10)

is to be further explored and a new ecclesiology may be developed against the Patristic insight that 'Eucharist makes the Church even as the Church makes the Eucharist'.[21]

3. The Council's strong support for the abundant use of the Word of God in the liturgy (SC24 et al.) should lead to making liturgical celebration a process of proclamation.[22]

4. The essentially communitarian character of liturgy has to be properly interpreted: that liturgy is not only a communal celebration, but also more particularly a community-building process; hence smaller communities to be preferred to larger congregations.

5. A renewed and inculturated liturgy envisaged by the Council requires ordained ministers who are 'prophets' and not mere priests who are 'ritual performers' *(pujaris.)*.

Concluding Remarks

In the foregoing discussion we have tried to highlight the way the Council, mainly through its Document SC has endeavoured to make the liturgy participatory. This endeavour concerns directly and in the first instance the Roman Rite; but indirectly and implicitly also all other Rites as hinted at in SC 4.[23] This effort of the Council has been followed up by two other very important Post-Vatican documents from Rome, namely the Apostolic Constitution *Missale Romanum* of Pope Paul VI promulgating the revised Order of the Mass, and General Instruction of the Congregation for Divine Worship, properly introducing the new missal. Among the various expressions regarding the relationship between liturgical celebration and the nature of the Church, these two documents highlight again the participatory nature of the liturgy. Anybody who pays attention to the Order of Mass will find the presence of people expanded at every point and its many actions described in detail; this is all the more significant when we see that in the Pius V's missal the people were practically ignored. Likewise the General Instruction also, while introducing the missal time and again stresses the ecclesial nature of the celebration with full and active participation of the people (See for example GI 5,7,24, 43, 75, 75, 82 etc.). This is also true of the Instruction *Eucharisticum Mysterium* of the Congregation of Rites which came out in 1967, that is between SC and the said General Instruction. All these documents are greatly forward-looking in this matter of a people-oriented liturgy, compared to the Instruction *Redemptionis Sacramentum*.[24]

Endnotes

[1] The Council had been planned, conducted and completed in three phases, called (i) Preparation, (ii) Celebration and (iii) Implementation in which the second means the actual sessions conducted with deliberations and decisions; the other two seem to be self-explanatory.

[2] These four objectives are taken from the words of the late Pope John XXIII, which he often mentioned in his speeches. For example. The Allocution of Jan. 25,1959; the Apostolic Constitution *Humanae Salutis* of Dec.25,1961; the Allocution *Gaudet Mater Ecclesia* which opened the Council (See Rev. A.Bugnini & Rev. C.Braga Ed **The Commentary on the Constitution and on the Instruction on the Sacred Liturgy,** Benzinger Brothers, New York, trans., 1965, pp.52-107 (52).

[3] The essentially pastoral concern of the Document is clear from its insistence on the important part, the people have in the whole range of the liturgy – in the Holy Mass, the sacraments, sacramentals, the Divine Office and the Liturgical Year (See J.D. Chrichton, **The Church's Worship,** Geoffrey Chapman, London, 1964, pp.52-75 (53).

[4] *Ecclesia in Asia (EA* 25).

[5] For example, nos. 14, 27, 30, 41, 50 etc.

[6] The time between Vat.I and II (1870 – 1962), was one of great freedom movements in colonial countries, and newly freed countries like

India had more indigenous bishop-representatives for the first time in an Ecumenical Council like Vatican II.

[7] This text no.48 together with no.14 gives a summary reference to the priesthood of the lay people. In no.14 we read "Such participation by the Christian people as a 'chosen race, a priestly kingdom, a holy nation, a redeemed people '(I Pt.2:9; see also 2:4-5) is their right and duty by reason of their baptism". The OT people as a whole were a 'priestly people': They had first the Tabernacle, then the Temple, a priesthood set apart and a liturgy laid down by Yahweh himself. They were the 'gathered Church', God's assembly (Qahal Yahweh), which in the NT becomes the *Ecclesia*. And when in the NT, Christ becomes the New Temple (Jn 2:18 & //s) and the people are built into it to become temples of God's Spirit (Eph. 2:19-22; I Cor. 3:9-17). Peter and Paul envisage here the whole community as a 'priestly people', not merely bishops or priests. Read further in Chrichton op.cit., pp.64ff. All this would better explain the use of terms such as 'celebrating community' or 'celebrating assembly' in the liturgy about which the Instruction *Sacramentum Redemptionis* of Roman Curia has sounded caution (see no. 42 therein). One can also read profitably in this connection the two booklets: Celebrants **All**, published by Indian Liturgical Association, Bangalore, 1990; **Together in One Priesthood**, ed. By Puthanangady, Bangalore, 1991.

[8] Cfr. A.J.Chupungo, **Liturgies of the Future**, Paulist Press New York, 1989, pp.57-61.

[9] Ibid. p.62.

[10] Ibid. p.63.

[11] In Art. 4 of SC there is a solemn declaration of the equality before the Holy Mother Church, of all rights of the different Rites legitimately recognized by the Church. "Legitimately recognized" refers not only to the Rites already existing, but also to Rites which might be recognized in the future. To signify this possibility, the text which formerly read "legitimately existing" was changed before the final voting to "legitimately recognized" (Cfr. A. Bugnini et al, op.cit. p.58).

[12] Chupungo, op.cit. pp.70f.

[13] Joseph Cardinal Cordeiro, "The Liturgical Constitution: Sacrosanctum Concilium", in *History of Vatican II* Ed. Joseph A, Komonchak, Orbis Books, 1997, p.187.

[14] Cordeiro, ibidem, p.189.

[15] Cordeiro, ibidem, pp.189-91.

[16] Gerwin Van Leeuwen, "Liturgy in India After Vatican II" in *The Church in India after the All-India Seminar 1969: An Evaluati*on, Ed. Paul Puthanangady, Yesu Krist Jayanti 2000, pp.243-269.

[17] The latest among such restrictions from Rome may be found in the Instruction Redemptionis *Sacramentum* referred to above in No. (7).

[18] Cfr. *Making Liturgical Celebration A Proclamation*, (Papers presented on the occasion of the XI General Body Meeting of the Indian Liturgical Association (ILA), held at NBCLC, Bangalore, 13-16 October 2004).

[19] Cfr. "The Syro-Malabar Liturgy and Liturgical Renewal" in Star Publications No.3, 1980.

[20] Louis Malieckal, "Liturgical Inculturation and the Mission, in *Inculturation and the Syro-Malabar Church*, Ed. Bosco Puthur, LRC Publ. Kakanad-Kochi 2005, pp.183-205 (203-204).

[21] Cfr. Gerard J. Bekes OSB, "The Eucharist Makes the Church: The Ecclesial Dimension of the Eucharist", in *Vatican II: Assessment and Perspectives, 25 Years After*, Vol.II Ed. R. Latourelle, Paulist Press, N.York,1989, pp.347-363.

[22] The booklet referred to in no.18 above discusses this point in detail.

[23] Cf. A.Bugnini et.al Ed. op.cit. p.58.

[24] Rene Latourelle, Ed. op.cit. pp.3-26.

Chapter 9

Post-Vatican Liturgical Inculturation in India:
Contribution of Dharmaram College

Introduction

The late Fr. Gerwin Van Leuwen, O.F.M, who was closely associated with the NBCLC and its Post-Vatican liturgical movement from its beginning till the year 2000, gives an assessment of it, in which he shows that a serious effort was made to implement the thrust of the Council's vision of liturgical inculturation in general and also points out the efforts made specifically by the Roman Rite in India towards developing an Indian Order of Mass, which were later beset with controversial issues.[1] As the Council's vision of *aggiornamento* (renewal and adaptation) was aimed at the whole Church comprising all the Rites in it, the Oriental Rites in India, especially the Syro-Malabar Rite also began to consider the question of liturgical inculturation. Composition of new liturgical texts was an essential part of the immediate post-Vatican liturgical renewal movement. Even in an official

Roman document we read: "Texts translated from another language are clearly not sufficient for the celebration of a fully renewed liturgy. The creation of new texts will be necessary."[2]

It was in such a context that attempts to compose new anaphora(s) began to be considered by the Indian Church. In a letter of the Sacred Congregation for Divine Worship addressed to the Chairman of the CBCI Commission for Liturgy dated April 25, 1969 mention is made thus: "The proposal to compose a new Indian Anaphora in collaboration with experts in different fields is most welcome."[3] Accordingly, the three Ritual Churches in India went about the task but differently in accordance with their particular perceptions of the matter:

The Historic Event of All-India Seminar 1969: Its Impact on Inculturation

Soon after the promulgation of the Council's *magna carta* on liturgical renewal and adaptation, (*Sacrosanctum Concilium* – hereafter SC) there was a lot of ferment of it growing in the Catholic Church all over the world. In India too a lot of thinking and talk at various levels went for quite some time, though nothing concrete was put forward by anybody. Assessing the general trend, the CBCI commission for Liturgy stated thus in the year 1968:

> There is no more discussion as to whether we should adapt or not; adaptation has to be done and there is no need to prove it. The whole problem is first of all how to go about it; secondly, what is to be adapted; and thirdly how far we can go in the process of adaptation.[4]

It was the time of huge preparations in the whole Church of India in view of the proposed National Seminar on "Church in India Today."[5] High on the agenda was naturally the theme of liturgical inculturation. And here, of the three questions mentioned above the most crucial one was "how to go about it" as far as the starting of the programme was concerned.

It was in such a situation that a group of staff and students of Dharmaram College, Bangalore set themselves to the task in response to the Council's vision of a possible 'radical adaptation in the liturgy' (SC 40) and in support of the declared policy of the CBCI Commission for Liturgy in favour of inculturation. At a time when many of the bishops favourable to this matter were still groping in the dark on "how we must go about it", the leadership given to it by His Eminence the late Joseph Cardinal Parecattil of happy memory who was at that time President of the undivided CBCI of all the three Ritual Churches, is worth remembering. His efforts in this direction for over two decades are well known and documented.[6] Nobody in the Syro-Malabar Church dared to take the risk of scandal and criticism in the absence of some guidelines to follow. The Cardinal himself was waiting for some light from anywhere. Certainly he advised and encouraged individuals who approached him for light, for permission. Individuals here and there in the Latin Church were trying out something, without giving much publicity. The NBCLC was just beginning to function and the Late Fr. Amalorpavadass, its founder director had not yet given shape to any Indian prayer model but only seriously thinking about it.

Towards an Indian Order of Holy Eucharist: Dharmaram Contribution

It was under such circumstances that the said small group of staff and students which included this writer as well, under the leadership of Fr. Mathias Mundadan, then Professor of Church History and Master of Students of Dharmaram, with the blessings and encouragement of the late Cardinal Parecattil, set themselves to the task of giving shape to something like an

"Indian form of worship". The first attempt was a simple one in the form of 'para-liturgy' or 'Bible Service' that was getting currency in those days after the Council.[7] This was done in an entirely novel manner, using worship signs, symbols and gestures congenial to the local culture and with such spontaneity and devotion that the participants were highly impressed. It evoked spontaneously the cultural sensibilities of the participants who therefore were able to resonate deeply with the spiritual message of the celebration. Many of the so-called 12-point adaptations [8] which were soon to be formulated by Fr. Amalorpavdas for the CBCI Liturgy Commission and later proposed by CBCI for implementation in different dioceses according to the discretion of individual bishops, had actually been anticipated in that pioneering celebration.

When this simple 'Indian form of' para-liturgy was celebrated next in Dharmaram during the forthcoming CBCI meeting, the bishops were highly impressed by its originality, as they probably had a feeling of having seen what they were looking for. Among those who spoke words of high appreciation were the two Cardinals Valerian Gracius and Joseph Parecattil. It was then presented at the request of Fr. Amalor in NBCLC on the occasion of the AILM –II (All India Liturgical Meeting) of January 1969. The response of those liturgy experts showed that they were not only impressed but also provoked to try out similar models.[9]

Setting up a Team and its Committed Work

Soon after the CBCI meeting at Dharmaram, Cardinal Parecattil, then President of CBCI asked Fr. Rector of Dharmaram to entrust to a select group of staff and students the task of preparing a complete order of the Eucharist in the Indian style in view of the forth-coming All-India National Seminar on "Church in India Today" in May 1969.[10] Accordingly the group set to work, studying the Eastern/Indian character of the Qurbana (Holy Eucharist), Hindu ritual worship, bhajan singing and Vedic prayer-recitation, classical Indian music etc. For this purpose we, Deacons together with Fr. Vineeth got special permission and stayed for a few days in the famous Vinoba Bhave's Ashram called Brahmavidyamandir in the diocese of Chanda, Maharashtra.

Our stay in that Ashram, sharing meals with the Ashramites, doing the house-work (*Ashram seva*), praying with the inmates, listening to the way they are reciting prayers and chanting bhajans, and above all trying to understand the Hindu world-vision, through reading and discussing with them, we got confidence to venture upon the task of shaping an Order of the *Qurbana* in the Indian style and idiom. From the very beginning the prayers, hymns and the music were conceived in tune with the S. Indian and particularly Kerala language and culture. It was based on sound principles of adaptation keeping in mind the recommendations made by the Council.[11]

From the Vinoba Bhave Ashram the team moved to Carmel Vidyabhavan Pune, where Fr. Sylvester was Rector of the CMI Study House at that time. It is there that the team completed the work of formulating the text of the Qurbana, writing the hymns and composing the music. While the text was drafted mainly by Fr. Vineeth, this writer did the writing of the lyric (Malayalam text) for composing the music of most of the hymns. For composing the music of a few hymns, we had to depend on an outsider (one Bro. Pinto) from De Nobilee College, Pune. The rest was borrowed and adapted by this writer from Hindu bhajan singing and temple music.[12]

The Draft Text and Its Salient Features

The new text of the Eucharist thus prepared was Indian, Eastern and Christian at once: Indian in its language, signs, symbols, gestures and postures, music, recitation and the whole prayer-atmosphere; Eastern, following basically the structure of the four-fold 'inclined prayers'(Gehanta) of the Addai-Mari anaphora text, modified/ adapted to the Hindu mode of worship; and Christian, because it was conceived as far as possible, in continuity with the essential elements of the genuine Judeo-Christian liturgical tradition, while at the same time expressing the Christian thanksgiving in forms and thought-patterns harmonious with the Indian culture. In writing the hymns, wherever possible inspiration of Vedic texts has been imbibed and incorporated. In the prayers the cosmic vision of Hindu worship has been blended with the historical dimension of the salvation mystery in and through Jesus Christ.

The All-India Prospects of the Dharmaram Text

The text thus prepared was in use for several years in the Liturgical Centre of Dharmaram College from 1969 to 1974 in hand-written form. During this period it underwent several revisions and adaptations in language and rites,[13] while it continued to be celebrated in a select group at Dharmaram. An English version of it was made in view of presenting it at the IV All-India Liturgical Meeting (AILM-IV) organized by NBCLC, from 2-8 Dec. 1973. "It was then unanimously decided that this Indian Order of the Mass would be adopted by the CBCI Commission for Liturgy, and be widely circulated for further experimentation and be submitted to the Catholic Bishops' Conference of India for their approval for use in the whole of India, common to all the three Rites."[14]

It was later printed for private use (*pro manuscripto*) in the same year 1974, when this writer was the director of Dharmaram College, Liturgical Centre (1969-75) until he left for studies in Louvain.[15] Copies of it were supplied on request to some formation houses and liturgical experimentation centres, including Kurishumala ashram. In most places the text later went into disuse and hence gathered dust perhaps due to the so-called 'prohibition from Rome'.[16] However, it is heart-warming to see that in the Kurishumala Ashram, Kerala it continued to be used for week-day celebrations. However recently when a revised computer typed version of this Mass came out, with Malayalam and English texts side by side and with the publisher's own Introduction, he seems to have forgotten the original source of the Mass text. He has made no acknowledgement of the Liturgical Centre, Dharmaram College, which is the original publisher of the text. Interestingly he claims that he has introduced in this Indian anaphora "the structure of the Anaphora of St. James", and then he adds that "Our Indian Liturgy is thus related to the Church of Jerusalem, which holds pride of place in the Syrian Liturgy." I am surprised at this claim of the publisher, because, if anything, the structure has been inspired by the anaphora of Addai-Mari, as this was used by the Syro-Malabar Church in the late 1960's when this text was composed by us. But no explicit quotation or structural dependence can be seen in this composition. In fact, the central prayer (anaphora) is a unique synthesis of Eastern (East-Syrian) and Western, Hindu and Christian conception of 'sacrifice' or Divine worship. What the Kurishumala publisher claims may be due to the affinity between West Syrian and East Syrian thought and language.[17]

Concluding Remarks

If the Council's programme of *aggiornamento*, "updating" of the Church was concerned with all the areas, structures and institutions of it, certainly the most visible and vibrant aspect was inculturation in general and liturgical inculturation in particular, especially in the Third World countries. Hence from the beginning Indian Church was caught up with it, which was evident in the preparations, celebration and implementation of the historic national seminar," Church in India Today", as was explained in these pages. All the three Rites in India were involved in it, although at different levels of earnestness and enthusiasm. As Cardinal Parecattil was fired with the Council's idea of indigenization, naturally the Syro-Malabar Church, at least those who thought like him that in the liturgy signs and symbols, gestures and postures have to be truly indigenous, prayers have to breathe in the spirit and flavour of the local culture, took great interest initially in the process of liturgical inculturation. But soon this ferment subsided and almost died out mainly for the letter of prohibition from Rome, communicated by the CBCI Standing Committee, as noted above. Unfortunately, it was misunderstood as well as misinterpreted. The context of the letter was the proliferation of *Anaphoras* (Eucharistic Prayers) brought out in some of the countries in the West, like France, Belgium, Germany etc., freely interpreting the Council's idea of liturgical renewal based SC 37-40. That is why, Fr. Amalorpavdass, after mentioning this letter adds, "While this letter forbade for the time being the use of the Eucharistic prayer for India even in experimentation centres, experimentation in those centres could continue with the rest of the new orders of the mass."[18] As Dharmaram was an 'authorized liturgical centre', as already explained above, and since its scope was much broader than mere making of an Indian order of the Mass, it could have continued to function, with the blessings of authorities concerned, if they were ready to follow the examples of their predecessors.[19]

Endnotes

[1] Gervin VanLeeuwen, OFM, "Liturgy in India after Vatican II", in Paul Puthanangady Ed. *Church in India After the All India Seminar, 1969: An Evaluation,* YESU KRIST JAYANTI, 2000, pp.243-269.

[2] See *Introduction of the Congregation for Divine Worship,* No.43, quoted in D.S. Amalorpavadass, *Towards Indigenisation in the Liturgy,* NBCLC: Bangalore (no date), p.47 (Hereafter Amalor, *Indigenization*).

[3] See Amalor, Indigenization, p.48.

[4] Cf. *Word and Worship,* Bangalore, Dec. 1988, p.158; see also Amalor, *Indigenization,* p.26.

[5] It was a huge gathering in which more than 600 participated - cardinals, bishops, priests, sisters, brothers and a good number of lay people. The main venue was Dharmaram College and St. John medical college. The different areas of Church renewal – education, communication, pastoral, social, evangelization, liturgy and so on were under discussion, deliberation and decision-making.

[6] Cardinal Parecattil, *Syro-Malabar Liturgy As I See It (Malayalam),* publ. by Fr. Abel, EKM, 1987, trans.by K.C. Chacko; Mathias Mundadan, *Cardinal Parecattil: The Man, His Vision and Contribution,* Star Publ., Alwaye, 1998; Louis Malieckal, "Liturgical Inculturation in India: Problems and prospects of Experimentation", *Jeevadhara,* July, 1988, pp.279-292.

[7] The occasion was the Rector's Day, when the late Dharmaram visionary Bp. Jonas Thaliath was Rector.

[8] See Amalorpavdas, op.cit. pp.31-53, where we have first the letter from Rome permitting the use of the proposed new symbols, gestures and postures, which mentions also the said 12-points of adaptation (pp.31-33),; then we have a "Commentary on the First Stage of Adaptations in the Liturgy" (pp.33-36); next we have explanations of the 12-points of

adaptations (pp.36-44) and finally introduction to the 2nd, 3rd and 4th phases of adaptation (pp.44-53).

[9] I still remember what one of the big shots of that assembly told us who conducted that service: "Please wait let us also come." This comment clearly shows that the Latin Church had not yet made any concrete step so daring till that time in the direction of liturgical inculturation.

[10] The team consisted of seven members: Frs. Mathias Mundadan, Francis Vineeth (Indologist) and Sylvester Pudussery (liturgiologist); Seminarians (Deacons) - Prsasanna Bhai, Abraham Thuruthumali, Varghese Kottoor and myself (Louis Malieckal).

[11] SC 23.

[12] Just for one example: The famous bhajan *Om Jagadisvara Sadapi Chinmaya......*is a Hindu temple hymn in pure Sanskrit, which was adapted and christianized by this writer for our purpose. And it seems to be one of the oldest Christian bhajans still very popular at least among those who love indigenization.

[13] In this period of experimentation, revision and re-writing of text and composing more music between 1969-1974, several seminarians who were associated with the Liturgical Centre had been very helpful. Some of them who became later priests are Frs. Thomas Kochumuttam, Thomas Kandathil, Cherian Kunianthodathil, Jose Kuriedath and others.

[14] Amalorpavdass, New Orders of the Mass for India, NBCLC, 1974, p.63.

[15] It may be noted that this Liturgical Centre, being run with the explicit permission of Dharmaram authorities, was an animation centre in general, where different meditation methods, prayer models, bhajan singing etc were being practiced in which students also with proper permission would come to participate. Original publication in Malayalam is thus: *Bhārata-sabhakyoro-pūjākramam,* Dharmaram Liturgical Centre (Pro Manuscripto), 1974.

[16] The prohibition referred to here is a letter from Cardinal Knox, Prefect of the Sacred Congregation for Divine worship. On the ground of this letter, communicated through the CBCI Chairman of the Commission

for Liturgy, the CBCI Standing Committee published on 20 Oct. 1975 the following: "Until and unless the CBCI gives its explicit approval, the use of the above two (viz The Indian anaphora and Readings from non-Biblical Scriptures in the Liturgy) is forbidden to all, whether in private or in public, even in authorized centres for experimentation." See Amalorpavadass Ed. *Report of the Fifth All-India Liturgical Meeting*, NBCLC: Bangalore, 1977, p. 14. (Hereafter Amalor, Report. For a slightly different version of this prohibition see Puthanangady, op.cit. pp.252f. Emphasis added).

[17] For the full text (in English) see Francis Kanichikattil, CMI, *To Restore or to Reform* ? Dharmaram publ. Bangalore, 1992, Appendix (I) pp.139-161, and for its original Malayalam text see Appendix (III) pp.177-201. Moreover what is given in Appendix (II) is the text of the Indian Order of the Mass prepared by NBCLC. There is also an Appendix (IV) which contains a Malayalam text called Bharathiya Puja published by the Ernakulam Liturgical Centre.

[18] Amalor, Report, p.104.

[19] The allusion here is to the blessing and support of Frs. Mathias Mundadan, Jonas Thaliath, John Chethimattam and others. Fr. Chethimattam, however, because of his great devotion and loyalty to the hierarchy of the Church, was constrained in openly supporting the centre lest he should displease the watchful eyes of some higher Syro-Malabar Ecclesiastical authorities. At the same time, for a comprehensive assessment of Fr. Chethimattam's position in this regard, see my article, "Approaches to Inculturation and Liturgy", in Kuncheria Pathil Ed. *Contributions of J.B. Chethimattam to Indian Theology (Jeevadhara* Vol. XXXVII, No.220, July 2007, pp.381-95).

Chapter 10

Fr. John Britto Chethimattam's Approach to Inculturation and Liturgy

Introduction

Fr. Chethimattam's reflections on the question of inculturation spans a wide spectrum of areas like Christology, Missiology, Dialogue, Theology of Religions, etc., and as such border on the themes of indigenization and contextualization of theology as well. On the other hand, he has not written much directly on liturgical inculturation, as far as I have gone through his writings. Probably in this matter he was rather constrained in expressing his mind freely, because it appeared to him very sensitive in itself and so he did not want to displease the watchful eyes of some higher ecclesiastical authorities especially of the Syro-Malabar Church, of which he was a very devoted and faithful son. At the same time we can see that his ideas about theologizing in context and inculturation in general must have logically led him to give a much stronger and clearer articulation to liturgical inculturation

as well. Whatever be the case, he has left behind enough food
for thought on how to go about inculturation in matters of
liturgy.

Culture and Religion: Their Mutual influence and Impact

From a Christian point of view inculturation may be broadly
understood as a process of cultural adaptation of the truths of
Christian religion. Therefore in our enquiry about the author's
reflections on inculturation let us start with his understanding
of this twin subject – culture and religion, and their interaction.

In his article "Religion the Cutting Edge on Culture"[1] our
revered writer admits that culture according to sociologists is
the sum total of values, customs, rituals and laws transmitted
from generation to generation to define a community's collective
identity; that religion on the other hand is the expression of
the ultimate4 concern of human life.[2] Elsewhere he states that
'there is much confusion about culture itself', and after referring
to Clifford Geert, Durkheim, Weber, Freud and Malinoski, he
quotes Clifford to say that "Culture denote4s an historically
transmitted pattern of meanings embodied in symbols, a
system of inherited conceptions, expressed in symbolic forms
by means of which men [sic] communicate, perpetuate and
develop their knowledge and attitudes towards life.[3]

He then goes on to examine and explain their mutual impact:
Culture is a larger reality than religion. It may enshrine many
values, even negative or anti-religious values, and thus it may
distort religion. However religion is one of the most prominent
elements that will make up culture, even as culture will remain
as the means and medium of religious expressions. Citing the
example of Christmas celebrations in the West, Dr. JBC (as he

was fondly known among his theology students) shows that it manifests the structure of an alienated society/culture which tries to compensate for its alienation by a sort of 'gift-giving practice' among nuclear families. In this process the notion of the Church as a great fellowship in which members stand in solidarity and mutual support, is conveniently overlooked. Instead the existing practice of a mass of isolated families being engaged in a great shopping spree is a caricaturing of the Church as a community. In other words the western celebrative culture gives a distorted meaning to the religious festival of Christmas.

However, this is not the case in the celebration of the Easter. Easter continues to mark the change and renewal in the socio-cultural order. The crucified Jesus continues to represent the rejection of a sinful world and to rage against a corrupt social order. Resurrection stands as a promise of transcendence of the human spirit and re-constitution of a new humanity. The Easter celebration thus places emphasis on the Church as the new socio-cultural unity in the place of the nuclear families. In other words there is 'instrumentalization of religion by 'culture' both in its negative and positive aspects.[5]

JBC then points out the impact on society when religion settles down for an unholy alliance with culture. Thus the firm grip that a patriarchal culture has on religion and its values is shown by the interior place assigned to women in most of the religions like Hinduism, Judaism, Christianity and Islam. For example in Hinduism a woman in her childhood is subject to the father, in marriage to her husband and in later life to her son; hence is the preference for a male child in a Hindu family. For Judaism and Christianity, God is the father, not mother. The Bible was written from a male perspective. Hence the woman

(Eva) was created out of a rib of the man (Adam). Catholic Church excludes women from getting ordained to priesthood on the pretext that God became incarnate as man (not woman). "But it is not clear", JBC here makes a veiled attack on the official Church, "why the other specific conditions of Christ, like race, religion, time, economic situation etc. are not taken as restrictive of the priesthood." If all these cultural aspects, he seems to underscore, are not obstacles to priesthood in the Church, why should only gender be an obstacle, which is also a cultural factor.[6]

Criticizing the Marxian way of relating religion and culture, JBC says that one has to distinguish between mystifying religious ideologies which justify the existing social order (culture) and the future-oriented religious ideologies which challenge the existing social order and encourage people for social transformation. In the encounter between religion and culture, no religion including Christianity, he says, is a pure ideology which could be applied to any situation like a Platonic world of ideas. The Gospel of Jesus Christ can be communicated to any culture, live in it, transform it and achieve in it a new self-expression; but the same cannot be said about Christianity or Catholicism. For, Catholicism itself is a particular embodiment of the Gospel, a religious culture. We are here closer to the mind of the author regarding the question of inculturation. Each religious culture provides doctrinal frame work and community organization in order to impel and direct people to act. In the face of a new situation these ready-made frame works have to be left behind.[7]

However the history of all religions, he explains, presents a different story: In trying to communicate ones religious insights to others, every religion has been militant because of its identification with a particular culture or political structure.

The story of the spread of Buddhism in India and Srilanka during the reign of king Ashoka, and its later disappearance from India during the time of Hindu kings is a classical example of militancy. He goes on to show that Christianity and Islam which arose in the shadow of a foreign culture eventually became militant for their own survival, each with the convicti0on that its secret doctrine was the only true and necessary means of salvation whether in Europe, Middle East or America.

Indigenous Theology Or Theological Contextualization

JBC in his article, "Inculturating Our Theological Thinking"[8] gives us to understand still better his mind regarding the question of inculturation. He says that as late as 1999 when the late Pope St. John Paul II released in Delhi the Roman Synodal document *Church in Asia*, the word 'inculturation' was frequently used by different speakers in radically different meanings: For some it stands for a "mere strategy to make Christianity look less offensive to Asians" in the sense of "inter-culturation, confrontation between different religions set in radically different cultural framework, each believing itself culturally superior to others and trying to make itself understood by the other." For some others, "inculturation is limited to stating one's religious doctrine in the categories and symbols of the other." But JBC is not happy with these meanings of culture and so quotes the words of Cardinal Dharmaatmaja, the President Delegate of the Synod for Asia from his concluding words of the ceremony of releasing the Roman Document mentioned: "Being Church in Asia to day means participating in the mission of Christ the Saviour in rendering his redemptive love and service in Asia, so that Asian men and women can more fully achieve their integral human development.......bringing the good news into all dimensions of human life and society, and through its influence transforming humanity from within and making it new..."[9] And by way of summing up the thought s on this matter, he adds that, "here rarely there is effort made to step into the cultural shoes of the other and walk with him up the religious path."[10] Hence we can say that for him inculturation is "the effort made to step into the cultural shoes of the other and to walk with him up the religious path."

He then shows that the NT writers, unlike their contemporary Greek writers did not fall into the temptation of enquiry into the ontology of God as a rational justification for a life of faith, instead, they "inculturated the Gospel message into the concrete situations they encountered. They did not attempt an ideological presentation of Christ and his teachings, but only faced the actual socio-cultural situation in the light of Jesus' faith and resurrection."[11]

For better models of this type of inculturation, says the author, we have to go back to the origins in the first century, when the Kingdom of God broke into history through the life-intervention of Jesus Christ. The apostles who received this message and had a direct encounter with the Risen Lord took this message to the different parts of the world, to concrete situations of life. And when this message was committed to writing, it was not in the form of a systematic treatise but as presentation of the Christ-event to actual contexts. In other words, the Gospel was not proclaimed as an ideology or a program of action. Rather, Jesus Christ the Word of God was dynamically proclaimed and actualized in different socio-cultural contexts which gradually gave rise to different 'theological manuals' of the New Testament. This diversity of ways in which the one Gospel of Jesus Christ was actualized and Jesus, the Word of God was presented in the documents of the NT answers the question of how Jesus can be presented in the modern world, because he is not an ideology nor a program of action, says the author. In the 27 documents of the NT the same Jesus, the Word of god is presented as emerging out of radically different human situations as the divine answer to human basic concerns, as the explosion of God's rule and kingdom.[12]

Contextualized Christology

JBC in his article "Asian Jesus: The Relevance of Jesus Christ in the Asian World of Religious Pluralism,"[13] while explaining the historical fact that Christianity had spread in the Greek world in the very centuries after Christ, attributes its reason mainly to the work of inculturation or contextual theologizing of the Gospel message. He says, "The early preachers of the Christian Gospel in the Greek world like Paul and Luke were forced to adopt a philosophical thought pattern and style of spirituality of the Greek, taking care however to maintain the Jewish core of Christ's teaching.......What happened in this passing of Christianity from the Palestinian Judaic back ground to the Greek world was a contextualization of the image of Christ."[14]

Liturgical Inculturation

As was mentioned earlier, we have to understand the mind of JBC regarding the question of inculturation as such and liturgical inculturation in particular sense against the back ground of his reflections above on contextualization, religious dialogue etc. He holds that the word inculturation is very ambiguous and so people try to avoid its use for various reasons: Some avoid because it implies the denial existing Christian culture.

Some others who consider it unavoidable, try to interpret it in Pre-Vatican II paradigms like, 'conversion', 'Church founding,' 'acculturation', 'assimilation' and so on. For yet some others it is the readiness to get rid of colonialism and ethnocentrism, and recognition of the other as the principle of identity for the Church. The basic principle, he thinks, is, "see reality, make a theological judgement and act pastorally."[15]

According to the author, the process of inculturation is oriented to a better treatment of the human beings rather than a better understanding of God. Hence the value of religion should be seen in so far as it makes human culture hospitable to God's children. Therefore it must lead to the removal of the oppressive nature of the religious practices. All this shows his dislike for ritualism and for mere cosmetic cultural 'facelift.' And so he would he say, "Worship centers in God in order to bring people together in fellowship as his children or seekers of the Ultimate Reality," and so he considers, "this element of fellowship as the fundamental aspect of worship."[16]

Creating the world, God entered into his own creation; worship and ritual/liturgy attempts to re-capture and repeat the original irruption of the Divine into human history. Therefore he observes, in our search for the eternal in the temporal, worship symbolism has become the point of this passage to the transcendent, and adds, "For this very reason, symbols have to be fully human, expressing human aspirations, needs and pre-occupations, and at the same time contain a certain guarantee of God to whose worship they tend."[17] Besides, JBC makes a reference to the Council and warns the liturgists of two dangers in the words of Louis Bouyer: "Taking refuge in an immobile traditionalism, in which liturgy would petrify, and of rejecting altogether the domain of the sacred, the force of tradition and the sense of reverence."[18]

Fr. Chethimattam's view expressed above seems to be guided by the principles of Vat.II concerning liturgical adaptations, because the document says, ".....Liturgy is made up of unchangeable elements divinely instituted, and of elements subject to change. These latter not only may be changed but ought to be changed with the passage of time." (SC21). 'Elements subject to change' are what JBC calls 'the human side of the ritual'. These will have to be changed, adapted to suit the particular cultural variables of peoples life so that the liturgy become relevant and meaningful. 'The unchangeable elements [in the liturgy] are of divine origin and so cannot be replaced. About these JBC would say, 'they have the stamp of God's self-disclosure to man [sic], and so have to remain so unchanged forever. In order to explain further the writer's point of view we may consider an example here: Jesus instituted the Eucharist in the form of a meal/food which involves both eating and drinking. This form is basic to the Eucharistic mystery and its celebration in signs and symbols, whereas the concrete elements of the meal/food may have to be changed depending upon the socio-cultural context and the life-style of the people concerned.[19]

Moreover Chethimattam also makes clear that 'worship should not be an escape from the duties of a secular world and of social justice; it should be rather the act whereby the reality of God is made present and the resonance of that reality is made in our communities and in our personal lives, dominating the instability of the times.[20] To put it differently, and citing another quotation, "Though the liturgy is the worship of God, it is not to take man [sic] from his world, to escape from the tensions of his life, but to make him sensitive to the community, one with his brother next to him."[21] Another aspect of cultural adaptation in liturgy, he would want to impress on us may be noted. He reminds us that liturgy is a kind of play or drama. Any play has its time, dress-code and a form distinct from ordinary life. Similarly liturgy is something special. It is not for the sake of something else, but for the unique experience it contains. It is purposeless but meaningful, pointless but significant. Participating in liturgy means foregoing maturity with all its purposefulness and confining oneself to play.[22] What he wants to say is this: Any process of liturgical inculturation must not have goals outside of liturgy itself, namely to make it more modern, colourful, impressive etc. but to facilitate the unique experience of the Divine it can impart. Otherwise, over-enthusiasm to make liturgy closer to the feeling and mood of the people of[23] the day, may become self-defeating, losing the vertical dimension and ending up as mere socializing process. The human and sacral dimensions of the liturgical symbolism should be well-integrated in order to safeguard the wholeness of man, says the author.

He goes on to add that in any cultural adaptation of liturgy, one has to keep balance between spontaneity and regularity, particularity and universality. The Council's liturgical reform policy has taken note of this double aspect. It has allowed some spontaneity in the celebration, for example, in the case of the 'Prayer of the Faithful', 'Exchange of Peace' etc., while it is decreed that the liturgical texts should be approved by the appropriate authority. Briefly, he says, in all religious traditions, cultic symbolism implies a holistic approach to man [sic]. It combines the divine self-disclosure and the human thirst towards the Absolute: the actual concerns of the present moment in history and the deposit of the whole past; the action of the individual and the self-expression of the faith-community. In any liturgical renewal and adaptation, these two aspects, he holds, have to be constantly kept in mind.

Besides, quoting Louis Bouyer, he warns both traditionalists and progressivists in liturgical matters: Liturgical traditionalists are like the Monophysites, he says, because they take all ecclesiastical institutions as equally sacred and immutable; they forget the fact that liturgy spontaneously arose in the Christian communities as the product of many individual efforts, gradually elaborated and continually evolving within the community from which they came.[24] Similarly those who fail to see the divine self-disclosure in the liturgy, he adds, and consider it as a syncretic product borrowed from different religious traditions are caught in a sort of Nestorian dualism, because do not see the unique event of salvation that forms the original source of the cultic movement. And the same is the case with those who would reject all sacrality in worship and consider it a mere celebration of the secular world.[25] Also those who try to find in the Incarnation a wholly new sacredness that came down entirely from heaven will not escape a similar dualism.[26]

Concluding Remarks

In the foregoing few pages we have examined Dr. Chethimattam's reflections and insights on culture and inculturation in general, and on liturgical inculturation that emerge from there in particular. We have noted that his approaches to inculturation has touched several disciplines in theology, apart from liturgy. From these studies we can understand that he had a strong and consistent view about the question of inculturation. He has rightly observed that the power of religion is the power of symbols, the ability to convey something other than itself; that religious truths do not exist in the abstract, rather they do so in particular cultural mode, and hence the need of culture for religion. But culture also may contain harmful elements that may distort religion and religious values. Today's Christmas celebrations in the West is a case in point, as pointed out by JBC. In that connection he has made a strong point in favour of women ordination, because the fact that God became Incarnate as a male cannot be entertained as a valid reason to deny ordination to women from a cultural point of view; gender role, just as race, religion, time, economic situation are also cultural factors, and these are not taken as restrictive of priesthood in the Church.

He has further shown that only faith can be inculturated, not religion, because the latter is already a cultural factor. So, Christianity or Catholicism, as a particular embodiment of the Gospel of Jesus, is a religious culture with its proper ethics of governance. The missionaries from the West made mistake of transporting this religious culture from the West to all its colonies instead of bringing the faith in Jesus and inculturate it.[27] Here the primary purpose of inculturation is to make religions relevant to the actual life of the people, bringing about the reign of God in a particular time and place. This is the work of a prophet, he says, because in such 'inculturation process' there is a "dialectical encounter between an existing way of doing things and the new insights brought in by the prophet by his living faith."[28]

From the above discussion, we can see that his reflections on liturgical renewal is a natural sequel to his thoughts on cultural dynamics. He seems to add that it has to be the work

of a prophet, not of a priest as a ritualist (temple pūjāri). Only
a prophet will be ready to die for the cause he espouses, as was
the case with Socrates, who, for having accused the corrupt
Athenian society for its unjust actions had to pay for it by his
life.[30] His reflections on the 'human aspect of the religious
symbol', that 'in the liturgy a language of gesture is used',
that 'dance is the most original and most universal form of
worship' - these and other similar ideas of JBC definitely show
that he was very much for making liturgy a genuine place of
experiential encounter of humans with God by making use of
culturally relevant signs and symbols in it. Moreover we also
notice that for him 'liturgy is not only worship of God, but
also fellowship of the people' in the light of Vat. II. To put
it differently, as he does," liturgy is worship centred in God in
order to bring men [sic] together in fellowship as his children."
Similarly he seems to hold that inculturation is oriented to a
better treatment of humans rather than a better understanding
of God or again inculturation must lead to the removal of
the oppressive nature of religious practices. In other words,
inculturation has to aim at liberating the devotees from the
clutches of ritualism.

Briefly, as I pointed out in the Introduction above,
Chethimattam has left for us some very important and valuable
insights through his writings on the questions of inculturation
of faith and doctrine on the one hand, and of liturgy as a
natural sequel to it on the other. Finally I have a feeling that a
more comprehensive collection of his writings, especially those
in Malayalam, may give us a more accurate understanding of
his stand on liturgy and liturgical inculturation.

Endnotes

[1] *Jeevadhara* vol 30 (2001)349-365.

[2] Ibid. p.349.

[3] Clifford Geertzz, "Indian Culture and Christian Civilization", Francis Kanichikattil Ed. Church in Context (Essays in Honour of Mathias Mundadan CMI), Dharmaram Publications, 1996, pp.139-152.

[4] Ibid. p.351.

[5] Ibid. p.353f.

[6] Ibid. pp.355f.

[7] *Jeevadhara* 29(2000) 419-443.

[8] Here Dr. JBC first gives a summary of the different approaches to the practice of inculturation by different people; he is not happy with any of these approaches, and then proposes his own way of understanding it; see p.419.

[9] If we look at his 'definition' of inculturation closely we can see that for him the process of inculturation involves two steps, first a dying with the local culture of the other (stepping into the shoes of the other) and secondly a rising with him (walking with him up the religious path), namely the process requires an incarnational annihilation and a rising up in the power of resurrection.

[10] For example, he considers the Gospel of Mathew as a "Manuel of righteousness", that of Mark as a "Manuel of the Suffering Servant", that of Luke as a "Manuel of Compassion" and that of John as a "Manuel of the New Christian Community", see Ibid. pp.427-435.

[11] Having discussed first the different patterns of inculturation of the Gospel when the early disciples of Jesus moved out of the Palestinian context to the Greek, Roman and other world cultures, the writer takes up the question of proclaiming Jesus in India (see pp.427-436).

[12] *Jeevadhara* 26(1997)299-310.

[13] Ibid. p.300. While discussing the western contextualization of Christology, JBC points out the draw backs of the Greek thinking in accommodating the Hebrew thinking: In accommodating the Hebrew idea of the broad notion of the "Son of God" to the demands of the conceptualist thinking, Christian thought ran into great difficulties. The Greek answer to this problem was the concept of a mediator who would bridge the infinite gulf or distance between God and the material world.

Thus presenting Jesus as the Mediator, the 4th-5th century theologians argued against Arians, Appollinarians and Nestorians, and safeguarded the divinity and humanity of the one Mediator, between God and the human beings. And yet the tendency was to picture Jesus as a Creator-God, a sort of Demiurge by the side of the Supreme Being. Similarly, as the Greek thinking did not have a proper place for myth and legend as presented in the Bible, something between mere fantasy and truth, the Greek fathers went for a literal interpretation of the Biblical narratives, like the six-day creation, sin of the first parents by eating the forbidden fruit etc. Besides, in this Greek contextualization of Christianity Jesus became part of an ideology or creed to be confessed than a person to be encountered and experienced. This led to the Christian absolutism of the Middle Ages and the consequent religious conquest of the colonial period.

[14] See his article "Religion the Cutting Edge of Culture", cited in fn 117 above, p.357.

[15] See his article, "Nature and Scope of Inter-Religious Dialogue To day", *Jeevadhara* 21(1992)331-355.

[16] Ibid. p.337.

[17] Ibid.

[18] Although JBC has not explained this point giving the above example of the Eucharist as meal etc. I think that his very progressive ideas about contextualization and indigenous theology etc. logically leads to such radical liturgical inculturation as well, of course with necessary approval of the required authority.

[19] See "Symbolism and Cult in World Religions", *Jeevadhara* 5(1975)329-334.

[20] R.Weakland, "Music as Art in Liturgy", *Worship* 41(1967)5-15.

[21] Chethimattam, "Symbols and Cult in World Religions To Day" op.cit. p.338.

[22] Cf. Ibid. pp.340-44.

[23] Cf. Ibid.p. 344 and Louis Bouyer, *Rite and Man: Natural Sacredness and Christian Liturgy*, trans. M. Joseph Costelloe (Notre Dame Uni. Press) 1963, p.6.

[24] It may be noted that JBC here does not belittle the importance of social feasts and festivals like the feast of Fools in medieval Europe and Holi in India. In his article on "Man and Feast", Jeevadhara 6(1976)405-417, he on the one hand examines the natural origins of seasonal festivals as

re-juvenation of time and celebrations of life-situations, but on the other explains very well the meaning of such human and secular celebrations: Hew says, "In celebrations man [sic] proclaims his transcendence over, and freedom from, all his worldly pursuits and asserts his right to be himself, his capacity to rise above time and perceive its eternal meaning." He goes on to add, "What makes man different from animals is his capacity to celebrate, and this is rooted in his ability to understand what he is and what he is doing. Even when he celebrates the mysteries and events of gods and deities he knows fully well that God does not need the human celebration; it is for man....." (pp.412f).

[25] See the author's article "Symbolism and Cult in World Religions Today", cited in no. 22 above, and Louis Bouyer op.cit. pp.7-11.

[26] During the heated liturgical controversy in the Syro-Malabar Church in the 190s and early 90s, Dr. Chethimattam seems to have written some articles in Malayalam, criticising those bent on a blind Chaldeanization process of the liturgy. One such article is "Tradition is not Fetters" (Pāraμbaryaμ KoochuvilaGgalla – See *Karmla Kusumam*, August 1986). In this article, he directly supports liturgical renewal and say, "Tradition is not Fetters. Faith is handed down to us through historical tradition. However it is only a general model. Only such a Church can survive in today's world, which, without prejudice to the Gospel message, tradition and thought patter, would proclaim the Gospel and celebrate the liturgy, making necessary adaptations to the needs and requirements of persons, institutions and cultural contexts...........The printed prayers of the liturgy do not make liturgy; liturgy has to be a combined celebration of the priest and people.......It has to be different according to the nature and stature of the participants. Only then will be lively and active celebration.......... Similarly only when it is celebrated in tune with the needs of the people, time and place, the sacred rite will be liturgy. Church proclamation and liturgical celebration are not exhibition of archaeological findings; rather it is the self-manifestation of the people of God who are called by Word and Spirit of God." (My translation from his original Malayalam).

[27] Dr. Chethimattam, "Religion the Cutting Edge of Culture", op.cit. p.363.

[28] Ibid.

Chapter 11

Culture-Dynamics: Impact of Inculturated Formation for Mission

Introduction

The whole question of inculturation, put forward very strongly by the Council of Vatican II may be approached from different complementary perspectives. The present study is from one such perspective, namely formation for mission. This study is not intended to deal with questions like what inculturation is? The need and relevance of inculturation etc. These are taken for granted, although it may be necessary to make one or two remarks clarifying the underlying concepts. But, before we come to that, let me say a word about how this presentation has been organized. After giving the clarifications mentioned, we shall proceed to a short discussion of the theme "inculturation and formation" as it emerges from some important Vatican II and Post-Vatican II documents. Next we shall consider the theme from the perspective of official Church teaching in India after the Council. Thereafter we shall cast a bird's eye view of the *statu squo* regarding inculturated formation in India. Finally we shall devote some time for some critical reflections and constructive suggestions in view of inculturated formation for mission.

Culture and Inculturation

As we have explained earlier,[1] the root word in Latin 'colere' of culture means both "to worship" and "to cultivate", and the two nouns derived from *colere*, namely *cultus* and *cultura* mean "cult" and "culture". Culture evokes a wide spectrum of human accomplishments, difficult to convey all of them by one definition[2] In spite of all such elaborate definitions of culture, a very important dimension of human life is still not reflected in them. It is the dimension of human struggle for life and liberation. A threefold aspect of this struggle - economic, social and political – forms the basic structure of a human culture.

Consequently inculturation shall not be restricted to the field of worship (cult), and that too confined to mere ritual aspects, like waving flowers, incense and/or light called arati. Beyond the use of such ritual forms, we have to go a long way to make worship or liturgy expressive of the struggles and aspirations of the local people. Life and liturgy are deeply related and so cannot remain in isolation. For example, we do not really hear the word of God proclaimed in the liturgy, as long as we are deaf to his calling us in the life-struggles of the people. We do not in reality partake of the one bread and one cup to become one body of Christ (Cf. 1 Cor. 10:17), if we are not sensitive to the glaring inequalities and injustices within the parish community or in the society at large. In this respect, inculturation in the present study with its liberative thrust is considered as deeply intertwined with all institutions and structures of religious and priestly formation.

Inculturated Formation According to Vat.II

The Council which had its starting point in the late Pope Bl. John XXIII's insight on 'Aggiornamento' (updating) was very much a Council of renewal and up-dating of the Church. All its 16 documents bear the marks of this experience of the Council Fathers. We are concerned here only with those bearing on formation of religious and of priests in particular.

Vat.II on Religious Formation

The Spirit of God who continues to evoke new spiritual movements among the people of God, is constantly urging the religious to reflect seriously so as to discover how their institutes could and should be adapted to ever more perfectly to the changing circumstances of their own times. And so the Council in its decree on the "Appropriate Renewal of Religious Life (Perfectae Caritatis) gives principles of renewal so that religious life "may achieve greater good for the Church". Of the two fundamental principles stated in the decree, vi 1 return to the sources of Christian life and charism of the Founder, and 2) adaptations to the changed conditions of the times, we are particularly concerned about the second one, for which a "deep awareness of the contemporary human conditions and needs of the Church has to be created among members of the religious congregations (PC2). In particular the Decree prescribes the following:

> The manner of living, praying and working should be appropriately adapted to the physical and psychological conditions of today's religious…… to the needs of the apostolate, the requirements of the given culture, social and economic circumstances anywhere, especially the missionary territories(PC 3)

In the case of communities devoted to external works of the apostolate, the rules of enclosure have to be revised so that can better discharge the apostolic tasks assigned to them (PC16). So too religious habits have to be simple and modest, poor and becoming as well as suitable to the kind of services being discharged (PC 12). The Decree also envisages suitable programme of training for the new members, for, "The up to-date renewal of institutes depends very much on the training of the members......" (PC 18).[3]

Vatican II on Priestly Formation

The Decree on "The Training of Priests" (*Optatam Totius*) in tune with the spirit of *aggiornamento* "up-dating" of Vatican II, insisted that in each nation or rite a program of priestly formation should be undertaken so that universal laws of training might be adapted to the special circumstances of time and place, and thus priestly formation would answer the pastoral needs of the area in which the ministry would be exercised (OT1). Besides, when the Decree specifies a threefold training to be given, namely (1)" for the ministry of the word", (2) "for the ministry of worship and sanctification", and (3) "to undertake the ministry of shepherd" (OT4), there is in it at least an implicit reference to contextual adaptation in the training being imparted.

Post-Vatican II Church Teaching on Inculturated Formation

We are concerned mainly with the two major Apostolic Exhortations of the Pope – *Pastores* Dabo *Vobis* and *Vita Consecrata*, which came out following the Synod of Bishops, one on Priestly Training and the other on Consecrated Life in 1993 and 1994 respectively.

On Inculturated Religious Formation

This Apostolic Exhortation emphasizes that formation should involve the whole person and include every aspect of life: human, cultural, spiritual and pastoral. Moreover Vita *Consecrata* *(VC)*, rightly says that God the Father is the first formator: "Formation then is a sharing in the work of the Father, who through the Spirit fashions the inner spirit of the Son in the hearts of the young men and women."(VC 66).

Besides, comparing religious consecration to the Messianic consecration of Jesus on being 'sent by the Father', VC puts forward the idea that religious consecration is essentially "for mission". That the religious are "in mission" by their very consecration is a contribution of this Synodal document to the thought on religious life of Vatican II. Speaking about the methods of carrying out the task of proclaiming Christ, VC says that "conversion that is full and sincere adherence to Christ and his Gospel" implies inculturation and interreligious dialogue (VC79). Making Christ present to the world through personal life witness is primary mission of the religious (72-73), but to do this effectively religious life needs to be properly inculturated so that through its prophetic dimension it becomes "Gospel level, within a culture, purifying and perfecting it (VC80). Following the example of Jesus who proclaimed the Good News to the poor (Lk 4:18-20), the demand of inculturation for religious life implies also their social commitment, with preferential option for the poor, for those "in situations of great weakness (VC 81).

On Inculturated Priestly Training

Pastores Dabo Vobis (PDV is an elaborate study of the various aspects of priestly vocation, training and ministry appropriate to the present day. We are particularly interested in chapter five which discusses mainly the theme of priestly training. Preparation for priesthood, says PDV, essentially consists in responding from the heart to Christ's basic question: Do you love me ? (Jn. 21:15). And the proper answer to it can only be a total self-giving. "What needs to be done is to transfer this spirit......to the social, psychological, political and cultural conditions of the world today" (PDV 42). Moreover, it is significant that PDV considers human formation as basis of all priestly formation. The priest should mould his human personality in such a way that it becomes a bridge and not an obstacle for others in their meeting with Jesus Christ the Redeemer of man [sic]" (PDV 43). Of special importance is to have a capacity to relate to others, to be a "man of communion" etc. In these and similar guidelines of PDV we can see a great concern of the Pope and the Synodal Fathers to inculturate priestly formation in the "circumstances of the present day."

Inculturation in Formation: Scene of the Church in India

We consider here briefly the official thinking and teaching of the Church in India regarding inculturation in formation during the past few decades after Vatican II. First we shall see formation of the religious and the mind of the Conference of Religious in India (CRI), and then priestly formation and the guidelines of the Catholic Bishops Conference in India (CBCI).

Inculturated Formation of the Religious

My short reflection hereunder is based on a CRI publication,[4] written by Vanda Mataji, herself a religious well inculturated in dress, food habits, lifestyle and thought pattern. First of all, there is a common awareness that we in India (whole of Asia as well) have to consider "formation of a people who have a dual cultural heritage – Christian heritage and own national heritage. In Europe, America and Australia the culture is Christian. In Asia it may be, Hindu, Buddhist or Islamic. This is where inculturation plays a big role in formation."[5] Also it is generally accepted that "for formation to be effective, it has to be rooted in the existential situation of each country and culture."[6] For India these challenge are mainly 1) poverty and exploitation, 2) pluralism of many types (religions, cultures, traditions etc.), 3) communalism and regionalism. We have to take these challenges seriously, if our inculturation program is to be realistic.[7]

'The Chinese proverb: "Find your roots and take wings", observes Sr. Vandana in the above book, 'sums up the chief qualities of Asian formation to day.'[8] Surely it means that religious formation in India and Asia has to be adapted to our own cultural genius. Only so can we become creative, being rooted in the existential realities of our country. The characteristic notes of this Indian genius are value of silence, awareness of the Presence, loving obedience to the Guru, single minded pursuit of God experience even in the midst of work (nishkamakarma), value of renunciation, and simplicity and transparency in the lifestyle.[9] Needless to say, these are the more difficult objectives to realize by inculturation of religious life in India.

Inculturation of Priestly formation in India

The CBCI Commission for Clergy and Religious has brought out a book, *Charter of Priestly Formation for India*, after a number of seminars and consultations in preparation for it.[10] While speaking about the various aspects of (Major) seminary formation, sections 3.1.5. and 3.1.7. of this charter make short references to cultural aspects of formation. In particular emphasis has been laid on 'regionalization of formation' so that "this will make it possible for the seminarian to be thoroughly educated in the language and culture of the people of the region of his future ministry." (3.1.5). And the document adds: Through his formation the seminarian should be given opportunities to interact with and respond to contemporary Indian reality, especially the struggle of the masses for fundamental human Looking back at the present scenario of inculturated formation, one will have some mixed feelings - feelings of satisfaction and also disappointment. Satisfaction, because to a great extent westernized atmosphere with regard to structures and formation/administration personnel, academic matters etc. has changed. Lot of local flavor and colours in these areas have enriched many of the seminaries and formation houses. Moreover, some attempts to introduce regional languages, apart from English, as the medium of instruction, and some importance given to the study of subjects related to Indian religions and cultures are indeed quite welcome. Similarly adoption of Indian methods of prayer, bhajan singing, use of indigenous signs and symbols like bowing and prostration in liturgical celebrations (instead of kneeling and genuflection) have become more or less common.

At the same time the past post-Vatican II inculturation drive has not made much headway after 1980's. The 12-point formula of adaptation/inculturation highly recommended by the CBCI has taken a back seat in many places after the initial enthusiasm. This is particularly the case with regard to the following four areas, recommended long ago as major dignity and justice."(3.1.7).[11]

Status Quo of the Program of Inculturated Formation in India

Areas of inculturation.[12] These are the four areas specified for inculturation in seminaries:

1. Study of Philosophy and Theology, 2. Prayer, Liturgy and Spirituality, 3. Culture, Social Realities and Life-Style, and 4.Mission and Ministries.

Philosophy and Theology

With regard to inculturation in this area, we may note that under the influence of Liberation Theologies of different shades and Dalit Theology of India, study and teaching of theology have become somewhat in tune with the cultural context of our country, but pretty little has taken place in the case of philosophy, much less an integration of philosophy and theology from a unified vision of the Indian tradition.

Prayer, Liturgy and Spirituality

In this regard only inculturation in external signs and symbols has taken place, but not in vision and attitude, and so the third element here, namely spirituality with its significant values of silence, awareness of the Presence etc. has become only least adapted in the seminary context.

Culture, Social Awareness and Life-Style

Concerning this point, 'social awareness' is increasing. Due to people's movements at the grass-root level against glaring socio-economic disparities between the Christian masses and the Church personnel, attempts are afoot here and there to change the secluded type of seminary training and to expose the candidates to the harsh realities of people's life. The so-called action-reflection-action programme as part of 'doing theology', introduced in some seminaries is worth mentioning here; but nothing serious has taken place in change of life-style: food and clothing, building structures and other facilities and amenities of life still cry very much for simplification in tune with ordinary people's life.

Mission and Ministries

In this case not much has been done in any seminaries to initiate seminarians to special ministries (other than the traditional ones like education pastoral ministry etc.) like dialogue with other religions, adult literacy etc. or frontier ministries like, ministry of prisoners, rag-pickers, HIV aides, railway plat-forum dwellers etc. which are very much needed in our socio-cultural context. But this needs vision and conviction that these are genuine acts of evangelization/inculturation.

Some reflections and Suggestions for future action

In this last section we try to share some reflections in the light of a long time experience and efforts in the fields of inculturation and formation. We shall try to offer some suggestions for an effective inculturation of formation, centred on the mission ahead.

We have seen that the official Church, universal and local has published documents and provided guidelines encouraging inculturation in seminary formation. For the past several decades attempts were being made in inculturated seminary formation in response to the official guidelines. But it is a sad fact that the process has been peripheral and less than satisfactory. As a conclusion of his study on "Priestly Formation in the changing Society of India", Fr. Vallipalam makes the following significant observations:

Apart from a certain amount of adaptation, no inculturation or contextualization has taken place in the system of seminary formation in India. The reasons are several. First of all, these concepts are still not very clear to all. Secondly, not all those who are responsible for formation are convinced of them, and so look at them suspiciously. A third point is how to initiate the change and who will bell the cat. The whole question is therefore at a standstill. ......However a determined attempt must be made in this direction, since the seminarian holds in his hands the future of the Church.[13]

The above observations of Fr. Vallipalam are certainly relevant; but I think there is a more fundamental reason for the lack of depth and zest in the inculturation programme, namely, the goal of inculturation is not clearly perceived and defined.

It is here that we can profit from the Jesuit experience of the inculturation programme which began in the early 1980's with a fourfold objective of 1) vernacularization, 2) regionalization, 3) contextualization in life-style and manner of training, and 4) integration or harmonization. But after a period of 10 years, when the programme was evaluated in the 1990's, it was found that there was "an unresolved tension in Inculturation Commission Report's understanding of "culture" in India. Which culture is to be the basis? – folk culture or classical culture; little tradition or mainland tradition? etc. Further they discovered that "a critical analysis of the social context of our mission must be made before we can answer such questions as what culture or whose culture must we be inculturated into? And so it was finally settled that "like formation, inculturation cannot be considered apart from mission. It is in the concrete context of our mission that the tensions underlying the process of inculturation must be resolved."[14] Finally the 32nd Congress of the Society defined its mission to day as follows

The mission of the Society of Jesus is the service of faith of which the promotion of justice is an absolute requirement. This is so because the reconciliation of men and women among themselves, which their reconciliation with God demands, must be based on justice." GC 32, D.4, no.2).

And this general decision about the Society's mission was re-interpreted for India and S. Asia without any ambiguity in this way:

> This task demands to day an option for the poor......By the poor we mean all socioeconomically marginalized groups, particularly, the Dalits, the Tribals, women, unorganized labour, illiterates. Our work with other groups is justified to the extent that it contributes to the empowerment of the poor.[15]

When inculturation of formation is linked to mission, particularly in its social content, then the whole question of inculturation of seminary formation will assume deeper significance. Since mission thus determines formation, and since structures and practices will also be in view of mission, the different dimensions of training – human, intellectual, spiritual etc. will have to be tuned accordingly. We shall now consider some of these dimensions in relation to the demand on inculturation.

Consider first the human formation: The Synodal Fathers rightly placed it as the "foundation of the whole work of priestly formation". And so in PDV the Pope makes mention of a number of virtues and qualities that make a priest truly human. These are love for truth, respect for every person, sense of justice, reliability, compassion, integrity and especially well-balanced judgment and behaviour (PDV 43). These qualities would make him a "bridge and not an obstacle for others in their meeting with Jesus".[16] This means, just as Jesus through his incarnation came closer to us helping us to encounter God the Father, a priest as a truly human person or inculturated person (assuming the incarnational qualities), also becomes a medium or sacrament for others to encounter God.

Truly human formation will make him very like Jesus, especially closer to the poor. He will better understand the full implications of the phrase "option for the poor". He will first of all understand that without opting for the poor, he cannot opt for Christ, that he cannot love the poor well except with the heart and sentiments of Christ. Secondly he would understand that option for the poor means feeling with them as they live a life of rejection and forced silence. Thirdly it would mean for him to read and interpret the socio-economic-political reality through their own perception and feelings, and thus espousing their causes. Fourthly it would require of him to denounce as immoral structures that oppress the poor. Further it would demand from him a re-definition of all his ministries in favour of the poor and a life-style that is expressive of this choice. Fifthly he would conscientize them of the mechanisms and structures that oppress them and deny their rights.

But living as they do now in most of the present model of seminaries and formation houses, with their huge structures, superfine arrangements, upper class comforts and conveniences, no seminarian, barring very few exceptions, will be able to understand and appreciate the above-said implications of the catchy slogan "option for the poor". For, examine the source of inspiration of many entertainment programmes in seminaries – the mass culture or the elite fashion? As Fr. Velamkunnel has rightly said, "There seems to be an organized formation mechanism through which the religious are gradually being inserted into the elite culture and made to feel that their rightful place is in the elite society."[17] A sign of this organized mechanism is the so-called 'spoon-fork' culture. Where do we find these 'eating gadgets'? In the ordinary homes of the masses? Or in highly westernized families? Surely in the latter cases, and also in five star hotels, and of course in the houses of the religious and the clergy. Think of the value judgment inculcated into the minds of the young candidates on their admittance to religious/seminary life, when they are meticulously instructed about the 'decent way' (spoon-fork use) of eating. Truly," our cultural consciousness is heavily overlaid with foreign elements since our formation has been in terms of a foreign idiom".[18]

This calls for a suitable theological method to transform our habitual patterns of thought through a constant interplay of experience-reflection-action. Then theological reflection will be rooted in the experience of people's struggle for life, the cause of their unjust and oppressive situation which is critically analyzed and reflected upon in the light of faith -commitment. Our idea of theology has changed and is changing, because our idea of faith is no longer the same: It is no more mere assent to a body of revealed truths handed down to us in the form of creeds and dogmatic definitions. It is rather the experience of a living relationship between God and the human.

As relationship, it can grow through commitment to realize the plan of God. Theology then is an attempt to become more deeply aware of this faith-experience, and to discern action plan in response to the concrete context of life. Inculturation of theology then is not merely a process of translation and adaptation, but a constantly renewed programme of understanding life in all its historical and cultural complexity and diversity.[19]

And this approach to theological education will call for a spirituality of involvement /struggle, of praxis or reflection-action process, of solidarity with and liberation of the poor and the oppressed. Since holiness is said to be wholeness, it is a process of becoming a person in the fullest sense by discovering himself in relation to others, whom one wants to serve. As Fr. Rayan says, "To be whole and to make the world whole, spirituality must break out from its merely individual limits and become corporate.[20] The experience of encountering God in the human and social realities will exert a transforming effect on the seminarian, who will be challenged to deny himself, shattering his "domestic idols", like craze for fashionable dress and greed for delicious food and comforts.

Naturally we come to the question of life-style in the seminary. In India the most characteristic trait of a person of God is simplicity of life. It is not only sign of renunciation, but a positive mark of total freedom. Hence it attracts as well as liberates. It attracts others to the person who practices it, precisely because he/she has become a liberated person due to it.[21] So a life of simplicity in India today concretely means life of a common man/woman in clothing, housing, food, recreation, travel etc. life of a liberated person who is happy with what he/she has (a *sadhaka*). And it also means living like Jesus. Thus inculturation of seminary life-style means instilling into it the incarnational values.

Concluding Remarks

We started the discussion with a supposition that the effect of any culture by way of inculturation will exert great influence on forming religious and priests suitable for the mission. However in the process of our enquiry into the matter we discovered towards the end that we have to work rather backward from mission to inculturation, because both inculturation and formation have mission as their raison d'etre. Linking the three together, we may now say, "for our mission, the Incarnation is its inspiration, and inculturation must be modeled after Jesus' example, if our formation has to be for his mission."[22]

Moreover, in spite of repeated Church decisions and declarations in favour of inculturation in formation, we have seen, the process remains at a skin-deep level. Based on the Jesuit experience in this matter,[23] we have argued that the programme of inculturation must take seriously the content of social mission, although it may be a surprise, if not a new insight, for many to integrate liberation with inculturation. Otherwise our inculturation may slip into the classical elitist culture, oppressive and dominant; instead we need to inculturate into the subaltern culture of the poor, the Dalits and the Tribals.

Once this is assured in the seminary formation/house set-up, in the life-style of the staff and students, in its structures and institutions, in theological education and spiritual formation, then the other aspects of inculturation, viz in prayer and worship, celebrations and commemorations will follow spontaneously.

Endnotes

[1] See Introduction to this volume.

[2] We can find definitions by anthropologists which include people's beliefs and morals, customs and manners etc. to the traditional list of ingredients like fine arts, performing arts, literature, sculpture and architecture. Similarly sociologists make their contribution to it adding people's dreams and aspirations, norms values and ideologies that give direction to the cultural process.

[3] Cf also *Ecclesiae Sanctae* 33; *Evangelica Testificatio* 51.

[4] Vandana, *Formation of Asian Religious*, Bangalore: CRI Publications, 1975.

[5] Ibid. p.3.

[6] Ibid. p.3.

[7] Ibid. p.7.

[8] Ibid. p.17.

[9] Ibid. pp.18-41.

[10] CBCI Commission for Clergy and Religious, *Charter of Priestly Formation for India*, 1988; *Priestly Formation in North India*, Navsadhana; *Consultation on*

Priestly Formation, 1982; *Program of Priestly Formation for India*, Commissio Technica, not dated, etc.

[11] CBCI Commission for Clergy and Religious, Charter of Priestly Formation, pp.10f.

[12] Peter Fernando Ed. *Inculturation in Major Seminaries*, Pune, Ishvani; Indore, Satprakashan Sanchar Kendra, pp.13-16.

[13] Mathew Vallipalam, *Priestly Formation in the Changing Society of India*, Mumbai, St.Pauls Publications, 1989, p.264.

[14] *South Asian Assistancy, Formation in Mission: The Final Report of the Formation Review Commission (FRC) and Conclusions of JCSA, 1992, 11-13.*

[15] FRC, p.136.

[16] PDV 43.

[17] J. Velamkunnel, "Formation of Religious and Service of the Poor", *Vidyajyoti*. August 1980, p.321.

[18] Mathew Vallipalam, op.cit. p.259.

[19] M. Amaldoss," Inculturation and Theological Formation", P. Fernando Rd. op.cit. pp.52-64.

[20] S. Rayan, "Spirituality Today" Catholic Priests Conference in India, Aug. 1990, p.19. See also Felix Wilfred.

[21] A story is told about the Greek philosopher Socrates: He was living a simple life in every aspect of it but he was a happy and contented person of high thinking. He was found often going to the weekly market in the village. He would go around looking at and enjoying the many goods and products displayed in different stalls. But he would not buy anything. A friend of him who noticed this behaviour of Socrates, asked him one day: Dear friend, why do you come to the market regularly, but without buying anything any time? Then he is said to have replied thus, "Yes, I come regularly to the market, not to buy anything, because I am happy with what I have already; but to know without what all things I can be happy, when I look at the new goods and gadgets displayed."

[22] FRC 12.

[23] Other religious congregations also who have tried like the Jesuits will have similar experience. For example, as a CMI formator in the major seminaries for several decades, I can say that the momentum of inculturation has remained at the peripheral level, because Jesus' incarnation as its source of inspiration has not touched deep enough to translate its values in the life of the missionaries.

Chapter 12

Interface of Culture and Gospel: Total Inculturation as Mission of the Church in India Today

Introduction

The term inculturation is relatively new, but soon gained currency on the label of the Post-Vatican II theological thinking, although the idea is an old worry of the Church.[1]

Like the catchy phrase "option for the poor", inculturation is also very much a slogan bandied about in clerical circles, but deprived of its deeper meaning and significance. It is sometimes reduced to liturgical adaptations in its ritual aspect, like waving flowers, incense or light called aarati, or bowing with folded hands in holy places etc. Many fail to see that beyond these ritual aspects, we have to go a long way to make liturgy expressive of the struggles and aspirations of the people which are the life line of a people's culture.

In contemporary missiological discussion, inter-faith or inter-religious dialogue is considered a major method of evangelizing mission of the Church. Similarly action for justice and development of the people is taken as a necessary component of evangelization.[2] And inculturation of the Gospel of course, has been a burning issue in the Church down the centuries. This analytical approach to the question of mission of the Church in the past was helpful in so far as it highlighted the praxis from a particular angle or perspective; it became an obstacle to the holistic vision of mission. In other words the proponents of religious dialogue, social action and inculturation, each person being limited in the particular field of action, exaggerated own field and failed to see their common points of convergence.

This presentation is a modest attempt to show a synoptic view of three approaches pointing out their lines of contact and complementarity. We would call it a total inculturation agenda of the Church. In order to arrive at it, first we shall have a bird's view of the mission context of India, which calls for the kind of total inculturation. Secondly we shall look at culture and its constituents from a broader perspective leading to a fresh understanding of the process and dynamics of inculturation. Finally we shall point out certain aspects of inculturation required with a double focus on the Church on the one hand and on the Kingdom on the other.

Context of Mission in India

It is generally accepted that the Indian mind is 'context-sensitive' in the sense that it sees each thing as part of a whole or in a particular context without which it cannot be understood properly.[3] Consequently it is able to hold together seemingly contradictory aspects of reality as complementary parts of a whole.[4] This Indian insight is also helpful in understanding the nature and function of 'mission', when this is projected against the North Indian context, where it is to be realized. Some of the characteristics of this context are said to be massive poverty, religious plurality, caste universality, cultural diversity and communalist-fundamentalist calamity.

The massive poverty in India which persists even after 70 years of economic planning, is an obvious stark reality. It has been made more visible and striking because it exists side by side with fabulous wealth. The contrast that strike the eye instantly boggles the mind too – a contrast between sprawling slums and posh mansions, between pavement dwellers and palace revelers, the miserable landless and the miserly land lords and so on. In spite of the political and social reservations provided for the SC/ST and OBC, India is still ruled by high caste politicians and bureaucrats. The upper class-caste combination grabs about 80% jobs of the bureaucracy like, the IAS, IPS, IFS etc. Such concentration of social, economic and political power in the hands of the high caste minority results in the marginalization of the weaker and backward sections - the Dalits, Tribals, women and children, as well as agricultural labourers and farmers.[5] The systematic exploitation of the Indian people, leading to a sharp polarization of many poor and a few rich, is plainly visible. It takes forms familiar to us in the denunciation of the biblical prophets – cheating in trade (Amos 4-6), the corruption of justice (Is. 10:4), the concentration of land holdings (Is. 5:8-9), loans at exorbitant interest, leading to debt slavery or bonded labour, as it is called in India (Amos 18:6), all this within a system which offers little protection to the powerless because it is wholly controlled by those who exploit them. Poverty in India is the result of injustice; it is therefore is not merely an economic issue, but a moral and theological one.[6]

The impact of the government policy of globalization and economic liberalization on the poor is bound to be negative. In the new scheme only a limited number of new jobs and that too skilled jobs will be created. Perhaps the only hope for the poor is the so-called "trickle down" theory.[7] The NDA Government's Demonetization and GST policy has certainly not been in favour of the poor and the marginalized. The chief beneficiaries of these measures will be upper and lower middle class, almost to the exclusion of the poor, the informal sector.

Environmental degradation is a global problem, as we know, affecting all countries and peoples, but its special mention here is because of the relationship between ecology and the poor of North India. The poor directly depends on natural resources, like Tribals on forest, fisher folk on water resource, agricultural laborers on land. The often have their own wise way of sustainable use and management of these resources. But the unbridled market forces will deprive the poor of access to them and upset the mechanism that keeps the ecological balance. Thus the continued over-exploitation of the nature by the rich causes further and further marginalization of the poor.

Variety and multiplicity of forms of religion is perhaps nowhere else in the world so conspicuous as in India - a pluriform Hinduism, all the world religions, numerous primal religions of the aboriginal tribals, as well as new psychedelic cults around some Gurujis. It would be wrong to consider poverty as the root cause of this pervasive religiosity, as text book Marxism would have us believe sometimes. India has been so deeply religious through its history in the ancient times of Asoka and Chandra Gupta, famous for wealth and plenty, as well as in more recent times of foreign invaders/colonizers, notorious for their exploitation and looting of resources. On the other hand an attitude of dialogue and tolerance is at the root of this religiosity and religious pluralism. However this age-old virtue is under considerable strain to day.

In modern times we have been witnessing strong revivalism in the Hindu majority community. Though in principle this is harmless and desirable, it is in fact becoming increasingly vitiated owing to communal tendencies. Communalism in the Indian context essentially amounts to organizing an exclusive religious group on the basis of hostility towards other groups at the social level.[8] This communal tendency has reduced the spirit of revivalism into fundamentalism, which promotes conservatism and stagnation, breaks the basic unity of the people in a pluralistic society like India. A shift of accent from Hinduism as a religion to Hindutva as an ideology, is increasingly visible today. While the former stresses a certain other-worldly spiritual dimension of human life, the latter is a vision of a welfare Hindu state to be brought about through political power and domination over other religious groups.

As far as the Christian community is concerned, this development is a great threat to our mission, which was quite clear during the visit of Pope John Paul II to India in connection with the beatification of Sts. Chavara and Euprasia. A major section of the Hindi press covering the entire North Indian Hindi-belt was quite critical about the papal visit.[9] This utterly negative reaction of the Hindi print-media is symptomatic of some grave disease, viz our very poor influence on the religio-cultural context of the Hindi-belt, which in fact is the vast field of our evangelizing mission.

The context of religious pluralism in the North cannot overlook the fact that North India is the birth place of great religious founders like Buddha, Jina, Kabir, Guru Nanak. This region has produced many saints and sages who are highly respected the world over. Centres of Hindu revivalism, like the Ramakrishna Mission are found in all major cities ; Shivananda Ashram, Rishikesh, TM centre of Maharshi Mahesh Yogi, Rishikesh, Rajneesh Ashram, Pune etc. are attracting thousands of bhaktas from different parts of the world

Similarly, religious pluralism has to reckon with the long tribal belt of the Hindi heartland. About 60 million (7.8%) of the Indian population forms this group of aboriginals with their own numerous languages and dialects, traditions and worship patterns. The "Little traditions" of the Dalits and the marginalized sections of our society form a very important factor of this religious pluralism.

Another major factor of the mission context is the age old Hindu caste system. Caste norms and hierarchy are still prevalent in 90% of the communities, and it is overtaking the tribal society.[10] Whatever be the origin of the Hindu caste system, in its present form it is a social catastrophe mainly because, Dr. Ambedkar has rightly observed, it enjoys religious sanction. This sanction divides not only labour but also labourers into four rungs of the social ladder with absolutely no possibility for the lower rungs to move upward. And this assumes a most deplorable form in the 'untouchability' of the outcastes or Dalits. In spite of strong Constitutional safeguards and many enlightened laws of the State to protect their rights and promote their socio-economic conditions, the overall effect of these measures so far have been marginal. Caste discrimination continues unabated, especially in rural India.

From One Culture to Many Cultures

After having highlighted in the above few paragraphs the major components of the present context of the Church's mission in India, the next question to deal with is this: What is the most relevant response to this context? First of all we may note here that the major components of this context are in fact also the important aspects of the present Indian culture. Therefore the first thing to do is to understand the nature and dynamics of this culture in some depth so that this understanding will tell us what is the proper response needed. And we shall see that the answer is total inculturation.

This requires a broader discussion of what is culture, how mono-culturalism of the Christian West gradually gave way to multi-culturalism of the post-colonial period etc. After Tylor's (1832-1917) classical definition of culture,[11] there have been hundreds of similar definitions from different angles and vintage points.[12] But their significance will loom large only against the unitary concept of culture that was prevalent till that time.[13] Almost from the 4th to 16th century, there was only one view, one term to denote culture, namely "western culture" in its original Latin words like *Romanitas, Nobilitas, Humanitas* etc. Any human society or civilization outside the purview of this Western culture was called *Barbaritas* (barbarism) for many centuries.

This was a mono-cultural (Western) world view in which unity of Christian faith was safeguarded by appealing to the uniformity or rather unicity and static nature of this culture. Christian dogmas were considered unchangeable not so much because they were revealed truths as because the culture and its categories of formulation were understood as permanent, giving immutable meaning to them.

During the great western missionary wave of the 15/16th century under the protective umbrella of Western colonialism, it was this culture that the missionaries tried to transport to the New World as is evident from the notorious slogan "The faith is Europe and Europe is the faith" of Hilaire Belloc.[14]

Viewed in this way, one of the welcome aspects of western colonial expansion is that it helped to explode the age-old myth of the mono-cultural western world. Gradually, a pluralistic understanding of culture emerged thanks to this expansion and mutual contact of world civilizations of East and West, North and South, because this expansion brought first European and eventually American missionaries as well as political thinkers like Montesquiew (1689-1755), social anthropologists like E.B. Tylor (1832-1917) face to face with the reality of cultural pluralism. And this was finally accepted at least in theory, when political freedom began to be granted by or demanded from the colonizing countries to these newly discovered cultural groups since the middle of the 20th centuries.

Tylor's classical or first definition of culture, mentioned above is the first sign of this shift of culture-view from a uniform, static and changeless one to a pluriform, dynamic and changing view. "Culture is a complex whole", says Tylor, as he then narrated a wide range of human activities and accomplishments as part of it, and this is clearly pointed out in a long descriptive definition given by Vat. II[15] We can find in this description of culture by the Council elements from academic disciplines like, sociology, ethnology, anthropology, human accomplishments like arts and crafts, beliefs and practices of religions, languages and philosophies etc. Finally the concept of culture embraces also the history of human struggle with its triple dimension – social economic and political. In fact this struggle determines the very fabric of human culture, whereas myths, arts and other symbolic forms only faithfully reflect this struggle. Briefly, culture is the way of life of a social group; it embraces every aspect of human life, has reference not only to the present, but also to the past as its collective memory of the heritage, and to the future as the goal to achieve.[16]

From the above description of culture, what is clear is that today culture is not an absolute concept, and culture is not a monopoly of any one social group, because no social group can represent human nature adequately. There is only one human nature, but there are many human cultures, and in modern cultural anthropology, the dichotomy between nature and culture is superseded. The very nature of man/woman is cultural; he/she is a cultural animal or culture is the specific manner being human. Empirical and environment al factors, historical struggles for life and dignity, coupled with the normative values of religion do create manifold cultures. Hence comparison between cultures is odious, though there can be primal and evolved cultures, ancient and modern cultures etc.

Among the manifold components of a culture, religion stands out as the most important one. Ever since Tylor's work *Primitive Culture* showed this unique relationship between the two, no ethnographer has reported any primitive society without religious beliefs and practices.[17]

There are at least three ways in which religion and culture may be intimately related: In the first case, both may be co-terminus. Religious beliefs and practices taught and maintained as part of the natural scheme of 'enculturation', namely the normal process of acquiring competence in one's culture and gradually getting incorporated into it. This is the case with ethnic and tribal religions in general. In the second case, a dominant religion will be associated with the birth of a culture, later however, one or more immigrant religions may contribute to the growth of the host-culture. For example, Christianity at the birth of the western culture along with later religious groups from the East, another example is Hinduism (rather Vedism) at the birth of Indian culture along with later religious groups, like Christianity, Islam etc. In the third case, one prominent world religion may contribute to the growth of several cultures. For example, Christianity, Islam or Buddhism, because each of these has contributed to the growth of several cultures. Christianity's claim that it can be at home in any culture[18] belongs here. Inculturation, therefore gives not only another indigenous expression of faith, but also through that expression, Christian religion and host- culture are enriched.

Inculturation

Having analyzed at some length the complex reality of culture as embracing all human social life including the socio-economic and political structures, life struggle etc., we are now in a better position to understand the deeper implications and dynamics of inculturation.

First of all the concept of inculturation as understood in the Church circles has several precursors, like adaptation, accommodation, assimilation, indigenization etc., following the Council's concept of updating (aggiornamento). The process, as these terms suggest, consisted in adapting or borrowing some customs and practices from other cultures which are not intrinsically bound up with error or superstition, and not against Christian faith and morals. The defect of this approach may be noted: It presupposes that Christian faith is a pre-existing reality that can be easily dressed up and presented in the garb of another culture. Naturally this will disregard the deeper aspects of both faith and culture.

It is in the light of this awareness that surfaced in the Post-Vatican II positive attitude to other cultures and religions, that we have to understand the emergence of the term inculturation, [19] which has replaced the other terms mentioned earlier. In the present context even this term is considered by some as insufficient for the purpose, because they say, that it seems to imply culture in a limited sense, namely embracing only the areas of creative and performing arts, like music, dance, dramatics, and consequently that the question of inculturation may concern only the Churches of the Third World, which are considered to be culturally alienated because of the colonial heritage. On the other hand, more recent theological reflection on the question, taking the redemptive incarnation of Jesus as the proto-type of inculturation, would show that the Western [20]Churches of the First Two Worlds need it no less than those of the Third World. For, the Gospel message confronts any culture not in its restricted sense, but in the full sense of the total context of human life, where the Gospel message has to be incarnated. Though some writers prefer the term 'contextualization,[21] inculturation seems to be still in vogue and probably the best choice if two conditions are fulfilled (1) if culture is taken in its total or inclusive sense, (2) if Incarnation is taken as the original and unrepeatable model or archetype of inculturation.[22]

These considerations would give a simple definition of inculturation. It is a critical encounter and ongoing dialogue between Gospel and culture. The process starts in the particularities of both Gospel and culture. At least three stages may be considered for it. In the first stage Gospel in the particular cultural idiom (language, symbols etc.) of the evangelizer (missionary community) learns the local language and custom. Meanwhile some of the local people may accept the Gospel message, although in a foreign garb. This stage is called sometime the **translation stage.** In the next stage, the recipient culture, through a process of discernment, assimilates the essence of the Gospel and tries to express it in the life and signs of the local people. Thus a local community of Jesus disciples (Christ-bhaktas) is born; it remains rather passive or defensive to the native culture for reasons of survival in the midst of opposition from various quarters. This stage is called **assimilation stage.** The third stage is that of the **transformation** of the recipient culture, assuming a new spirit and orientation from the Gospel on the one hand, but also an enrichment of the Gospel message in terms of this new cultural expression, which expands its catholicity on the other. The transformation process of the host-culture will involve removal of elements which cannot be absorbed by the Gospel. For example, the system of bonded labour, caste discrimination, practice of Sati or widow-burning etc. Similarly the Gospel's cultural garb also has to give up its foreign elements in order to assume the new expression., for example, early Jewish Christianity had to shed its Jewish ethnocentric conception (circumcision for Gentile Christians) in order to assume Greek cultural forms. In a similar way, the symbols and doctrinal formulations of Western Christianity based on Graeco-Roman thought-forms have to die and give them a new expression in the religio-cultural idioms of India.

The interaction between Gospel and culture involving a sort of dying and rising again to new life implies that inculturation goes the way of the Paschal Mystery of death and resurrection of Jesus. Whereas the paradigm of Incarnation would emphasize the need for transformation and identification with the local culture like the Logos at Incarnation (Phi. 2:5-11), Jesus did more than that: He also questioned meaningless practices, criticized unjust laws and empowered weak human kind by words as well as deeds, His own resurrection being the greatest among them.

Comprehensive Agenda of Inculturation

Having discussed the meaning of culture and inculturation as well as the context of mission that calls for inculturation of the Gospel, we have to consider in this last section, concrete steps for the whole process of inculturation as the real mission of the Church in India.

In any serious endeavour half—hearted measures will not deliver the goods, and this is true in the present case of the inculturation agenda as well. The Church/Churches in India has/have to make an all-out attempt for it, have to embark on a total program of inculturation, starting with the easier ones and going on to more difficult ones. Pope Paul VI who is well-known for his consistent and extensive teaching on cultural adaptation of the Gospel has pointed out on different occasions quite a few areas of inculturation; they are said to be the pastoral, ritual, didactic and spiritual activities of the Church.[23] Or the faith, liturgy, ecclesiastical organization and catholic action.[24] Or again areas of catechesis, theological formulation, secondary ecclesial structures and ministries.[25] What the Pope would want to emphasize here seems to be that "the whole of Christian life as well as the whole process of evangelization must be adapted to the genius and disposition of each culture."[26] In other words the Pope calls for a total or comprehensive agenda of inculturation, although he pinpoints only three major areas – liturgy, theology and catechesis.

Now, a pre-requisite or essential condition for the success of such a total inculturation agenda is a change of heart on the part of the Church or the evangelizing community. The heart must be set on things Indians. It cannot be denied, there are still Indians with a slavish mind-set, which is a heritage of the colonial past, dreaming about the "flesh pots of Egypt." But we Christians must not only avoid this temptation, but also set the good example of patriotism. We must show that our 'hearts' are here, because of our 'treasure 'is involved with the life and destiny of this great land and its people. Fr. Felix Wilfred has observed thus: "Whether we like it not, in the perception of our country men and women, Christianity, though apparently in the soil, seems however bent outward in the name of universality, like a coconut tree bent outward and yielding its fruits elsewhere."[27] So we have to cultivate a positive attitude and good will to appreciate what is Indian and indigenous without hankering after foreign goods and services.

If we develop this attitude it will be manifested in our love and thirst for ingredients of the national heritage – saints and sages irrespective of their religious persuasions, "little traditions" with their colourful stories and songs, languages and dialects etc.[28] Similarly, this appreciation will not allow us to close our eyes to the wanton misuse and misappropriation of national wealth and resources, like land, rivers, forests etc. because such misuse would not only upset the eco-system but also result in untold suffering and hardship to the poor. We cannot claim to be genuinely Indian by merely adopting some local customs, signs and gestures into liturgy alone or by putting on saffron clothes alone or by switching over to vegetarianism alone, although all these may be required according to circumstances, but more than all these we must be involved in the struggles of people for life and liberation. In other words, "we must liberate every man and the whole man," as the saintly Pope of inculturation Paul VI used to say. It may be noted here in passing that this Pope who has spoken so much about the process of evangelizing cultures and people, has almost identified it with that of inculturation and considered both as the mission of the Church.

Moreover, if inculturation is understood and carried out as the mission of the Church in India as explained above, it will be a fitting Christian response to the present trend of 'religious nationalism' and mono-culturalism on the one hand, and also to the many evils of the economic globalization, which is tied up with a particular ideology of free market economy. What should concern us here is peripheralization of the vast majority of the poor, neglect of local cultures and indigenous values, and refusal of the variety and diversity of cultural expressions. From a Christian point of view, inculturation is an antidote to all these evils: It insists on the importance of the local and the contextual, calls for the defense of the poor and the oppressed and welcomes pluralism of cultural expressions.

Theological inculturation is certainly another area, difficult but very important. As the late Fr. (Dr.) Soares Prabhu has said: "Because Christian theology is …..profoundly alienated from the Indian situation, it needs to be inculturated in the proper sense of the word. The move from alienation to inculturation is thus the basic challenge faced by Christian theology in India today."[29] He further notes in this way: Because there is a triple challenge of alienation, namely alienation from ordinary human life context, alienation from Indian intellectual life and alienation from the pastoral concerns of the Christian people, all these are mainly because of the kind of theological education obtaining in Indian seminaries, which, barring some minor modifications after Vat.II, is still ghettoish and away from actual life context.[30]

Further we have to note that "an inculturated theological reflection must necessarily be done in a local language" for obvious reasons. However such theology will not simply be "translation in a local language of eternal truths, nor will it be "merely a comparative study that reveals elements similar to Christian ones in other religions." Rather it will be a creative reflection born of the dialogue of faith with life of a community in all its cultural and religious complexity."[31]

The kind of inculturation we are talking about aims at accelerating the process of building up the local Church, through a process spearheaded by power centres of the basic Christian communities. And conversely, if we build up a truly local Church, its inculturation will have happened spontaneously. But this would imply more than establishing a local Christian community. In fact the process involves a twofold mission activity: 1. Building up a local Christian community rooted in a particular people, culture, history, socio-economic structures etc. Such a community is a minority everywhere, even in the so-called Christian countries of the West. 2. This group is supposed to prophetically influence and transform, as leaven in a dough, the life of the whole people. For example, Christian influence on some of our illustrious country men like Gandhiji, Tagore, Vivekananda, was not due to direct Christian preaching, but through other factors like distribution of the Bible and other Christian literature, Christian education abroad, foreign leaders etc. So the task of mission inculturation is twofold: incarnating the Church locally through a kenotic process, and extending the Kingdom by transcending the particularities of the local. In other words, dynamics of inculturation implies the growth of a small Christian community and the gradual emergence of a larger human community based on the values and challenges of the Kingdom.[32]

Concluding Remarks

Each culture and the whole culture comes within the scope of inculturation or evangelization, as the saintly late Pope Paul VI has clearly stated. From the foregoing discussion, it may be seen that inculturation includes socio-religious great traditions as well as little traditions of the people; it also includes socio-religious structures, every sphere of personal and family life, economic and political systems, as well as the classical areas of culture like arts, architecture and sculpture. Further it includes the history of human struggle with its threefold dimension – social, economic and political. Finally it covers the formation of local Christian community with its own theology, spirituality, liturgy and disciple. In other words, the scope and range of inculturation is all – embracing.

We have not dealt with the entire sphere of inculturation. Some very important areas have been highlighted, but others have been only pointed out. We have indicated that 'total inculturation' as a method embraces in its broad sweep other dimensions of mission like religious dialogue, liberative action for the poor. Thus this approach will have common points of convergence, but it will not be reduced to either dialogue alone, or action for justice or even to inculturation in its limited sense.

Endnotes

[1] It may be noted that in the past Bernard de Sahgun in Mexico in 1524, Matheo-Ricci in China in 1583, and Robert de Nobilee in India in 1606 caused ripples and even sometimes waves in the Church by proposing and experimenting on it. –Cf. Examiner, Mumbai, April 9, 1994.

[2] The 1971 Synod of Bishops, *Justice in the World*, Introduction.

[3] Cf. A.K Ramanujan, "Is there an Indian way of thinking:? An Informal Essay", *Contribution to Indian Sociology* 23(1989)41-58.

[4] Cf. Soares Prabhu, "From Alienation to Inculturation", *Bread, and Breath*, Ed. T.K John, Gujarat Sahitya Prakas, 1991. For a deeper understanding of the relation between a whole and its Parts in the Indian thought, see Louis Malieckal, *Yagna and Eucharist*, Dharmaram Publications, Bangalore, 199, pp.1-12.

[5] Cf.Mihir Desai, "The Need for Reservations: A Shouri and Others, *Lokayan*, July-October, 1990, p.4.

[6] Soares Prabhu, op.cit. p.64.

[7] In simple terms the theory means this: In a free market economy faster growth can be expected. The benefit of course will be first reaped by the rich higher strata of the society; but gradually the lower strata also will get a share, as the benefits "trickle down" as the top layer containers are filled to overflow.

[8] Bosco Puthur "Mission of the Church in the Context of ..... Dr. Arulsamy Ed. Communalism in India, Claretian Publications, Bangalore.

[9] Louis Malieckal, "Syro-Malabar Mission: New Challenges in Perspective", Ed. G.H. Ambooken, *Mission and Community Building*, (CMI-CMC Publ.TVM,1990), p.163.

[10] K.L. Singh, "People of India Project" The Profile of a National Project", *Current Sciences*, Vol.64, no. 1 (Indian Academic Sciences 1993).

[11] E.B. Tylor, *Primitive Culture*, p.1 (quoted in J.P. Pinto, *Inculturation through Basic Christian Communities*, pp.1-2 (ATC Bangalore, 1985).

[12] Around 300 definitions have been included in the book, *Culture: A Critical Survey of Concepts and Definitions*, by Kroeber and Kluckhohn (New York, 1952).

[13] Among the urgent tasks of Propaganda Fide in Rome, on its establishment in 1622 was dissociating Christian faith from the tarnished image associated with the colonial powers. The following text speaks volumes for it:

The following quotation from a letter of Propaganda Fide to its Vicars Apostolic, written in 1659 makes the point clear; ".........What could be more absurd than to transport France, Spain, Italy or some other European country to China? Do not introduce all to their practices but faith......It is the nature of man to love and treasure above every else their own country and that which belongs to it. In consequence there is no stronger cause for alienation and hate than an attack on local customs and especially when these go a venerable antiquity.......Do your utmost to adapt yourselves to them." (J.P. Pinto, op.cit. p.60).

[14] It is his own book titled *The Faith is Europe and Europe is the Faith*, TAN Books, 3r Edition 1992 (1st ed. In 1920).

[15] Cf. GS 53, EN 20 and the final message of the Synod of Bishops 1977, no. 5.

[16] Cf. C. Illickamuri, "Inculturation in liturgy, A. Narikulam Ed. *Inculturation and Liturgy* (Star Publ. Always, 1992), p.76.

[17] Cf. Majumdar and Madan, *An Introduction to Social Anthropology*, Mumbai, 1956, p.151. See also Fuchs, *Origin of Religion*, Alwaye, 1975, p.17.

[18] The very program of inculturation of faith by the Church is based on this basic principle.

[19] Cf. Julian Suldana, I*nculturation*, (St. Pauls Publications, Bangalore, p.9-11.

[20] Cf. Illickamuri, op.cit, p.79.

[21] Protestant writers general prefer this tern 'contextualization', but this term speaks all about context, and very little about the text or the Gospel message. Cf. J.P. Pinto op.cit. p.10.

[22] In this sense inculturation calls for kenosis or self-emptying, death and resurrection of the culture of the evangelizer as well as of the evangelized.

[23] J. Mananthodath, *Culture, Dialogue and the Church*, (Intercultural Publications, New Delhi, 1996), p.137.

[24] J.Mananthodath, op.cit. pp.138f.

[25] EN 63. See Mananthodath, op.cit. p.137.

[26] J. Mananthodath, ibid.

[27] F. Wilfred, "No salvation outside globalisation", *Jeevadhara*, Vol 25, no. 145, 1995, pp.79-92.

[28] See Ibid. chapters 3-7, especially 3.

[29] Op.cit. p.58.

[30] Ibid. p.71-75.

[31] Michael Amaladoss, *Making All this New: Mission in Dialogue*, (Gujarat Sahitya Prakash, Gujarat, 1990), p.70

[32] M. Amaladoss, *Mission To day*, (Gujarat Sahitya Prakash, Gujarat.1990), p.114f.

Chapter 13

Liturgical Inculturation and Mission

Introduction

The Syro-Malabar Mission Assembly that was held in November 1999 had highlighted the mission thrust of this *sui juris* Church on its entry into the New Millennium. In chapter III of its Working Paper, with the caption **Jesus' Mission the Church's Reason to Exist a** brief presentation of the triple point – liturgy, inculturation and mission had been made, which makes up the title of this presentation. The Mission Assembly (MA here after) had understood the process of inculturation, including liturgical inculturation, as intimately related to the mission thrust.

Apparently this mission thrust seems to be absent in the present seminar,[1] as it appears from its thematic title. Therefore in my presentation the attempt is to bring this mission thrust into focus, while discussing the question of liturgical inculturation.

Because there is no other mission but the redemptive mission of Jesus Christ (*mission Dei*), which is to be carried forward by the Spirit in and through the Church, making her "missionary by nature" (AG 2), and because the sacred liturgy is a symbolic expression as well as memorial celebration of that same mission, bearing on Syro-Malabar liturgy and mission.

Mission Yesterday and Today

The Council inaugurated a great paradigm shift in the concept of mission:

First of all the expression 'missions' was replaced by 'the mission'. Namely, for a long time before the Council, those countries or territories were called 'missions' where the (Roman) Church had not been established, and where consequently the then Propaganda Fide (presently Congregation for Evangelization of people) used to send regularly its chosen missionaries to do that work. In that perspective mission was not an ecclesial act, as a faith-community's common witnessing and sharing the Good News. Rather, it was considered the task of individual zealous Christians for the expansion of the (Roman) Church.

The Council on the contrary re-discovered the true nature of the Church and declared: "The Church on earth is by her very nature missionary, since according to the plan of the Father, it has its origin in the mission of the Son and the Holy Spirit (AG2). Thus the whole Church is in mission everywhere through concrete acts of the faith communities, namely individual as well as local Churches. Mission is the basic duty of the entire people of God (AG 35; EN 43).

The bishops of Asia meeting in Taiwan in the year 1974 described mission or evangelization as the local Church being in dialogue with the Asian realities. They spelt out these realities as the poor and the marginalized, the great cultures and the great religions,[2] since then mission as a threefold dialogue with the poor, the cultures and the religions has become a usual way of describing it. However these are not to be taken as three separate activities of mission. The truth is that they pre-suppose and involve one another in a process of integral mission. "One cannot authentically liberate the poor from the poverty by changing the economic and socio-political structures without transforming the way they look at God, the humans and the world, and the value system that guide their relationship to them, that means without a cultural change. One cannot profoundly change culture without the help of religion that speaks of ultimate concerns and values. Dialogue with other believers is meaningless if it does not lead everyone to realize the presence and action of God in their life and community, and to listen to God in challenging culture and religions themselves and in doing justice through the defense and promotion of common human and spiritual values. One cannot change the way people think and the values they live by without changing the economic and socio-political structures that keep them enslaved. An integral evangelization therefore has to engage in the liberation of the poor, through transformation of culture in collaboration with believers of other religions."[3]

Context of Syro-Malabar Mission in India

There are some important factors that make up the present context of our mission in In India. A. Underdevelopment and Liberation Movements, B. Communalism and Religious Nationalism, C. Ecclesial Pluralism and All-India Jurisdiction

Underdevelopment and Liberation Movements

The widespread poverty of millions of our less fortunate brethren is largely due to the unjust and oppressive economic and sociopolitical system in which a powerful small group dictates terms to the rest of the population keeping them in perpetual bondage. Since for every action there is an equal and opposite reaction, in recent years we also have been witnessing awakening of peoples movements in reaction - Dalit movements, Tribal movements, most recently Kisan movement (of Maharashtra) to resist this oppression and to break out of bondage.

In such a situation, as messengers of the Gospel, we cannot remain passive spectators, while people are fighting and dying for justice sake. It is true, sporadic efforts to fight for their cause by some individuals - priests and sisters - are afoot, but this is not enough, we need to respond to this systemic evil through more concerted efforts in systematic ways.

Communalism and Hindu Religious Nationalism

The context of mission is being increasingly vitiated by communal violence triggered by hardcore Hindu nationalists who, under the influence of the RSS philosophy of mono—culturism and mono—religionism, which seeks to eliminate Islam and Christianity from India. Signs of this bigotry began to raise its head, in connection with the Papal visit in the year 1986 for the cause of beatification of two Indian venerable – St. Alphonsa and St. Chavara. In those days a section of the Hindi Press, covering the North Indian Hindi-belt was very critical about the Pope's visit. One Hindu fanatic challenged the Pope: "Let the Pope make a unilateral declaration that all religions are true." At its face value this challenge may appear too offensive to Christians. But we have understand that its main point runs like this: "Does Christianity recognize Hinduism as an authentic religion."? And we know that, ever since the

Council and its document Nostra aetatae in particular, we have
no difficulty to give an emphatic reply "yes of course" to that
question. At the same time we also have to confess that by
and large such a recognition of Hinduism (and of any religion
for that matter) was not possible before the council. Therefore
we have to consider below ways and means of responding to
this challenge.

Ecclesial Pluralism and Rome's Recent Statement about SMC's All-India Jurisdiction

Already for a few years now SMC has been experiencing the
challenge implied in the letter of the late Pope St. John Paul II
dated 28 May 1986 and sent to all the bishops of India. In the
tenor of that letter which in fact is only affirming the Council
statement in OE3, SMC has the same rights and obligations
with respect to preaching the Gospel to the whole world as
any other Church. But it is quite known that in practice this
point had not been recognized by the Latin bishops in India
in general. Subsequently there had been also efforts by SMC
bishops, including the one during an *Ad Limina* visitation
in this direction, but all of them had failed to produce the
desired results. It is in this light that we have to consider the
latest statement by Rome, accepting for all practical purposes
the ancient Church regulation of SMC's right of All-India
Jurisdiction. We have to wait and see how SMC is going to
implement this right in the present scenario in a prudent and
relevant manner on the one hand, and how the Latin Church
would respond to it in a sensible and brotherly manner on
the other.

A Three-fold Orientation to Facilitate Relevant Response in the Given Scenario

These orientations are conceived as three kinds of dialogues between the SMC and the particular challenge of the context

Church in Dialogue with the Poor and the Oppressed

What is meant by 'dialogue with the poor' is becoming increasingly a poor Church, and not merely a Church for the poor in terms of raising funds for development activities in their favour. To become poor, however, does not mean to become miserable, but lowly in the spirit of Incarnation. Pope Francis latest Encyclical *Gaudete et Exultate* (Rejoice and be Glad), while explaining how to be holy in the contemporary world, makes this point clear as well. For this to happen, the Church has to move away from the de-personalized and institutionalized model. When a new mission starts attention should be focused on preparing persons who would animate and build it, and not on the structures to be put up there. The poorer the mission is the stronger will be signals of the Kingdom's message emitted from it, and so will be less suspect before the religious bigots.

Certainly developmental activities are not ruled out ; perhaps this is an area where different Churches can easily join hands forgetting their 'imperial boundaries' and move forward in the perspective of the Kingdom. In any case our work will be more effective, if we are poor ourselves, because our motive will be purer, mind clearer and hands freer.

Church in Dialogue with Other Churches and Religions

In the present scenario, if one Church goes ahead with its programmes of frontier expansion, asserting its newly obtained freedom of movement for evangelization in India, while the other Church withdraw all support and cooperation, or worse still, set up road blocks, this can create an impasse in the long run with regard to the whole task of evangelization. What is needed is not mere peaceful co-existence either, but real pro-existence so that the Gospel witnessing may not suffer.

In order to realize the full scope of the evangelizing mission, we need to have a new look at the inner relationship between the institutional Church and the Kingdom/Reign of God. The goal ahead to realize must be clear; it is not the Church, but the Kingdom. The former is just a symbol of the latter, and then mission is the concrete way the Church symbolizes the Kingdom. Therefore it would be wrong to imagine that the Church exists first in concrete structures before it pursues its mission. Perhaps this wrong conception emphasizes the idea of jurisdiction leading to territorial claims and quarrels, making it a multinational company or a show—piece of commercial propaganda. All Churches exist as servants of the Kingdom for its progressive manifestation by the work of the Holy Spirit. Hence the real bond that unites the three - Church, Mission and Kingdom – is not human plans and programmes, but Divine Providence. Only in this Divine perspective can we overcome all our petty and narrow boundaries – geographical, ritual, ethnic and linguistic.

Similar is the case of dialogue with other religions: India saw a sudden spurt of anti—Christian violence during the past few years. In the new dispensation of the NDA government supported and even dictated terms by the Sangh Parivar outfit this situation is likely to be on the increase. There may be many reasons behind this hostile attitude, one of them of course is prejudice and misunderstanding, because they identify us with the colonial Christianity with an absolute claim of truth and salvation. It is here that genui9ne interreligious dialogue in the sense as introduced by Martin Buber[4] will be very helpful. In the multi—religious context of India, to be in dialogue and harmony with every religion seems to be a genuine mission of the church in India. The Pope's visit with some 200 religious leaders of seven major religions of India -- Hinduism, Islam, Buddhism, Sikhism, Jainism, Judaism and Zoroastrianism – in Chennai, during his visit in 1986 was a unique event in field of inter-religious dialogue.[5]

Church in Dialogue with Cultures

It seems that this is something that should concern the SMC mission in North India as its top priority. The Council Decree *Ad Gentes* has spoken long ago very clearly on the interaction of the word of God with local cultures giving rise to new ecclesial communities (AD 22). In the NT perspective founding of a new ecclesial community is not simply reproducing an existing Church through its apostles or missionaries rather it is a new Event, a new encounter of the Gospel with a given socio—cultural milieu, and so very like the process of a seed growing into a tree, even as in the vision of AG22 (see also LG 26). This concept of the local Church being rooted in the culture and soil of the land, shows that, what we try to build up in North India, shall not be carbon copies of the so-called 'Mother Church' in Kerala. The historic letter of the Congregation for Evangelization (the Propaganda Fide) written in 1659 to the Vicar Apostolic in China may be recalled here:

> What would be more absurd than to transplant France, Spain, or Italy into China? It is not his that you must transplant but faith, that faith which does not reject or abolish the customs of any nation, but on the contrary wants them to be safeguarded and preserved carefully........ [6]

Thus is a serious matter for us to consider in respect of SMC mission in India: Do we/do we not transport/transplant Kerala or worse still Chaldea to the mission outside Kerala? Does it happen in our personal life style, in modes of communication, use of signs and symbols in prayer and worship, culture superiority complex etc. Whatever be the historico-ecclesiastical politics that hinder the shaping of a relevant liturgy for our home Church, it is imperative that the Church's mission in the North take a bold step in this matter and go ahead with the incarnational dynamism of inculturation which is in the very nature of growth of any local Church.

Liturgy and Mission

The Council that declared that the activity of the Church is centred on liturgy as its source and summit (Cf SC 10), has also stated that liturgy marvelously fortifies the faithful in their capacity to proclaim Christ (Cf. SC 2). These two texts make some significant statements connecting liturgy and mission. The late Fr. Amalorpavdas, who was counted as a champion of liturgical inculturation in Post—Vatican II Church in India, has interpreted this connection in this way:

> Now the mission of the church expresses itself best and reaches its climax in the Eucharist. The Eucharist is the greatest epiphany of the mystery of the Church and the climactic moment of the fulfillment of the mission. It is not simply bread and wine that are consecrated, but the whole mankind [sic], the universe and all the realities of the world and human existence that are assumed in Christ and consecrated to God and become united with him.[7]

A Close Look at Liturgy for Mission

A liturgy for mission has to own up and express in signs and symbols the process of building up the new community of freedom, fellowship and justice which is the primary goal of mission. In principle every liturgy, Eucharist in particular, symbolizes the New Testament assembly of the people of God, called by and sent out by him with a mission mandate.

Just as liturgy is the community celebration of the saving act of God in Christ, so also mission is the community proclamation of the same salvific activity. Celebration and proclamation are both rooted in the day-to-day life of the community. In every liturgical gathering of the faithful there is also a sending or mission of the assembly. The faithful listen to, participate in, and experience the *Mirabilia Dei,* "wonderful works of God". And this ecclesial Christ experience is shared, recounted and proclaimed to others, which is authentic mission. When the word of God is listened to, broken and shared in the liturgy, it imparts a twofold experience of the Paschal Mystery: sinfulness and brokenness of the human race on the one hand, and divine forgiveness, compassion, love and communion on the other. Every celebration is meant to deepen this two—fold experience so that the departing community at the end of the celebration becomes a "missionary people", a people living the personal experiential message to share and proclaim, similar to the experience of St. Paul on his encounter of Jesus on the road to Damascus.

The content of proclamation is the first hand Christ-experience as this is testified by John the Evangelist (1 Jn 1:1-5). This experience is ritualized and sacramentally realized and communicated in liturgical celebrations. Whereas Christian dogmas and doctrines are articulation of Christian faith in appropriate categories of thought, liturgy imparts and keeps alive this faith for personal fulfillment and communal proclamation. It was in the liturgical action of "breaking bread" in memory of Jesus action at the Last Supper (1 Cor. 11:23-27) that the disciples' faith became alive as in the Emmaus episode (Lk 24: 14-25). The Eucharistic liturgy which is the community prayer of the "new people" (a people who are 'converted to Christ' or who have accepted his mind in accordance with Phil. 2:1-6, is to be celebrated in the "new temple" which is not made of brick and mortar, but spontaneously emerges wherever people gather in the name of God, wherever communities are created sinking divisions and factions, as one Body of Christ (1 Cor. 12:12ff), uprooting evils of injustice and exploitation. In course of time, when ritual celebrations of the Eucharist also will take place in all such situations, there will be also authentic expressions of Christian fellowship. In this vision of mission which is rooted in a deeper understanding of liturgy (Rahner's liturgy of life), the missionary community's priority may not be to celebrate Eucharist wherever proclamation of the word takes place, but to give shape to basic human communities, which will eventually call for the liturgy of the Eucharist (liturgy of the Church according to Rahner) as their authentic symbol and holding centre.[8]

Viewed in this way, the Eucharist is the marvelous epiphany of the mystery of the Church and the glorious fulfillment of the Church's mission on earth. As we have noted earlier in the words of Fr. Amalor, consecration of the Eucharistic elements is not simply the transformation (transubstantiation) of bread and wine into the body and blood of Jesus; it is also the transformation (transignification) of the whole universe into the body of Christ; all material realities and human lives are assumed into Christ and consecrated to the Father. In Rahner's theology of worship, liturgy of the Church (ritualized worship) is a real symbol of the liturgy of the world (responsible Christian life/ active response to the plan of God). And this is what the Eucharist is in its double dimension as symbol and reality: It is both the body of Christ glorified, and at once symbol of the cosmic or universal body of Christ, or the eschatological community which is the final goal of all mission.[9]

Teilhard de Chardin's Vision of the Eucharist

The scientist-theologian Teilhard De Chardin makes similar reflections on the unity of the cosmos in Christ with the Eucharist at the centre stage. This unity of the cosmos in Christ for Chardin is not figurative, but very realistic; it is the basis of his further reflections on the Eucharist. So he writes:

> The Incarnate Word could not be the supernatural (hyper-natural) Centre of the universe, if he did not function first as its physical, natural centre. Christ cannot sublimate creation in God without progressively raising it up by his influence through the successive circles of matter and spirit. That is why, in order to bring all things back to the Father, he had to make himself one with all – he had to enter into contact with every one of the zones of the created, from the lowest earthly to the zone that is closest to heaven.[10]

It may be seen that underlying this thought of unity of the whole created order is an echo of St. Iranaeus' thought of 'recapitulation' (*anekaphaleosis*) of everything in Christ, which is originally due to St. Paul (cf. Eph.1:10). In Chardin's thought the universe is an organic whole and all its parts are vitally linked to one another and to the whole to form a totality. Consequently, in the Eucharist the sacramental species is not only the elements of bread and wine mixed with water, but the totality of the world. Hence the time required for the consecration of the 'extended sacramental species 'is what is called the time of creation. In other words, the material for the Eucharistic offering is the totality of the world, not an isolated part of it, because since the unique event of Incarnation, the world has become a sacrament.[11]

St. John Paul II's Cosmic Vision of the Eucharist

It may be seen that Chardin's cosmic role of Christ's incarnation, which had not found favour with the Pre-Vatican II Roman Church, has made entry into the saintly Pope's Encyclical *Dominium Vivificantem.*[12] Hence, going a step further the Pope in a later Encyclical, having recollected the numerous times, places and contexts in which he has celebrated the Eucharist during the 25 years of his Pontificate, makes the following statement on the cosmic dimension of the Eucharist:

> ....This varied scenario of celebration of the Eucharist has given me a powerful experience of its universal, and so to speak, cosmic character. Yes, cosmic! Because, even when it is celebrated on the humble altar of a country church, the Eucharist is always in some way celebrated on the altar of the world. It unites heaven and earth; it embraces, permeates all creation. (No.8)

Liturgical Catechesis and Mission

Christian faith must be appropriated, and not just repeated by formula-recitation, by every generation anew. Appropriation is a free, dynamic, personal and context-friendly reception of faith, and the process goes through several steps of interpretation, inculturation/contextualization and celebration, leading to handing over (*paradosis*) or proclamation. In the context of mission this means that without proper liturgical catechesis transmission of faith will be sterile, static and not context-friendly. In fact creative catechesis challenges perpetuation of the status quo, if this has become irrelevant and unjust, and proclaims the message of liberation to all.[13] Catechesis as a process of faith-interpretation brings in inculturation in every aspect of life of the community, including liturgy. Hence it is important to remember that catechesis does not simply mean teaching faith. As the Council points out, it is interpretation of faith, which means deciphering authentic signs of God's presence and purpose in the happenings, needs and desires of the people, distinguishing and discerning the many voices of our age and judging them in the light of the divine word (GS 11 & 44).

Whereas catechesis is thus interpretation of faith in the religio-cultural background of the people, liturgy is the celebration and affirmation of the same faith in terms of relevant signs and symbols. It is here that the question of re-interpretation of the existing religio-cultural symbols and signs arises.

Now, culture and religion are intimately united like language and thought or body and soul. The symbols therefore have to acquire cultural meaning under the influence of the religion or religions underlying the culture. Hence they need to be re-interpreted in the light of the Christian faith, and in this process we may also have to make a prophetic critique of the existing cultural garb, bringing out both positive and negative elements in them.

A related question is also to be noted: Can we separate signs and symbols neatly as cultural and religious? Given the close link between culture and religion, as explained elsewhere, ambiguities are possible. Moreover, "If we recognize true and holy elements as seeds of the Word not only in other cultures but also in other religious traditions, and if today we go a step further to see the Spirit of God operative in other religions" (RM 28), what is wrong in integrating even religious elements, provided they are not mixed up with superstition, but in fact help to express more adequately the mysteries that we celebrate? Therefore some amount of Hinduization/

Islamization etc. maybe even normal and be expected. As a matter of fact we have modern Indian theologians who consider themselves "Hindu-Christian."[14] It is only through dialogue with religions that the religious value of the indigenous signs and symbols can be understood, and a Christian meaning and orientation be given to them.

Inculturated Syro-Malabar Liturgy and Mission

Liturgical celebrations are not neutral experiences; they are symbo9lic affirmations of the human and spiritual values which the celebrating community treasures as most precious heritage. They influence the feeling and thoughts, emotions and aspirations of the community, and they are the ways in which the members of the community become open to God's saving action, responding to it in faith. However, this task of the liturgy will be effectively realized only if its celebration is properly inculturated, only if the signs and symbols, gestures and postures, language and setting etc. of the liturgy are in tune with the given culture of the people concerned. Viewed in this way, Syro—Malabar liturgy cannot be considered sufficiently inculturated in order to be effectively at the service of the mission of this Church in India.

History of Inculturation of Syro-Malabar Liturgy

We may consider here different levels and times of cultural adaptation of Syro-Malabar liturgy: 1. Cultural Adaptation at the Origin of the Thomas Christian communities, 2. From Adaptation to Alienation at a later period, 3. Post-Vatican II Inculturation Attempts: Problems and Prospects.

Cultural Adaptation at the Origin of St. Thomas Christian Community

If the Christian community in Kerala had an Apostolic origin with St. Thomas arrival in Kerala in 52 A.D, much like the other early Apostolic communities that sprang up in Greece, Rome, Egypt, Mesopotamia and elsewhere and had given rise to a life and worship according to local cultural forms – language signs, symbols etc., it has to be maintained that the new community in Kerala also was capable of celebrating its faith through meaningful signs and symbols taken from its own religio— cultural context. It is believed that these Christians lived like their compatriots in their socio-cultural environment, in their family and social customs, in the practices like processions, offerings and ceremonies connected with marriages, funerals, in the gestures and postures during worship and so on. The church architecture was like that of Hindu temples except for a cross on the top.[15] Moreover, with regard to such cultural at-homeness of these Christians of the period of time in question, A.X. Iyer comments: "It is almost certain they were old customs traceable to a time when Christianity was introduced into Malabar and accepted spontaneously without changing the indigenous character of the inhabitants."[16] Thus from the first to the fourth century, the community was quite at home in Malabar with local cultural expressions, in socio-political as well as religio-spiritual matters, although the exact nature and extent of use of particular worship signs and symbols is not known.

Period of Contact with Chaldean Christians (4th to 15th century)

With the arrival of Chaldean Christians and interference of the Church of Persia in the ecclesiastical affairs of the

Malabar Christians during the period of time in question the existing religious life and practices of the local Christians were affected to a great extent. Although this contact with the Persian Church helped to strengthen the church-life of the Indian Church because of the continued shepherding or pastoral care extended from Persia to Malabar, the religious life of the Christians was tampered with because of the introduction of many Chaldean practices replacing the existing socio-cultural practices in accordance with the declared policy of the Synod of Seleusia of the Persian Church that was held in the year 410.

Cultural Alienation during the European Colonial Period (16ᵗʰ to 20ᵗʰ century)

With the arrival of the Portuguese, especially after the historic synod of Diamper (1599), the already Chaldeanized St. Thomas Christian local liturgy was systematically Latinized, apart from having tampered with the socio-political customs and practices. It appears that the colonizers had several motives, religious and commercial in this process.[17] From the list of errors drawn up in preparation for the Synod of Diamper, which were condemned and hence forbidden to practice after the synod, we get a glimpse of the elements of cultural adaptations that still existed in the life and worship of the Christians of Malabar. No doubt, most of these elements gradually disappeared under the pressure of a double alienation of Chaldeanization and Latinization.

Post-Vatican II Inculturation Attempts: Problems and Prospects

The Indian Bishops had already raised this issue of inculturation in their petition to the Preparatory Commission of Vatican II.[18] That is why soon after the Council, the undivided CBCI

Commission for Liturgy declared, giving top priority to inculturation as follows:

> There is no more discussion, whether we should adapt or not. Adaptation has to be done and there is no need to prove it. The whole is, first of all, how we must go about it, secondly, what has to be adapted, and thirdly, how far we can go in the process of adaptation.[19]

Let me add here a personal note which seems to be unavoidable. It was in such a situation that a group of staff and students of Dharmaram College, Bangalore set themselves to the task in response to the Council's vision of a possible 'radical adaptation in the liturgy' (SC 40) and in support of the declared policy of the CBCI Commission for Liturgy in favour of inculturation. At a time when many of the bishops favourable to this matter were still groping in the dark on "how we must go about it", the leadership given to it by His Eminence the late Joseph Cardinal Parecattil of happy memory who was at that time President of the undivided CBCI of all the three Ritual Churches, is worth remembering. His efforts in this direction for over two decades are well known and documented.[20] Nobody in the Syro-Malabar Church dared to take the risk of scandal and criticism in the absence of some guidelines to follow. The Cardinal himself was waiting for some light from anywhere. Certainly he advised and encouraged individuals who approached him for light, for permission. Individuals here and there in the Latin Church were trying out something, without giving much publicity. The NBCLC was just beginning to function and the late Fr. Amalorpavadass, its founder director had not yet given shape to any Indian prayer model but only seriously thinking about it.

Towards an Indian Order of Holy Eucharist: Dharmaram Contribution

It was under such circumstances that the said small group of staff and students which included this writer as well, under the leadership of Fr. Mathias Mundadan, then Professor of Church History and Master of Students of Dharmaram, with the blessings and encouragement of the late Cardinal Parecattil, set themselves to the task of giving shape to something like an "Indian form of worship". The first attempt was a simple one in the form of 'para-liturgy' or 'Bible Service' that was getting currency in those days after the Council.[21] This was done in an entirely novel manner, using worship signs, symbols and gestures congenial to the local culture and with such spontaneity and devotion that the participants were highly impressed. It evoked spontaneously the cultural sensibilities of the participants who therefore were able to resonate deeply with the spiritual message of the celebration. Many of the so-called 12-point adaptations[22] which were soon to be formulated by Fr. Amalorpavdas for the CBCI Liturgy Commission and later proposed by CBCI for implementation in different dioceses according to the discretion of individual bishops, had actually been anticipated in that pioneering celebration.

When this simple 'Indian form of' para-liturgy was celebrated next in Dharmaram during the forthcoming CBCI meeting, the bishops were highly impressed by its originality, as they probably had a feeling of having seen what they were looking for. Among those who spoke words of high appreciation were the two Cardinals Valerian Gracius and Joseph Parecattil. It was then presented at the request of Fr. Amalor in NBCLC on the occasion of the AILM –II (All India Liturgical Meeting) of January 1969. The response of those liturgy experts showed that they were not only impressed but also provoked to try out similar models.[23]

A New Inculturated Liturgy in the Making

Soon after the CBCI meeting at Dharmaram, Cardinal Parecattil, then President of CBCI asked Fr. Rector of Dharmaram to entrust to a select group of staff and students the task of preparing a complete order of the Eucharist in the Indian style in view of the forth-coming All-India National Seminar on "Church in India Today" in May 1969.[24] Accordingly the group set to work, studying the Eastern/Indian character of the Qurbana (Holy Eucharist), Hindu ritual worship, bhajan singing and Vedic prayer-recitation, classical Indian music etc. For this purpose we, Deacons together with Fr. Vineed got special permission and stayed for a few days in the famous Vinoba Bhave's Ashram called Brahmavidyamandir in the diocese of Chanda, Maharashtra.

Our stay in that Ashram, sharing meals with the Ashramites, doing the house-work (*Ashram seva*), praying with the inmates, listening to the way they are reciting prayers and chanting bhajans, and above all trying to understand the Hindu world-vision, through reading and discussing with them, we got confidence to venture upon the task of shaping an Order of the *Qurbana* in the Indian style and idiom. From the very beginning the prayers, hymns and the music were conceived in tune with the S. Indian and particularly Kerala language and culture. It was based on sound principles of adaptation keeping in mind the recommendations made by the Council of Vat.II.[25]

From the Vinoba Bhave Ashram the team moved to Carmel Vidyabhavan Pune, where Fr. Sylvester was Rector of the CMI Study House at that time. It is there that the team completed the work of formulating the text of the Qurbana, writing the hymns and composing the music. While the text was drafted mainly by Fr. Vineed, this writer did the writing of the lyric (Malayalam text) for composing the music of most of the hymns. For composing the music of a few hymns, we had to depend on an outsider (one Bro. Pinto) from De Nobilee College, Pune. The rest was borrowed and adapted by this writer from Hindu bhajan singing and temple music.[26]

The Draft Text and Its Salient Features

The new text of the Eucharist thus prepared was Indian, Eastern and Christian at once: Indian in its language, signs, symbols, gestures and postures, music, recitation and the whole prayer-atmosphere; Eastern, following basically the structure of the four-fold 'inclined prayers' (Gehanta) of the Addai-Mari anaphora text, modified/ adapted to the Hindu mode of worship; and Christian, because it was conceived as far as possible, in continuity with the essential elements of the genuine Judeo-Christian liturgical tradition, while at the same time expressing the Christian thanksgiving in forms and thought-patterns harmonious with the Indian culture. In writing the hymns, wherever possible inspiration of Vedic texts has been imbibed and incorporated. In the prayers the cosmic vision of Hindu worship has been blended with the historical dimension of the salvation mystery in and through Jesus Christ.

The All-India Prospects of the Dharmaram Text

The text thus prepared was in use for several years in the Liturgical Centre of Dharmaram College from 1969 to 1974 in hand-written form. During this period it underwent several revisions and adaptations in language and rites,[27] while it continued to be celebrated in a select group at Dharmaram.

An English version of it was made in view of presenting it at the IV All-India Liturgical Meeting (AILM-IV) organized by NBCLC, from 2-8 Dec. 1973. "It was then unanimously decided that this Indian Order of the Mass would be adopted by the CBCI Commission for Liturgy, and be widely circulated for further experimentation and be submitted to the Catholic Bishops' Conference of India for their approval for use in the whole of India, common to all the three Rites."[28]

It was later printed for private use (*pro manuscripto*) in the same year 1974, when this writer was the director of Dharmaram College, Liturgical Centre (1969-75) until he left for studies in Louvain.[29] Copies of it were supplied on request to some formation houses and liturgical experimentation centres, including Kurishumala ashram. In most places the text later went into disuse and hence gathered dust perhaps due to the so-called 'prohibition from Rome.'[30] However, it is heart-warming to see that in the Kurishumala Ashram, Kerala it continued to be used for week-day celebrations. However recently when a revised computer typed version of this Mass came out, with Malayalam and English texts side by side and with the publisher's own Introduction, he seems to have forgotten the original source of the Mass text. He has made no acknowledgement of the Liturgical Centre, Dharmaram College, which is the original publisher of the text. Interestingly he claims that he has introduced in this Indian anaphora "the structure of the Anaphora of St. James", and then he adds that "Our Indian Liturgy is thus related to the Church of Jerusalem, which holds pride of place in the Syrian Liturgy." I am surprised at this claim of the publisher, because, if anything, the structure has been inspired by the anaphora of Addai-Mari, as this was used by the Syro-Malabar Church in the late 1960's when this text was composed by us. But no explicit quotation or structural dependence can be seen in this composition. In fact, the central prayer (anaphora) is a unique synthesis of Eastern (East-Syrian) and Western, Hindu and Christian conception of 'sacrifice' or Divine worship. What the Kurishumala publisher claims may be due to the affinity between West Syrian and East Syrian thought and language.[31]

Endnotes

[1] The theme of the seminar was The Possibilities of Further Inculturation of the Syro-Malabar Liturgy.

[2] Rosales and Arevalo, *For All People of Asia*, Orbis, Maryknoll, New York, 1992, pp.14f.

[3] M. Amaladoss, "Beyond Inculturation : Can the Many be One?, Vidyajyoti, Delhi, 1998, p.48.

[4] Cf. *I and Thou*, trans. By R.G. Smith, Edinburg, T& T Clark, 1923, p.4.

[5] Cf. Louis Malieckal, "Syro-Malabar Mission: New Challenges in Perspective", Ed. By G.H. Ambookan, *Mission and Community Building*, CMI-CMC Gen. Dept. of Publication, 1990, 172.

[6] Quoted in Joseph R. Levenson, *Confucian China and its Modern Fate*, Berkeley and Clos Angels, University of California Press, 1966, p.118.

[7] *Towards Indigenization of the Liturgy*, NBCLC, Bangalore, undated, p.20.

[8] Cf. Louis Malieckal, "A Liturgy for Mission that Proclaims Jesus Christ to all Cultures and Peoples, *Third Millennium*, April-June, 1998, p.16.

[9] Ibid.

[10] *Christianity and Evolution*, Harcourt Race, Jovanovich, N.Y., 1971, p.71.

[11] De Chardin Teilhard, *Hymn of the Universe*, Harper & Row, N. Y., 1965, pp.24-26.

[12] There we read "The Incarnation then also has a cosmic significance, a cosmic dimension. 'The first born of all creation', becoming incarnate in the individual humanity of Christ, unites himself in some way, with the entire reality of man, which is also 'flesh', and in this reality with all 'flesh', with the whole creation." p.50.

[13] Lorreno Fernando, "The Challenges to the Indian Church:: A Pastoral Perspective", *Vidyajyoti, 60(1996)743.*

[14] Cf. Michael Amaladoss, "Beyond Inculturation:: Can the many be one"?, *Vidyajyoti*, 1998, p.12.

[15] Placid Podipara CMI, "Hindu in Culture, Christian in Religion, Oriental in Worship", *Ostkirchliche Studien*, 8(1959)90ff.

[16] A. Cherukarakunnel, "Indenisation among St. Thomas Christians", *Jeevadhara*, July-August, 1971.

[17] Cf. Malekandathil Ed. *Jornada of Dom Alexis de Menezes: Portuchese Account of the Sixteenth. Century Malabar*, LRC Publications, Mt. St. Thomas, Kakkanad, 2003, xxxiii.

[18] Cf. Julian Saldana, *Inculturation*, St. Pauls Mumbai, 1987, p.47.

[19] Amalorpavdas, op.cit. ibid.

[20] Cardinal Parecattil, *Syro-Malabar Liturgy As I See It(Malayalam)*, publ. by Fr. Abel, EKM,1987, trans.by K.C. Chacko; Mathias Mundadan, *Cardinal Parecattil: The Man, His Vision and Contribution*, Star Publ., Alwaye, 1998; Louis Malieckal, "Liturgical Inculturation in India: Problems and prospects of Experimentation", *Jeevadhara*, July, 1988, pp.279-292.

[21] The occasion was the Rector's Day, when the late Dharmaram visionary Bp. Jonas Thaliath was Rector.

[22] See Amalorpavdas, op.cit. pp.31-53, where we have first the letter from Rome permitting the use of the proposed new symbols, gestures and postures, which mentions also the said 12-points of adaptation pp.31-33,; then we have a "Commentary on the First Stage of Adaptations in the Liturgy" pp.33-36; next we have explanations of the 12-points of adaptations pp.36-44 and finally introduction to the 2nd, 3rd and 4th phases of adaptation pp.44-53.

[23] I still remember what one of the big shots of that assembly told us who conducted that service: "Please wait let us also come." This comment clearly shows that the Latin Church had not yet made any concrete step so daring till that time in the direction of liturgical inculturation.

[24] The team consisted of seven members: Frs. Mathias Mundadan, Francis Vineeth (Indologist) and Sylvester Pudussery (liturgiologist); Seminarians (Deacons) - Prsasanna Bhai, Abraham Thuruthumali, Varghese Kottoor and myself (Louis Malieckal).

[25] SC 23.

[26] Just for one example: The famous bhajan *Om Jagadisvara Sadapi Chinmaya*......is a Hindu temple hymn in pure Sanskrit, which was adapted and Christianised by this writer for our purpose. And it seems to be one of the oldest Christian bhajans still very popular at least among those who love indigenization.

[27] In this period of experimentation, revision and re-writing of text and composing more music between 1969-1974, several seminarians who were associated with the Liturgical Centre had been very helpful. Some of them who became later priests are Frs. Thomas Kochumuttam, Thomas Kandathil, Cherian Kunianthodathil, Jose Kuriedath and others.

[28] Amalorpavdass, New Orders of the Mass for India, NBCLC, 1974, p.63.

[29] It may be noted that   this Liturgical Centre, being run with the explicit permission of Dharmaram authorities, was an animation centre in general, where different meditation methods, prayer models, bhajan singing etc were being practiced in which students also with proper permission would come to participate. Original publication in Malayalam is thus: *Bhārata-sabhakyoro-pŸjākramam*, Dharmaram Liturgical Centre (Pro Manuscripto), 1974.

[30] The prohibition referred to here is a letter from Cardinal Knox, Prefect of the Sacred Congregation for Divine worship. On the ground of this letter, communicated through the CBCI Chairman of the Commission for Liturgy, the CBCI Standing Committee published on 20 Oct. 1975 the following: "Until and unless the CBCI gives its explicit approval, the use of the above two (viz The Indian anaphora and Readings from non-Biblical Scriptures in the Liturgy) is forbidden to all, whether in private or in public, even in authorized centres for experimentation." See Amalorpavadass Ed. *Report of the Fifth All-India Liturgical Meeting*, NBCLC: Bangalore, 1977, p.14. (Hereafter Amalor, Report. For a slightly different version of this prohibition see Puthanangady, op.cit. pp.252f emphasis added).

[31] For the full text (in English) see Francis Kanichikattil CMI, To *Restore or to Reform*? Dharmaram publ. Bangalore, 1992, Appendix (I) pp.139-161, and for its original Malayalam text see Appendix (III) pp.177-201. Moreover what is given in Appendix (II) is the text of the Indian Order of the Mass prepared by NBCLC. There is also an Appendix (IV) which contains a Malayalam text called Bharathiya Puja published by the Ernakulam Liturgical Centre.

Chapter 14

Why or Why not Inculturation?

Introduction

By way of drawing to a close the above series of Essays, I would like to dwell on the topic 'inculturation' itself which has run through a major part of the above discussion. When opponents of inculturation often raise the question why we should undertake the work of inculturation at all or what is the purpose of inculturation, proponents of inculturation often put the counter question why not we undertake inculturation or sometimes give the answer that inculturation is for evangelization.

In one of the above Essays mention was made that Incarnation is the original model or proto-type of inculturation. We have to remember here that Incarnation is a unique historical event, even as it is a meta-historical event. In its meta-historicity it is unrepeatable, inimitable; but in its historical aspect, as part and parcel of human history, it may be repeated, imitated by humans, of course in a limited way looking at it as the highest ideal of human life.

As a proto-type for human imitation, Incarnation offers a double challenge: 1. Identification with the poor and the marginalized and 2. Confrontation with the powers that be. And the two challenges have the backing of two complementary symbols, namely the Cradle and the Cross, respectively.

Cradle as the Symbol of Identification with the Marginalized

John the Evangelist who recorded for humanity the revelation of God's descent, saying, "…the Word became flesh and dwelt among us…" (Jn 1:14), has amplified it adding, "God loved the world so much that he sent his only Son so that everyone who believes in him may not die but have eternal life."(Jn 3: 16). The Infancy Narratives of Mathew and Luke have painted for us the context of the birth of the Saviour, becoming one with us in all things but sin. Thus he was born poorest of the poor, wrapped in strips of cloth and laid in a manger of the cattle, not even in a room of an inn, or emergency night-shelter of travelers, because there was no room vacant in the inn.(Lk 2:7). He suffered experiences of rejection, nakedness and abandonment from Bethlehem to Calvary, thus totally identifying himself with the poor and the marginalized, which has been graphically recorded by St. Paul in Phil. 2:6—8.

This is the first phase of any genuine process of inculturation whenever the Gospel encounters a culture. The external support, the linguistic garb, the building scaffold of the evangelizer's culture in which the Gospel message has been enshrined, has to undergo first of all an 'incarnational descent, a dying to self' of the Logos in order to dispose itself for the assumption of the new cultural idiom of the people to whom the evangelizer was sent. In fact a meeting of two cultures (of the evangelizer and of the evangelized) and a crossing over from one to the other through a three-fold action, called **translation, assimilation and transformation** described earlier,[1] takes place here.

Cross as Symbol of Confrontation with Evil Structures and Contexts

The process of self-emptying of Jesus was only one aspect of the mystery of Incarnation. He became one with us in everything positive that human nature is capable of assuming unto itself. Thus he underwent all kinds of suffering and evil in body, mind and spirit in so far as they were not sinful. At the same time he questioned evils of the society, of the Judaic religious practices in so far as they were blatant violation of God's commandments and welfare of humans, especially of the poor and the marginalized. Though he did not project himself as a socio-political or religious reformer, his God-given task as the Messiah or Saviour of humanity implied confrontation with the rampant evils of the day and context in which he lived, and the gospels bear ample testimonies to this fact. Humanly speaking, it is this unavoidable face off with the ruling class of the time that finally brought him to the untold suffering and death on the Cross. And the Cross together with the Empty Tomb vindicated his uncompromising stand against all kinds of evils including death. Thus his triumph over sin and death raised human race from its fallen state.

This is the second phase of the path of inculturation, as we look at its proto-type, namely the Incarnation. When the Gospel encounters a new culture with its underlying values and religious beliefs as well as practices, the transformation process of the host-culture will involve removal of elements in it which cannot be absorbed or accepted by the Gospel values. For example, the system of bonded labour, caste discrimination, practices of child-marriage, Sati or widow –burning, dowry-bargain and subsequent persecution etc. Similarly the guest-culture of the Gospel also has to give up its foreign elements in order to assume the new cultural expression. For example, early Jewish Christianity had to shed its Jewish ethnocentric garb (Mosaic law of circumcision of all male Jews) in order to assume Greek cultural garb, when people of Greek origin became Christians. In the same way, the liturgical signs and symbols, doctrinal concepts and formulations of Western Christianity, based on Graeco-Roman idioms and expressions may have to give way to new expressions in tune with the religio-cultural idioms of India, for example. We have to understand and evaluate from this vintage point the earlier attempts of inculturation of those of Brahmabandha Upadhyay, Keshab Chandrasen, De Nobilee, Matheo Ricci and many more like them.

Inculturation, not Mission-strategy, but imitation of Incarnation-Pedagogy

Having dealt with the dynamics of the process of inculturation, we now come to discuss its rationale. Inculturation is not a mere method or much less a strategy for the evangelizing mission of the Church, just as its proto-type which is Incarnation, we said, was not a technique or mask used by God to appear on earth as a human person. The second Person of the Triune God did not just appear as man but became human, assuming the human condition in everything but sin so that he may experience the evil consequences of human sinfulness and remedy it in a unique way.

The Bible and inculturation

The mystery of the incarnation tells us that while God always communicates in a concrete history, taking up the cultural codes embedded therein, the same word can and must also be passed on in different cultures, transforming them from within through what Pope Paul VI called the evangelization of cultures.[2] The word of God, like the Christian faith itself, has a profoundly intercultural character; it is capable of encountering different cultures and in turn enabling them to encounter one another.[3]

Here too we come to appreciate the importance of the inculturation of the Gospel.[4] The Church is firmly convinced that the word of God is inherently capable of speaking to all human persons in the context of their own culture: "this conviction springs from the Bible itself, which, right from the Book of Genesis, adopts a universalist stance (cf. Gen 1:27-28), maintains it subsequently in the blessing promised to all peoples through Abraham and his offspring (cf. Gen 12:3; 18:18), and confirms it definitively in extending to 'all nations' the proclamation of the Gospel."[5] For this reason, inculturation is not to be confused with processes of superficial adaptation, much less with a confused syncretism which would dilute the uniqueness of the Gospel in an attempt to make it more easily accepted.[6] The authentic paradigm of inculturation is the incarnation itself of the Word: "'Acculturation' or 'inculturation' will truly be a reflection of the incarnation of the Word when a culture, transformed and regenerated by the Gospel, brings forth from its own living tradition original expressions of Christian life, celebration and thought",[7] serving as a leaven within the local culture, enhancing the *semina Verbi* and all those positive elements present within that culture, thus opening it to the values of the Gospel.[8]

As there have been heresies of Pelagianism as well as Gnosticism, and a variety of different shades between them, because all of them failed to understand and appreciate in one way or other, the mystery of Incarnation in its depth and breadth, so also we can find in the history of the Church's evangelizing mission, people who have misunderstood and misinterpreted the true meaning of inculturation. I would consider inculturation, therefore, a human imitation of the unique divine pedagogy of Incarnation. The divine act is unique, inimitable and unrepeatable in itself, I said earlier; but from a human point of view, we can look up to it and try to personalize it, just as we, as disciples try to personalize obedience to our Master, looking up to Jesus' unique obedience to the Father. Briefly, just as, for the Church to exist is to evangelize, so also for her to evangelize is to inculturate totally, in the footsteps of her Master's unique act of Incarnation.

If Incarnation was the full unfolding of divine revelation, which began with the act of creation, the Church's total inculturation,[9] will be an appropriate human response to it leading to the final fulfillment of the whole creation. Moreover, since the Gospel or the message of Jesus, cannot entertain any discriminatory sense towards any human situation or culture of the world, on the contrary has to be at home with all cultures, the process of inculturation is to be taken for granted in any encounter of the two – Gospel and culture.

Now, if this Gospel-culture interface takes place in a genuine spirit of dialogue, the result will be excellent witness value towards evangelizing mission of the Church. Thus we see that, although the purpose or direct goal of inculturation is not at all mission in the first instant, its overall impact cannot but be the acceptance of the Person and message of Jesus Christ at least partially, if not fully.

Concluding Remarks

We started discussing the above series of 14 essays, after presenting the semantic interface of two cardinal concepts – cult and culture, going back to their common origin in the Latin language root word *colere*, "to worship", "to cultivate", "to transform", "to develop", "to sanctify" etc. Thus, as we went deeper into the mutuality of *cultus* and *cultura*, we began to grasp that the two seemingly contradictory aspects of human life – secular and religious, material and spiritual are not so, but in fact complementary. In other words, ritual worship (worship in signs and symbols) and vital worship (worship by one's life/ by a responsible Christian life) are two inseparable sides of the same coin of human life.[10] Since human person is by nature a symbol-maker,[11] he/she expresses and/or communicates his/ her relation to God also in terms of symbolic/ritual gestures of allegiance, respect, adoration, love etc., as in personal or communal worship/ liturgy.

When we understand religious worship in this way as belonging to the essential nature of man/woman, religion will not be misunderstood as "opium of people", as has been branded in the Marxist-communist philosophy, but truly as liberative and salvific, as has been explained in the Essays 7 and 8 on" Liberative Potential of Christian Worship Symbols" and 'Liberative Potential of Religious Rituals". Similarly, in the Gospel-culture encounter, if this is practiced in a dialogical manner, both culture and Gospel will be beneficiaries, because Gospel values will help purify the culture of its alien and enslaving elements on the one hand, and culture will help increase the Gospel's catholicity or range of dissemination and acceptability, leading both to higher sense of fulfillment. Some of the Essays on Liturgical celebrations, Inculturation as well as mission have taken up these aspects of the cult-culture encounter and have shown that the two words - cult and culture - are not only etymologically connected, but also mutually complementary semantically, and together they contribute towards integral liberation and fulfillment of humanity.

Endnotes

[1] Cf. Essay on *Interface of Gospel and Culture*, pp.117-130, (125-126).

[2] EN 20: AAS 68(1976), 18-19.

[3] Benedict XVI, Post Synodal Ap. Exhortation *Sacramentum Caritatis* (22 Feb. 2007), 78.

[4] Cf. Ibid. 48.

[5] Pontifical Biblical Commission, *The Interpretation of the Bible in the Church* (15 April1993), iv.

[6] AG 22.

[7] John Paul II, Address to the Bishops of Kenya (7 May 1980), 6: AAS 72 (1980), 497.

[8] Cf. *Instrumentum Laboris*, 56.

[9] Cf. Chapter 12 on **Interface of Gospel and Culture,** especially pp.125-29.

[10] In Karl Rahner's terminology, they are called 'liturgy of the Church' (ritual liturgy) and 'liturgy of the world' (responsible human life in obedience to God's commands). The connection between the two liturgies - ritual and vital—will be clear when we see that in both cases what is given to God is 'worship', in one case in terms of symbols, gestures and postures (anjali *hasta, arati* etc.) and in the other case by obeying God's commandments. Here it may be noted that the word 'worship', coming from two old Anglo-Saxon words was originally written as 'worthship', namely value, worth, quality of the person concerned. Therefore in either kind of liturgy, what we are doing is to accept/recognize/ acknowledge God as our most valuable or worthiest person; this is done either in signs and gestures or by actually obeying God's commands etc.

[11] An embodied spirit or spirit-filled body, man/woman makes ample use of signs and symbols, gestures and postures to communicate among themselves, so much so that man/woman is said to be a symbolic animal also, apart from being defined in Greek philosophy as a rational animal. Thus in actual life he/she relies on symbols and symbolic gestures in order to express as well as communicate deeper values of human life, like love, respect, compassion, friendship etc.